Chapter 1

Ceto sat cross legged in an island of he.

Her space was nestled, tucked away at the edge of her garden. She had designed it to transport her from the lonely world she knew, to one filled with magic and mystery.

She read books here, watched films and listened to music. She dreamt here.

The patch was filled with blankets and pillows, bright flowers, hanging greenery and climbing ivy. She felt safe here, hidden by the swaying branches of a weeping willow and cocooned in the nature around her, as it changed slowly to orange.

This particular day, she was listening to a slow heartfelt playlist, happy to switch her mind off for a moment.

Closing her eyes and stretching out her legs, she leant back on an array of multi-coloured and mismatched cushions, her ink black hair falling over her shoulders like liquid, keeping her neck warm. She welcomed the gentle breeze brushing over her translucent exposed skin, with its autumn chill.

My favourite time of year. She thought to herself with a gentle smile playing around her lips.

After a while, she had the strange feeling that she was being watched. Opening one of her eyes a little and peering up through her long dark eyelashes, she spied a figure standing over her.

"I'm busy." Ceto closed her eye again and turned her head away from the figure. She felt the cushions move slightly as the figure sat beside her.

"Hi, Oscar." She sighed, pulling out her ear phones. She opened her eyes and sat cross legged again as she faced her only friend.

Though she wouldn't let her body language betray her, she was happy to see Oscar.

The two smiled at each other for a while until Ceto broke eye contact. She nestled her face in her red tartan scarf and

1

watched her hands as they absentmindedly played with the tassels.

"She's no better?" Oscar asked in his musically soothing tone. Ceto looked up, finding comfort in his familiar face. His auburn hair in its usual messy style, the spray of freckles across his long, crooked nose. He searched her with his hazel eyes in the way only Oscar could, concern etched across his beautiful face.

Ceto's high cheek bones tinged pink at the thought; Oscar had grown in to a beautiful person, inside and out.

They had met by chance at age eleven, when Oscar had made his way up the scary hill that no other child dared, and to her back garden.

Ceto had always thought of him as a brother, but over the past few years her feelings had become to change towards him and she wasn't sure what she was supposed to feel anymore. These new feelings embarrassed her.

Oscar smiled, creating deep dimples as he did.

"What are you listening to anyway?" He asked, changing the subject, knowing that she wasn't going to answer his question in this mood. He grabbed her phone and started to scroll through the playlist she had chosen, "Emotional." Was all he commented, a slight mocking in his tone. He raised his eyebrows and handed it back.

She reached for her phone, her ivory hand grazing his, a little spark firing off as it did.

Ceto always felt a little silly when Oscar asked her what she was listening to; he had always loved music, every genre, every style. It was his passion, one that she didn't share.

In the past, he would make her playlists for birthdays and Christmas', as gifts.

As they grew older, he would make her playlists intended to lift her spirits or change her mood. Just recently, the music he sent seemed to have hidden meaning. But Ceto quickly pushed that thought out of her head, knowing it was foolish to think this. Wishful thinking.

She still had the tapes he'd made for her when they were younger, and the CDs from when they were teenagers, now he would send them through the music app on their phones. They usually cheered her up, it was like having a piece of him in her pocket.

Oscar reached his hand out and placed it where her knee was under her blanket.

"Hey, what's happened?" Oscar asked, his smile gone and the concern returning.

"She's just no better, I don't think she'll get better." Ceto replied, scared to say anymore for the fear of crying in front of another human; nothing embarrassed her more.

He took a deep breath in and exhaled almost tunefully.

"She's inside?" He asked. Ceto nodded.

Oscar stood up, towering over her, he held out his long arm for her to take, lifting Ceto up out of her cocoon. They made their way from their hideaway and through the backdoor of Ceto's home.

It wasn't really a house, more of a wooden barn, but it was a home.

Closing the backdoor behind them, shutting out the cold and taking off their jackets and scarves, they made their way through the kitchen. It was filled with wooden tops and a rustic basin for washing. Pots and pans hung on the walls and shelves upon shelves of mason jars filled with herbs, vibrant liquids and pastes that seemed to move about.

They made their way into the living room which was simple but warm with its mismatched chairs, a wooden pallet Ceto's mum had made in to a coffee table and a couple of shabby lamps dotted around the room, casting a warm glow on a lady sat straight backed on the sofa.

She sat facing the TV, her milky eyes staring blankly at a

program currently playing with canned laughter. She wasn't really watching, she was a shadow of the mum Ceto had known.

Oscar made his way over to the sofa and sat next to the lady, as if nothing strange could be seen here.

"So, what are we watching Adara?" He nonchalantly asked, watching the TV himself.

"Oh, I've seen this one. It's the one with the toe." Oscar carried on the conversation as if Ceto's mum had acknowledged he was there, of course she hadn't.

"What was for lunch today, Adara?" He enquired warmly. There was no reply, he wasn't expecting one. He looked up to where Ceto still stood and smiled an encouraging smile, but it had a sad tinge to it.

"I'll make us tea." Ceto offered and made her way to the kitchen again, lighting the little camping fire and placing the kettle on top.

As she waited for it to boil, she glanced over at her mum and Oscar. Oscar still calmly having a one way conversation, Adara still gazing off into the distance, rocking gently from side to side.

Ceto shook her head a little at the memory of their first meeting.

Oscar had been spending the summer sneaking up the hill to where Ceto and her mum had been living alone for years. Adara had no idea that this strange boy had been making his way to their back garden for weeks now.

"Ceto!" Her mum had called. Both children froze in their playing. They jumped up and stood still, waiting for their punishment.

When Adara had emerged around the corner, she had frozen too, horror transforming her entirely black eyes into circles, her breath caught on an inhale.

"Who are you?" She'd demanded.

"Oscar." He'd replied, complete with a little curtsey. A curtsey that had Ceto bent double, clutching her stomach from the tightness that came with too much laughter. Seeing her daughter, having been alone for eleven years, quietly playing by herself, learning and taking on too much responsibility; seeing her pale face light up with joy at a simple action from this boy, with bruises on his knees and a swipe of dirt running from his jaw and up his cheek, seeing her laugh like this lifted Adara's heart.

"Hello Oscar." Adara composed herself and bent slightly so that she was level with the boy.

"Does anybody know you're here? Your mum, where does she think you are?"

"She thinks I'm playing with the other kids in the park. I heard Ceto playing and…" He shrugged as an ending to his sentence.

Adara thought hard, glanced over at her daughter, her crystal blue eyes shining with happiness.

"You may play in our back garden, stay away from the animals and off the raised beds." She smiled warmly at Ceto's first and only friend.

"I'm Adara." She formally held out her hand to shake Oscar's and they had seen each other most days from that moment on.

Ceto never did find out what had horrified her mum so much that day.

Adara wasn't a cold parent, she was controlling and careful, but she could be warm too. She worked hard raising the livestock and caring for the vegetables and herbs. Keeping whatever they needed and selling the excess at the little stall she owned down the hill on market day.

Adara didn't speak these days, she was simply a shell; breathing, eating and drinking when Ceto fed her, nothing more.

She once had eyes that were fully black, no whites at all, now they had turned milky. Her hair used to flow like liquid, as Ceto's does, but it wasn't black, it was a white blonde. But now it was a course and wispy grey mass that sat on top of her head.

The whistle of the kettle boiling brought Ceto out of her miserably tinged thoughts.

Oscar made his way over to the kitchen to help with the tea and spoke in hushed tones.

"I'm sorry I've not been around much, I wish I could help more." He began but Ceto held her hand out to stop his pity. His mum had died when he was a young teenager and his dad had checked out when they lost her, leaving Oscar almost as alone as Ceto.

"Don't, I'm fine." Ceto offered him a smile but he shook his head, knowing she was struggling more than she would ever say.

"I could ring the doctor for you?" He offered.

"You know she's never liked to use doctors." Ceto chuckled slightly as she raised her hand to slice through the air, displaying a shelf full of glass jars with odd liquids, ointments and herbs of different varieties. "She has a remedy for every illness."

The friends giggled quietly together at joint memories of oozing ointments being slopped onto cut knees, splinters, sprained wrists and any other childhood accident.

Oscar placed his hand, bony but strong, on top of Ceto's slender one that lay on the wooden counter top. His completely covering hers and a great shock jolted her heart, making her pull her hand away. She busied herself with pouring water in to three mugs and letting the tea bags brew.

"I am, I'm fine." Ceto said with a little more conviction this time, but not meeting his kind eyes.

The two friends drank their tea in silence on the sofa with Adara.

Ceto had tried to feed her mum some food but she had only mushed a couple of mouthfuls before she stopped opening her mouth for the next spoonful.

The sun could be seen setting through the glass in the backdoor.

"I'd better go," Oscar sighed. "But I'll be back early tomorrow and help you at the market?" He asked this as a question even though they both knew he would never let Ceto do that on her own, even if she refused. She smiled up at him and mouthed a thank you.

Oscar picked up Ceto's phone and scrolled for a few moments before returning it to her. She looked down at the screen, her heart jumped in her chest and glowed.

"A new playlist? For me?" Ceto beamed up at Oscar.

"You've been looking a little glum." He replied and gave a cheeky half smile before letting himself out the backdoor, waving behind himself at the two figures sat in the semi darkness.

Ceto went through her nightly routine of walking her mum slowly and awkwardly to her bedroom, laying her in her bed and tucking her in tightly.

"Night, mum." She whispered and she turned to leave the bedroom, heading for the sofa.

Ceto wrapped herself in an old blanket and huddled in an almost vertical position. She placed her ear phones back in and played Oscar's new playlist he had made, especially for her.

Ceto's heart glowed with every song, every lyric, every note change and she tried to decipher what he was trying to tell her, as if it were a secret language.

Sleep waved over her as the music played on and she drifted into a peaceful slumber.

Chapter 2

The next morning, Ceto jumped up to a tapping on the glass in the backdoor. She groggily flopped off the sofa and internally cursed herself for falling asleep in such an uncomfortable way, her joints stiff.

In her half asleep state, she had assumed the tapping was Oscar, here to help with market day. Rubbing the sleep away, her arm held out to open the door, she gasped and froze.

On the other side of the glass stood a dozen or so ravens. They were bigger than any Ceto had seen before and they stood eerily still, watching her.

Living at the top of a steep hill, away from other human's and with nothing but farmland and forest behind them, Ceto had grown up with an abundance of wildlife around. It didn't scare her, it usually calmed her. The same thing could not be said for these birds.

She slowly positioned herself to sit back on her heels and gently tapped the glass. The raven at the front tapped again, making Ceto smile; did the birds want to play? She went to tap again.

"CETO!" Came a high pitched screech from behind her, making her jump so much that she fell backwards and on to the floor.

"Get away! Go!" Ceto's mum croaked, wafting her arms in front of her, the shawl draped across her shoulders falling to the floor. The raven cawed loudly at her and then shot off in to the sky and away.

"Mum?" Ceto whispered, disbelief making her voice thick in her throat. Tears of relief filling her blue eyes.

"Mum, I've missed you."

But in the time it had taken Ceto to realise that her mum was finally herself again, she had reverted back to her shadow state and fallen awkwardly on to the sofa.

Frustrated tears spilled over Ceto's eyes and down her cheeks, furious with herself for feeling hope.

Ceto gathered herself together, swiped the tears from her chin and picked up her mum's shawl that had fallen. She wrapped it lovingly around Adara's bony shoulders.

"How about some breakfast?" Ceto offered, rubbing the now still figure's arms to offer comfort.

Comfort for the both of them.

She made her way to the kitchen, pottering about in a dreamlike state, making breakfast. The world outside still dark, a light patter of rain had begun.

Glancing over at the clock on the wall, she mentally noted how long she had until Oscar would be here.

Enough time, she thought.

Ceto carried her mum's breakfast of porridge over to the sofa and placed it down on the coffee table. Offering a spoonful, Adara sat straight and still again but she didn't open her mouth. Instead a single tear rolled down her gaunt face, dipping in to the hollow of her cheek.

Ceto hastily put the spoon back in the bowl with a tinkle and wiped her tear away.

"Do you remember when we went to the park in the village?" Ceto asked, as if her mum would answer.

"I must have been, what? Six years old, maybe seven?" She carried on, ignoring the familiar feeling of a one way conversation. Another tear escaped her mum's blank eyes and Ceto wiped that one away too.

"You wiped my tears away then, remember?"

She didn't know if her mum remembered or could even hear what she was saying, but Ceto remembered vividly. She remembered the way any child would recall a bad memory. The way it latches on to your brain and pops to the forefront, unannounced.

Ceto was a young child, Adara had promised to take her daughter to the park in the village for her birthday.

9

Ceto remembered skipping ahead, desperate to see this magical place that she'd been told so much about, her hair in pig tails bouncing behind her with every joyful bounce.

She didn't have a care in the world, she didn't feel anxious or unsure, she knew exactly what she wanted and she headed straight towards the swings.

Spinning around and planting her bottom down with a thud, expecting the swing to do the work.

She recalled her mum laughing in the light way she used to, and making her way over to show Ceto how to swing.

After a few moments, she was higher than the tops of the trees.

Mid swing, she noticed a group of children a little older then herself enter the park without a second glance at Ceto and her mum having the time of their lives.

She slowed the swing to a stop and looked up at her mum. "Mum, can I go say hi?"

Adara glanced over to the group of children around the seesaw and back to her daughter.

"Aren't we having a good time together?" Her mum had answered.

Nodding, Ceto slid off the swing and made her way to the slide on the other side of the park, a little closer to the other children.

She watched them, laughing together and fighting playfully. Her mum was at the bench, distractedly looking for something in her bag.

Mustering determination and courage, Ceto pushed herself down the slide and made her way over to the seesaw.

"Hello." She whispered, barely audibly.

There was no response from the children who seemed to tower over her.

She balled her hands into fists and willed herself to speak louder.

"Hello." She said again.

One of the children turned around, looking down at Ceto with pure hatred on their face. They reached out their arm and pushed her hard enough to knock her to the ground with a painful bump.

Ceto began to cry on the floor, the children had forgotten that she was there and began to laugh amongst themselves again.

The young Ceto had assumed they were laughing at her childish tears and she cried harder.

Adara scooped her daughter up and carried her over to their bench, placing Ceto on her knee. She covered the small child with her body, blocking out their surroundings. Her blonde hair falling from behind her ears and framing her soft pale face perfectly.

"Shh. I'm here, it's just you and me." Her mum soothed, wiping the tears away from her cheeks. She unwound her red tartan scarf from her neck and wrapped it around Ceto.

"Let's go home. I have birthday cake! Does that sound nice?" Looking back, Ceto realised her mum was probably trying to bribe her, but bribery worked in her young mind.

"Eat just one mouthful for me, I've put some honey in it for you, doesn't that sound nice?" Ceto now bribed her mum, bribery worked.

After a frustrating breakfast, Ceto made her mum comfortable and turned the TV on for company. She then went to her room to change, feeling scruffy for sleeping in her clothes.

Changing into dark jeans, a thick hooded jumper and comfy, warm boots, she gathered her mass of hair and tied it into a bun, odd strands of hair with their own minds spilling out here and there. She'd learnt long ago that her hair did whatever it wanted, she didn't have the energy to fight with it now.

Now dressed, she made her way to the kitchen, wrapped her mum's tartan scarf around her neck a few times, and stretched on her gloves and her thick coat. She took a moment to bury her face into the scarf for comfort; it had a scent that seemed to last, the scent of Adara.

"Won't be long." She called back to her mum, riddled with anxiety.

Ceto had done quite a few market days by now and Adara was always exactly where she had left her when she returned. But that didn't stop the feeling in her stomach, she felt as if something horrible would happen when she wasn't with her. She reminded herself that without the small profit she made from market day, they had no hope of living their simple lives.

With a sigh, Ceto pushed open the glass backdoor and stepped outside, her head bent forward to protect her face from the rain, and she got to work with stacking crates of produce onto a trundle.

After a while, Oscar had made his way up the hill, calling out a greeting in the almost sunrise.

The two grabbed everything they needed and started making their way down the hill.

"You okay?" Oscar groggily asked, obviously having woken up not long ago.

"You seem more away with the fairies than usual?" He waited patiently.

Ceto considered keeping from him the strange thoughts in her mind; her visit from the ravens and her mum's sudden and short improvement.

She reminded herself that Oscar had been a part of her life for twelve or so years, and a day hadn't gone by where she hadn't told him absolutely everything.

But things were different now, she felt exhausted from the

struggle with her mum, from keeping their home going, she also didn't understand these new feeling towards Oscar.

"I've had a strange morning." She decided to reply, but shot him a smile so he wouldn't worry.

There was silence on this crisp autumn morning, the only sound from the rain pattering around on the dusty ground under their feet. Silence whilst Oscar waited for more and Ceto gathered her thoughts.

"There were these birds in the garden…playful things." Ceto smiled at the memory of the game they had been playing.

"Playful birds? Can birds be playful?" Oscar asked, a little mocking in his tone.

"These ones were." Ceto smiled back, her face dropping before she carried on.

"My mum got out of bed by herself this morning and shouted at them." It sounded like a dream when she spoke it out loud; she wasn't entirely sure it wasn't anymore. It had happened so quickly and Ceto's memory of it had grown foggy through the busy morning. She wondered if Oscar would think it was a dream too.

He stopped dead and placed his gloveless hand on the bend of Ceto's arm, she noticed they looked painfully red from the cold. She had the sudden urge to grab them in hers, to warm them.

"What did she shout?"

"She was shooing them away. It happened so quickly, she hasn't said a word since then. I couldn't even get her to have more than a mouthful of breakfast."

Ceto had carried on walking now, her head bent low, partly from the rain, partly from the look of pity on Oscar's face.

"Ceto, I…"

"I'm fine." She flapped her hand, shooing away his wordless worries.

The two didn't speak for the rest of the trip down the hill. It wasn't awkward, they could happily sit in comfortable silence. Oscar was like an extension of Ceto, it was easy. Their silence was one of contemplation.

They worked silently as the sun began to show itself above the village houses, placing crates on the shelves of their stall. An array of different seasonal vegetables, a few bottles of goat's milk and Ceto had managed to collect a basket full of fresh hen's eggs this morning.

The morning went as it usually did, customers passing by Ceto to be dealt with by Oscar. People even waited patiently in a queue at a few points of the morning so they could be seen to by her helper.

She didn't give this a second thought, she was used to it. There was a time when she had tried to engage in conversation with the villagers but they had screwed their faces up as if it disgusted them to talk to her. One lady had even spat on the ground one morning.

That was the last time she tried to make conversation with the customers.

So instead, she busied herself sorting change, re-arranging the crates as the morning went on, and she would greet customer's dogs when they were waiting in the queue.

Often the dogs would be pulled away as if some disgusting monster was infecting their pet. She was comforted by the fact that the animals often whined a little, unable to be fussed over anymore by the nice lady that their owners strangely couldn't see.

Ceto enjoyed the company of animals more than humans anyway, at least they seemed to like her.

The low sun was at its highest point when they had sold out. Oscar came over carrying two coffees, handed one to Ceto and tapped the rim of his gently against hers, smiling up at her as he sipped.

"Well earned drink, we make a good team." He said, wrapping his arm around her, rubbing her arm up and down, she assumed to warm her but she was better dressed for the weather than he was. She didn't point this out, instead she let herself enjoy the closeness and comfort.

"Here." She wound her way out of his grasp and handed him some money from the locked box.

"Nah-uh." He replied, holding up his coffee free hand and shaking it slightly.

"Stop trying to give me money every time we do this, you're my *friend*."

The word *friend* seemed to vibrate through her, unable to hide the hurt feelings on her face. Oscar assumed she was hurt that he'd turned her offer down.

"I just meant...I don't do this for payment or a favour. I do this because we're a team. We're friends, I wouldn't see you doing this alone."

"No, no, obviously. I'd just feel bad if I didn't offer. You've given up your time and..." Ceto trailed off, hiding her face in her scarf. Why had it become awkward to talk to him sometimes, these moments of stuttering were becoming more frequent as time went on, she couldn't imagine a world without Oscar.

"Are you going to help me drag these back up the hill anyway?" Ceto asked, trying to sound jovial and light.

"Let me finish my drink!" Oscar acted hurt, the two laughed into their drinks, steam escaping into the cold air as they did.

Oscar helped Ceto up the hill, he apologised for having to leave her so soon. She knew he had his dad to check on and so she waved his apology away.

Ceto went through her day, seeing that her mum was warm and fed, doing the same with the animals and finally making some food for herself. By this time, the sun had already set and the darkness closed in around Ceto again.

As she sat next to her mum in the dark, she began to feel the pangs of loneliness and reached for her phone to speak to Oscar.

She patted down her pockets, checked in the kitchen, checked the garden, her hideaway, her phone was nowhere to be seen. With a roll of her eyes and a groan, she vaguely remembered placing it on a shelf under the stall.

She took an anxious glance at her mum.

"I'll be back in a few minutes." She explained to the empty air, deciding she would run down the hill and back up as quickly as she could. Not taking a coat and not bothering to lock the back door either. *I'll only be a minute.*

Relief washed over her when she saw her phone hadn't been taken during the day, pocketing it, she set off at another run, slower this time, up the hill.

Ceto slowed a little as an eerie feeling washed over her, something felt off about the quiet evening.

Suddenly, a blood curdling scream hit her ears, it ran down her spine and up through her veins. Everything about her went cold and her stomach felt as if it had forgotten gravity. Ceto's body stopped dead halfway up the dirt track, unable to move for a second or two. Her eyes staring blankly into the dark night. Her insides squirming, full of horror. Horror because the scream, which was still ringing in the air, had come from the top of the hill. It had come from the little barn.

"Mum." Ceto breathed, running up the hill as fast as her numb body would allow her.

Reaching the top of the hill, she paused at the sight of the open back door. She tried to quieten her rapid breathing. Suddenly, a flurry of black feathers flew past her and off into the night. She watched them as they grew smaller in the sky. Taking a few steps inside, she paused; she couldn't see her mum, she wasn't sat straight backed on the sofa.

Ceto's eyes slowly followed a trail of black liquid, her feet edging her further into the barn, her round eyes peering around the back of the sofa.

Blood.

There her mum lay. Unmoving.

She threw her hands to her mouth as if to stifle a scream that couldn't find its way out through the terror. Her wide eyes took everything in, unwillingly.

There, her beloved mum lay.

The woman who had been so full of light and laughter, who took care of her when she was sick or upset.

There, her one of a kind mum lay, the little light she had left now drained out of her slowly and completely.

There she lay with thick black blood escaping the wound on her head.

Her mum, her friend, gone.

Silent tears rolled down Ceto's cheeks as she fell down to her knees' next to Adara. She grasped her mum's hand in her own, squeezing it tightly.

So tight, in the hope some of her own life would be taken and given to her mum. Hoping she'd wake up happy and healthy. All the darkness taken away from the last few months, erased.

Suddenly, Adara's eyes snapped open.

They weren't the milky colour Ceto had become used to, but shiny and black once more.

She could see her own eyes reflecting back in them.

With another snap, Adara's back arched as if something was being pulled from her body. She took a great long raspy gasp of air, finally settling back down on to the cold dusty floor. Her face now looked peaceful. A strange wave of calm washed over Ceto. The darkness had finally left Adara.

Ceto grappled across the dusty floor to where her phone had

dropped by the door. With shaky hands and struggling to see through the constant assault of tears, she managed to call Oscar.

He answered the phone, Ceto couldn't open her mouth to ask for help, she knew if she did that she wouldn't just be fighting off tears, but sobs.

"Ceto?" Oscar asked, his voice almost cracking with angst. She still couldn't speak, she silently chastised herself for not getting her emotions under control before she had called.

"I'm on my way." It wasn't a question, it wasn't a warning, it was a statement. Oscar was on his way. The phone hung up. Ceto dragged her still numb body off the floor and slowly made her way to her hideout in the garden.

She had no thoughts, wasn't she supposed to have thoughts? All she had were tears, a waterfall of silent tears.

Sitting in her usual place amongst her cushions, she looked down at her hands and was surprised to find they were shaking quite visibly, she couldn't feel her limbs.

After a few moments, a figure ran past her as she sat alone in the dark. The figure skidded to a halt at the backdoor, opened it a little and poked their head into the gloomy room.

"Ceto?" It loudly whispered and then entered slowly to the silence.

Ceto could hear heavy boots making their way through the kitchen and to the sofa.

Then, silence.

"CETO?!" The figure bellowed, running outside to frantically scan the darkness.

Heavy boots running towards her.

"Ceto?" The figure breathed, wavering a little. Ceto looked up.

"Oscar." She said flatly. A sad confusion etched in to her face.

"What happened?" She whispered.

"Y-your mum. She…" Realising she was probably in shock, Oscar sat gently down beside her, wrapped his arm around her and guided her head to rest on his torso.

There they sat for a while, his heart thrumming under her ear.

"What happened?" Oscar asked this time.

"There…was a scream. I found her. Behind the sofa."

"Okay. Okay." Oscar lulled as he tried to make sense of this and wondering when it was best to suggest that they ring the police, knowing the mother and daughter had never had dealings with anyone like that, they seemed to avoid anyone but himself at all costs.

"Erm, Ceto. We should probably call someone…someone that might be able to help…with your mum?" He edged.

Ceto pulled away from him and made her way back into the house.

"Wait!" He called after her, following her in.

Ceto stood still in the kitchen.

"I don't want anyone to touch her."

"I can understand that." And he did. Oscar understood, he always did.

Ceto turned to look out into the night again.

"She needs to be out there, amongst the trees and the breeze. She loved the rain, did you know that?" The ghost of a smile turning up the corners of her mouth as she weakly made her way towards the doors.

"She loved to be outdoors. We could, maybe…" Oscar started to suggest having Adara cremated and scattered in the wind but he stopped at the sight of Ceto.

She stood with her eyes closed, head tilted up to the sky, arms spread wide, a peaceful look on her face. He considered placing his hand on her shoulder to bring the suggestion of calling the police to her attention again, but something made him wait.

A gentle breeze had started to gather in the barn behind

them, Ceto's beautiful hair flowed in front of her, her loose t-shirt flapping gently.

Then, a strong sand filled gust rocked both glass doors on their hinges and brushed its way past the two figures. Finally escaping into the night, dancing and swirling on the wind.

"Ceto?" Oscar whispered, placing his hand in hers, he was a little taken aback to see she was smiling, still crying, but smiling.

Her breathing became faster, her chest rising and falling, until uncontrollable sobs finally escaped her chest and she fell back into his firm arms.

"Bye, mum." She whispered between cries. Oscar looked behind them to the floor where Adara should have still been lying. He wasn't completely surprised to see that there was no sign of her. He'd always known there was something extraordinary about Ceto and Adara, but that didn't matter. Right now he had to be there for his hurting friend.

Ceto found herself with an overwhelming feeling of gratitude that she had met Oscar all those years ago.

Chapter 3

The friends sat in their hideout through the night, wrapped in blankets and each other. Each drifting off into a restless sleep from time to time.

As the sun entered the sky, turning the darkness to a golden orange, a spray of clouds followed. Beams of the golden light warmed spots of the dewy ground, casting a particularly bright ray across an alder tree in the distance.

Oscar gently shook Ceto from her half sleep.

"Come with me."

Ceto let herself be pulled up from the ground. The tears had now stopped, she supposed she was too exhausted to let anymore fall. Finding comfort in the soft way Oscar grasped her cold hand, she plodded next to him, both walking in silence.

When they reached the alder tree that sat on the edge of a wild pond, Oscar wrapped his arm around her small frame and guided her close to him as he had the night before.

"I can feel her." Ceto breathed, feeling the soothing of the breeze as it ran over her body.

"She was always kind to me. Do you remember that time my dad locked me out and it was raining? God, it was hammering with rain!" Oscar chuckled at the memory of his misery.

"I came here, she wrapped me up in warm blankets and gave me some of her special tea. Do you remember her tea? It would warm you right through." He smiled at the cosy recollection.

Ceto noticed he was talking to her as he would talk to her mum when she was ill. A one way conversation, just trying to fill the empty silence. He was good at that.

"I remember, she said it was *magic tea*." Ceto laughed at the absurdity of a magic tea but Oscar gave her a sad, knowing smile.

Ceto and Oscar stood listening to the breeze shuffling the

leaves on the trees around them and dancing through the long grass, enthralled in memories of Adara.

Ceto remembered a bleak morning at the market with her mum, it was before she had met Oscar. She sat on a stool behind the wooden stall, reading a book that she couldn't recall now.

Customers came and went, barely interacting with her mum. She would look up every now and then, her mum would look down at her and smile warmly.

"We won't be here much longer." She had softly said.

It was a winter's morning. Snow that had turned to slush lay in piles at the edge of the streets, fine rain now falling from the grey clouds, Ceto's button nose growing redder as the morning went by.

"Here." Adara had offered, pushing bits and bobs around in her bag. Furious with herself for forgetting to bring a warm drink for them. Instead, she handed Ceto some coins.

"Go across the road and buy yourself a pie, that'll warm you up." Pointing to a delightfully smelling shop close by.

Ceto remembered looking up at her mum, her eyes wide with fear.

"I can't go by myself. I can't do that."

Her mum bent down to her level, grabbed her arms tightly and peered right into her eyes and said with conviction, "You can do this."

The faith her mum had in her gave her confidence and willed her to be able to do it, she ached to make her mum proud. She looked down at the coins in her hand and back up to her mum.

"I have enough here for two?"

"Oh no, don't worry about me. I don't need one, get the one you want." She said with a smile and ushered her daughter away from the stall and in the direction of the bakery.

When Ceto entered the shop, it was empty. She made her way

to the glass case before her and placed her stiff hands on the slightly warm barrier. She walked up and down, taking in the different pies and pasties that she could buy.

"Step back from the glass please." Came a gruff male voice from above her and she jumped back at the command.

Stumbling over her words, shocked that someone other than her mum had not only noticed her, but spoken to her.

She held her palm up to the man, not meeting his eyes and asked for a cheese pie.

The man took the money from her hand and gave her some copper as change, finally handing her the food she'd requested.

The pie was warm on her small hand, a little grease leaking through the paper bag and on to her skin.

Muttering a small thank you, she scurried out of the shop and back to her mum.

She beamed with a sense of accomplishment and her mum beamed back with pride.

Adara had refused at first, but the mother and daughter shared the pie, both feeling a little warmer, a little fuller and a little happier.

That memory had always given Ceto comfort.

"What do I do now?" Ceto asked, flatly.

"We can figure that out together." Oscar squeezed her slight shoulder into his long torso.

Chapter 4

The next few weeks went by slowly and the days merged together for Ceto.

Oscar visited almost daily. He stayed as long as he could, but he had his own life to live. A couple of times he had nipped up the hill just to check on his friend. Once he'd found her freezing in her hide out under a bundle of frosted blankets, asleep. After he'd firmly asked her to never do that again, he found her in different states around the house; either huddled in a corner of the sofa, hugging her knees beside her mum's bed or simply standing in the dark kitchen.

Oscar let Ceto deal with the death of her mum in her own way for a few weeks but when she seemed to grow worse, rather than better, he decided it was time to interfere.

"Ceto," He had said one early morning, "I think it's time to have a tidy up?" Starting as a statement but ending in a wary question.

Ceto glanced up at him from the sofa, her eyes red and barely focusing. She then glanced at the state around her; various dishes in the sink from meals Oscar had prepared for her, books flung across the floor when she'd had a maddening search for her mum's favourite one, and only giving up when exhaustion overtook and the small barn floor was littered with literature.

Ceto groaned her way to a standing position and shuffled over to a wonky mirror on the wall, grasping for the edges of her oversized cardigan and pulling it taught around her, showing just how thin she had become, her body so slight to begin with. She pushed her unkempt hair behind her ear in an attempt to tidy it up a little, it didn't help.

"What a mess."

Oscar assumed she wasn't just talking about her appearance or the disarray around her, fresh silent tears falling down her face again.

Cursing himself for hurting his best friend, he rushed to her side.

"I'll help." He smiled at Ceto through the mirror and began to pick up books and papers from the floor. Ceto watched for a while until she found the energy to help, following Oscar's lead.

After a slow few hours, the kitchen had been cleaned, by Oscar, the surfaces had been dusted, by Oscar, the floor had been mopped, by Oscar. He didn't mind, Ceto had cleared the floor and lovingly placed the books back on the shelf where they lived.

Standing side by side, they observed their hard work and Ceto had to admit that the fog in her brain had cleared slightly.

"See, I don't know about you, but I feel better already." Oscar pronounced, always in sync with Ceto's own thoughts. She looked up and gave a meek smile in response, only to look away quickly, her cheeks growing hot at the thought of the chaos she knew was awaiting them in Adara's room.

"What?" Oscar craned his neck around a little to put himself in Ceto's line of sight.

"You haven't seen my mum's room yet." She answered with a nervous chuckle. It sounded hollow.

Oscar gave her another encouraging smile, took her hand and led them to Adara's room.

He stopped suddenly at the threshold.

"Ah." Was all he uttered.

Ceto shamefully remembered having a particularly difficult night in this room. She remembered the anger bubbling to the surface, the inability to control the situation happening around her and the insecurity for her lonely future.

She remembered grasping her mum's hairbrush and hurling the object across the room. The clatter it had made as it tumbled to the ground gave Ceto a small sense of power she had been lacking these last few weeks.

Before she knew it, she was breathing heavily on the edge of the bed, hands grasping the edges tightly, glancing around at the clothes and bedding strewn around the small room; curtains ripped off their poles, a small round mirror lay smashed on the floor, trinkets and anything else she could find, cast aside in a blur of sad rage. She had closed the door afterwards and hadn't entered again until now.

Oscar muttered something about a brush for the glass, leaving Ceto alone in the turmoil.

She stepped over the threshold.

"Sorry, Mum." She whispered to the empty space around her. Picking up whatever she came to, not sure where to start, grabbing bedding and clothing and slumping them on the empty bed.

Ceto picked up a handful of material, gasping slightly when a heavy object slid from a pocket and landed on the floor with a heavy thud.

She could feel a heat coming from the object and a slight clicking, like a beetle connecting its wings together.

A crease forming between her eyebrows, Ceto bent down to retrieve the object.

It was as hot as fire but at the same time as cool as the iciest sea, a small breeze seemed to brush against her hand where she held it.

The bronze object was circular and the size of her palm. At the top of the object sat an engraving of mountains, to the right sat a green leaf, the bottom had a single flame and to the left sat an engraving of two wavy lines. In the middle of the four symbols lay set a raised gem, pale green but with sparkles and marbling under the surface.

It was incredibly intricate.

Ceto couldn't imagine where Adara would have gotten this from or what she would have used it for. Their life had always been minimalistic, they had no need for fancy items like this. The only use Ceto could think of was a small paperweight.

"Ceto?" Oscar called timidly from the doorway, Ceto sucked in a breath and spun her head towards him. She had been in almost a trance, unaware of what was going on around her until now.

She slid the object into the pocket of her pants, feeling the warmth against her leg.

"Oh, thank you." She replied, taking a step forward and holding her hands out for the dustpan and brush, putting on a cheery façade so he wouldn't ask more questions.

Her front didn't fool Oscar but he'd known Ceto long enough not to prod for more answers when she did this. They fixed the room in silence from then on. Ceto's mind on the object she'd found, Oscar's mind on Ceto.

After a while, everything was back to where it should be, with the exception of the broken mirror.

Ceto regretted breaking the mirror. She often found her mum standing in front of it, seeming as if she could see *through* it, as if she was looking at something beyond the glass, longingly. But when Ceto had stolen a glance, all she saw was her confused and excited expression.

"I'll throw this away on my way out."

"No!" Ceto clawed at the bag full of broken mirror. Oscar pulled it out of her reach, his eyebrows coming together.

"I...it was my mum's favourite. I thought I might try and fix it." She stuttered.

Oscar wasn't convinced; he had never known Ceto to have dark thoughts, but she was in a bleak place at the moment and she did seem desperate to get her hands on a bag full of sharp shards. The worst thought did travel through Oscar's mind. But then again, he had known how attached Adara had been to the small mirror.

He handed the bag over, reluctantly.

"You think it's fixable?"

"I can at least try."

This didn't hinder Oscar's worries but he was nothing but trusting.

Oscar stayed a while, made them both a late lunch and they ate in silence. He tried to start a conversation or two, with no avail.

He selfishly missed his friend, she used to be so full of life, light and laughter, now she was a shell. Much like Adara had been.

He noticed her attention would constantly return to the bag of shards. This made him worry more, but he had an internal list in his mind of all the things he had to get done today, which he couldn't put off anymore.

"I'll come and check on you tonight." He tried to placate himself.

Taking Ceto's plate, he placed them in the sink without washing them, optimistically hoping Ceto would wash them herself.

He said his goodbyes and backed out of the glass door, checking behind him as he turned the last corner.

With Oscar gone and the empty barn silent again, Ceto pulled the object out of her pocket and sat back on the sofa, pulling her knees up and placing the object gently on her legs, feeling its heat through her pants. Its warmth filling her with a sense of safety and calm that she hadn't felt for, what felt like, an extremely long time.

Ceto didn't know how long she had been examining the object for, but the sun had just about set in the back garden, casting an auburn glow on the world around her.

Stretching out her stiff joints, she reached over for the broken mirror and tipped the contents on to the coffee table.

The back and the frame of the mirror were perfectly intact, only the glass had broken. With a scraping, she moved all the shards over to one side, placing the frame in front of her. Starting with the biggest pieces, placing and rearranging, shuffling and repositioning, she quickly had what resembled the majority of the mirror in place.

Excitedly scurrying for a hot glue gun that lay forgotten in a draw, she eagerly spread it across the back of the pieces. After a while, she had completed her task. An elation surged through her for an entire second, slowly ebbing away as disappointment at the lack of accomplishment took its place. She was sure it would have brought her more.

Ceto picked up the mirror, holding it at arm's length. She reluctantly took in her appearance; her sallow skin, her eyes turning dull, her hair frizzy and sticking out at odd angles as it lay tangled in a messy bun. How like her mother she had become. She was not going out the same way. A determined Ceto glared back from the mirror and then looked down to the bottom of the frame, confusion between her eyebrows. A round hole had appeared.

The strange object excitedly hummed in her pocket.

Certain the hole hadn't been there in all the years the mirror had been in Adara's room, she shakily reached for the object. Hands trembling slightly, unsure of what she expected to happen.

As she held it above the hole, it seemed to pull itself towards the mirror's frame, as if it was a strong magnet.

Clink!

It snapped in to place and Ceto's reflection changed into beautiful scenery.

It wasn't a picture, she could feel the breeze on her face, and she could smell the air, a scent of wild flowers and salt.

Before her lay a blanket of luscious green and the sound of insects buzzing.

"Mum?" Ceto was certain that her mum had a connection to this place. She placed a finger on the glass only to find that her finger went *through* it. She snatched her hand back and cradled it at her chest.

Ceto sat still for a while, the mirror lay on the coffee table, the swaying green still visible.

Ceto suddenly jumped up from the sofa and marched to her room.

She quickly changed into a pair of slack jeans and her heavy boots, a comfortable t-shirt and a thick zipped jacket. Grabbing a worn backpack, she raced around the barn, unsure of what to put in it. She threw in a wool hat, her tartan scarf, a spare pair of socks, plus a few odd items she picked up without a thought. Looking down at the arrangement of items, she concluded that this was enough. Flinging the back pack on her shoulder, wrapping her scarf around her neck and gliding over to the coffee table, Ceto held the mirror at arm's length again, relief washing over her when the green reflected in her blue eyes.

I hadn't imagined it. She smiled to herself.

Taking a steadying breath, Ceto poked a finger through the glass again, then her hand, her arm, elbow, shoulder.

Then a few things happened at the same time.

The mirror snapped back to reflecting the barn, Ceto's arm still inside the mirror, Oscar's pale reflection stared at the back of her as he watched her *enter* Adara's mirror, one hand still on the back door.

Then, the world around Ceto melted away to a brilliant white, a strong gust of wind gathering the hair that had fallen from her bobble into a whirlwind around her head, making her close her eyes and raise her arm to her face for protection. The wind stopped suddenly. There was nothing, not even a slight breeze.

Ceto opened her eyes to the whiteness around her, all that

stood ahead was a tangle of branches in the shape of an archway and through the tangle, lay a familiar scenery of green.

She edged her feet forwards, growing closer to the branches. The closer she walked, the more real the scene became. Her ears began to tune into sounds of birds and insects off in the distance, the wind dancing through the long grass. She could smell an array of sweet smelling flowers, a slight salty scent to the air.

As she came to stand on the threshold, she could feel the warmth from the sun, strong in the blue cloudless sky. It was summer here.

She took a longing glance behind her, from where she'd come; there was nothing there but blank white.

"Oscar." She whispered. A calm washed over her and she turned back to the frame.

Her home gone, there was no option now but to move forward. Ceto drew up her foot and placed it onto the meadow, a satisfying crunch underfoot as she disturbed the dirt below.

Chapter 5

A cool breeze instantly wrapped around Ceto's body, embracing her warmly. Feeling the urge to feel carefree, she yanked the bobble from her hair, releasing it to dance with the playful wind. She closed her eyes as a sense of freedom took over her pain. The bright sun beat down on her exposed skin as she began to remove her jacket. Its beams delightfully stroking her, welcoming her. She chuckled with genuine joy for the first time since her mum had left her.

Mum.

Her eyes snapped open as the memory flooded her senses, hitting her like a weight, bringing the familiar guilt with it. She took advantage of her open eyes to take in her surroundings. Bee's lazily frolicked from flower to flower, intertwining with butterflies of magnificent colours whilst crickets merrily chirped as if encouraging the dance above them. Fluffy seeds blowing this way and that, in time with the melody of the wind. Everything was intensely bright before her.

In the distance ahead, a mountain rested, seeming to stretch up to the sky above. The bright colours stopped at the foot of the mountain in the distance. She shivered as it seemed to loom over her

To Ceto's left she could just about make out the sea and if she squinted her eyes, she could make out a civilisation there on the water.

Maybe I should make my way there? She worried to herself.

To her right and not too far from her, lay trees that stretched as far back as her eyes would allow her to see and they stood all the way along to the bottom of the mountain.

Am I dreaming? Have I gone insane?

It all *seemed* very real.

Ceto stood alone near the tree line in the vast meadow taking everything in. Wondering what she was supposed to do now.

She glanced behind herself, trying to catch a last glimpse of the world she'd left behind but the white void had gone too. All that stood behind her was an archway of branches. Through the archway, the sky was filled with continuous streams of smoke shooting in to the bright blue sky.

Logic filled her mind and panic suddenly hit her, her heart grew cold. There was no way back now. She had no idea where she was, or if anyone or anything lived here. Would anyone help her? Did she need help? She sunk into her scarf. A gentle breeze glided through the long grass towards Ceto and washed over her, bringing with it a calmness.

She breathed to steady the thoughts that now attacked her. Turning her reluctant body around, wondering what to do and where to go, a rustle in the trees to her right caught her attention. Ceto froze, waiting for it the move again, never taking her eyes off the patch of forest.

There a figure stood, slowly swaying from out of the tree line and then it stopped dead just outside the forest, as if it was afraid to go any further.

The figure seemed to turn their head to one side and then the other, taking a long look at their surroundings before making a decision. After a pause, they moved towards her. As they came closer, she could see that they had a human form, although much taller than any human she had ever seen. They moved with a smooth rhythm, as if they were gliding.

Ceto moved towards the figure. She didn't think, her body was doing it for her, encouraged by the breeze at her back. A reflex had taken over her body, against her better judgment, and strangely she wasn't afraid. She was filled with an excited intrigue.

Still unsure of whether this was real or if she'd had a mental breakdown, she smiled and wondered if this was all in her head.

What a beautiful breakdown.

As the figure swayed closer, she began to piece them together.

Under the sun's bright light, their skin seemed to gleam with every fluid movement. Their body had a masculine form, tall and muscular. The outline of their physique visible beneath a drape of chiffon material. Ceto's mind tried to pinpoint the colour of the outfit but as she watched it, the material changed colour as if it were made of crystal, dancing around the wearer as if it had a mind of its own.

Trying to watch the colours hurt her head and she had to avert her eyes. She tilted her head upwards to the figures' face which was strikingly feminine, with their soft chin, sharp high cheekbones, plump lips, strikingly arched eyebrows and perfectly round eyes. Their eyes seemed to hold within them a magnificent milky way, which glared into Ceto's soul.

Their hair fell pin straight from the centre of their head and down into a pair of impressive wings. She was unable to see where hair stopped and wings began, as both were a brilliant white.

Their wings were held close around their arms as if for comfort. The feathers dragged along the floor behind the figure. Their feet stood firm and bare in the grass before Ceto.

She was speechless in the presence of this creature. She was sure she had never seen anything as flawless. She felt completely insignificant and small in their presence. They were a perfect mixture of formidable male and delicate female.

Ceto now knew that this wasn't fabricated in her head; she knew she would never be able to imagine a creature with this much grandeur and poise.

She dropped her gaze, finding it strange to meet someone who could see her. Not only see her but coming towards her rather than recoiling in disgust. She wasn't sure how to react, she found herself wishing Oscar could be here to guide her. She wanted to turn and run back to the tangled mess of branches she'd left behind, claw her way through them and find her way back home. But then the figure smiled.

"Ceto." A voice of a hundred bells. Deep notes, high notes and all the notes in between.

"You look just like your mother." They clasped their hands together and bowed their head slightly.

"I have been waiting in the tree line for your return home. Come with me, we will have tea. You look a little shaken." They offered their hand towards the forest, gently guiding Ceto.

She didn't move, her legs had finally given up, frozen. The creature gave her a pitiful look, smiled and then reached out their long arm to place their hand lightly on Ceto's back to guide her towards the forest.

One leg stiffly moved and then the other, there was silence as they both moved towards the trees, the only sound coming from the clump of Ceto's heavy boots in answer to the figure's soft rustle of wing and material against the grass.

It wasn't that Ceto was scared, in fact, she felt strangely at ease. Her silence was in response to the fact her brain was working overtime, trying to piece together the onslaught of information she had received in the last few minutes.

How do they know my name? Was the first coherent question that made it to the forefront of her mind.

Once she fought her way through the façade of calm, her instincts began, her stomach twisting with fear.

"No." She planted her feet on the ground and refused to move. Her body language defensive.

Surprise spread across the figures face for a split second, so quickly that Ceto wasn't sure she had definitely seen it. They looked towards the mountain over their shoulder and back to Ceto. Calm spread through her body again.

"Into the tree line, go." They whispered urgently.

Ceto looked at the surroundings for the danger they seemed so afraid of. But there was nothing.

She could tell that her questions wouldn't be answered in the meadow so she reluctantly turned and marched towards the forest once more.

When her feet hit bouncy forest ground, she defiantly turned to face the creature.

"Who are you?" She was embarrassed at the level of rudeness she was emanating, but she held her scowl.

"This way, please." They asked, a little less urgently now they weren't in the meadow.

They led the way deeper into the trees, Ceto followed. She absent-mindedly got caught up with their wings dragging across the ground, kicking up leaves and twigs as if brushing the forest floor, yet their wings stayed dreamily clean, her anger faded as she became entranced.

Chapter 6

After a while, Ceto and the figure arrived at an endearing cottage nestled away in the greenery. It was made of stones and a thatched roof, a small stream of smoke escaped the chimney; it felt familiar.

"Please?" The figure held their arm out towards the cottage. The cottage was unkempt with moss growing up its walls, the windows thick with dust and ivy growing sporadically. In spite of the rundown aesthetic the cottage gave, Ceto didn't feel threatened, she felt peaceful and comforted. Her mind void of urgent questions.

She obliged, ducking her head as she entered the little cottage. She turned to look at her captor once more, her mouth poised for a question but before she could speak, they asked, "Tea?"

Ceto sat on a stool in what she assumed was the kitchen. The house was all one level and it had no interior walls. The kitchen sat directly after the front door, a bedroom lay next to it which consisted of a dust covered bed and a wooden cot. The cot strangled with ivy.

"Can I at least ask your name?" Ceto sounded exhausted.

"Khepri." They answered whilst they filled two cups with tea that had been whistling on a fire, much like the one Ceto had at home.

She took the cup with a thank you, still waiting for them to snap their hand away as many other strangers did.

She took a sip, memories of her mum flooded her mind. This was the tea she used to make, it was refreshing and seemed to warm and soothe her.

"I assume you don't live here?" Ceto asked Khepri from behind her cup, in between sips. They didn't seem to fit in the cottage.

"No, the trees are my home." They chuckled at her question. This unnerved her. Rather than the disgust she had grown used to, was this new stranger going to laugh at her, poke fun at her ignorance, until she went away?

There was a pause whilst Khepri gathered their thoughts.

"This is your home." They waited for Ceto's response but she had become silent.

"I had expected you and your mother…" They trailed off as Ceto glanced down at the ground.

"Ceto?" Khepri's wings rustled with anxiety.

Ceto explained what had happened to her mum, from the first day she had noticed a small difference in her behaviour, the way she would find Adara staring at the distance before her. How she would seem to snap out of a trance when her name was called. How she had grown worse until she was unable to look after herself at all. Up to her mum's gruesome death.

Khepri's eyes darkened, their wings fell low on their back, sadness leaked from their every fibre.

"She was not ill. She had been taken by the man that lives in the mountain. It sounds as if she held on for a very long time, she was an incredibly strong soul. She had a lot of fight in her.

I just wish I could have foreseen this. I wish I could have prevented this." Khepri grew silent now, they both sat there in the gloom, the only light entering through the small front door.

Ceto grew fidgety under the watchful eyes of the magnificent creature before her.

"Urm," she twiddled with a tendril of hair, "how is it that you can stand to look at me?" She let her hair fall over her cheek.

"Stand to look at you?" Khepri asked, puzzled.

"Well, at home, I didn't have many interactions with people. They always seemed…repulsed." She glanced at the ground as every hurtful interaction swam through her mind. "You don't seem repulsed?" She whispered.

"Hmm." They shifted uncomfortably. "I taught Adara a spell of hiding before she left Natus with you. It was supposed to hide you in plain sight. Passers by simply would not be able to see you or interact with you.

But I suppose…" They placed their long finger on their smooth chin and tapped it gently, "if it was not performed correctly, then this would work too?" Khepri pondered for a moment. "Did these strangers forget about you once they had moved along?"

Ceto thought about this, forced herself to relive every interaction. "Yes." She replied in a whisper.

There was a silence as Khepri gave her a pitying look.

"I had a friend, though." Ceto fought back tears at the memory of the friend she had left behind. "He wasn't repulsed by me?"

"No spell is the same, dependant on who casts it and how it is cast. It did not work on your friend?" They said more to themselves than to Ceto. "Perhaps it was fate?" They gave Ceto a glare that leeched into her soul.

Ceto shivered.

"So, you knew my mum?" Ceto offered as a way to change the subject. A thought struck her like a thunderbolt.

"Did you know my dad?" She excitedly shuffled to the edge of the stool, trying to get closer to Khepri.

"Yes." They offered back, careful to leave out any emotion in their words.

Delight filled Ceto from the soles of her feet to the top of her scalp. Her mum had always side stepped her questions of her dad. Ceto had been so persistent one evening, she had made Adara sob achingly; she carried this night around with her always and she had never asked again.

Khepri was smiling down at Ceto now, their eyes full of happy memories and heartbreak.

"I knew your mother, she was magnificent." They whispered.

"I knew your father, he was fiercely kind and full of love."
Khepri frowned, appearing weary.

"It is time you learnt about *you*." They stood up as tall as they
could and ushered Ceto out of the house, she immediately
followed instructions.

Out in the forest, Khepri grew to their full height and
breathed in the clean air around them, their defined chest
rising and falling.

"This is Natus." They twirled, their arms open wide above
their head, and their wings stretched out, creating a gust of
wind that danced with them.

When they stopped, their arms brought down to their sides
with their palms still facing the sky as if absorbing the rays.
Their eyes closed, head tilted back. Ceto thought they looked
as if they had a child's excitement.

"Simply put, the Ignis people live in the south; they give us
light and warmth, they hold the fire and are made up, mostly,
of warriors." Khepri's hands clasped lightly in front of them
as they began to stroll through the forest, stepping over roots
and branches.

"The Azureus people live in the West; they are a calm people.
They live over the sea, offering medicines and *sight*. They
have seers, we used to rely on them to warn us of future
dangers." Their tone grew deeper.

"Used to?" Ceto inquired, but Khepri simply tilted their head
and smiled a smile a knowing teacher might give a very small
child, calming and reassuring.

"You're doing that, aren't you?" Ceto accused. "Calming
me?" She was becoming frustrated that she couldn't feel what
she wanted to feel.

"We are in the East." They carried on, ignoring her questions.
"We are the Folia. There aren't many of us left and we are a
solitary race. We are friends with nature. We play, we teach,
we calm the wind. We guide the seasons." Worry played on

40

Khepri's forehead. Ceto took advantage of their pause and asked, "What are you?" Rather ineloquently.

Khepri blinked in Ceto's direction, seemingly caught off guard.

"I am Folia." They offered to Ceto's eager expression.

Ceto held her gaze and willed them to explain.

"I am everything. Dark and light, male and female, old and young, I am the seasons, I am nature." They stretched their long fingers out before themselves, their nails beautifully pointed. "I am a human figure, but I do not have to be." They seemed confused at Ceto's question, as if they had never been asked this before.

"I'm sorry I interrupted." Ceto smiled.

Khepri rustled their feathered wings and carried on as if they hadn't been interrupted.

"To the North…" Khepri placed their graceful body to rest on a fallen tree, Ceto sat next to them. She understood that they were trying to piece their thoughts together and so she waited patiently in silence.

"The Ventus. They flew above us, kept watch over us. They mined and brought us rock for building and tools, they brought beautiful jewels. They grew herbs for food and medicine."

"Lived?" Ceto lingered on that word. It sent a shiver down her spine.

"There are no Ventus left…they are gone." Khepri explained, forlorn.

"They're *all* gone? They moved or…" She didn't want to finish that sentence.

"They lived in the mountain, until Krokar did."

"The man in the mountain? Did he…kill them?" Ceto could tell by their shoulders that this was a difficult subject to discuss.

"Since Adara…" They couldn't form the word, "Krokar has

41

been able to take over Ventus. I knew something had happened to her when the people of Ventus disappeared. The little strength I have is keeping him at bay for now. Adara was the first barrier." Khepri grew silent.

"Was my mum of Folia?" Ceto changed the subject.

"No, your mother was a seer in Azureus." Khepri proudly answered.

"Oh." She wasn't expecting that.

"Did you never wonder about her eyes?" Khepri asked, a little humour in their tone.

"Honestly, it wasn't until I was older that I started to realise they were different from everyone else's." Ceto chuckled humourlessly. She was beginning to realise that she hadn't known her mum at all.

"It is growing dark." Khepri announced, tilting their head to the stars beginning to glow through the canopy, and Ceto knew she wasn't going to get anymore answers today.

They walked together in silence back to the stone cottage Khepri started a small camp fire in the clearing and put together a meal of various edible plants, roots, mushrooms and potato's. Ceto devoured the meal hungrily and made her way to the small bed inside the house, shaking off the dust and sweeping away the debris to uncover a moth eaten patch work quilt. She shimmied her aching body into the bed and lay her exhausted mind onto her folded scarf. She quickly drifted off to sleep, her anxieties comforted with the happy thought of her mum sleeping in the same bed, keeping watch over a baby Ceto in the cot.

Chapter 7

The next morning, Ceto woke to the sun's gentle golden rays as they stroked her face, warmly waking her.

A clay pot of clean water sat warming above a small flame in the kitchen, a slither of material draped over the side, a sprig of mint leaf sat on the chair beside it.

Ceto gratefully splashed her face with the soothing water and chewed the mint leaf a little, before she made her way outside.

She hadn't forgotten what had happened to her, like the stories of her childhood would lead her to believe. It was all very clear in her mind, but she felt as if she was now gazing on Folia with fresh eyes.

Khepri wasn't around and so she took this opportunity to explore in her own time as she was used to; on her own and in silence.

Closing her eyes and taking a lungful of the sweet air around her. The wind seemed playful today, weaving in and out of her outstretched arms, sweeping her hair this way and that. She stepped to the left and the wind followed, she stepped to the right and the wind followed. She giggled, her shoulders moving up and down.

A feeling that someone was watching her tingled across her skin. She opened her eyes to find Khepri leaning against a tree, amused at Ceto and the wind playing like children. She thought they looked a little out of character to be leaning against a tree, they had seemed so in control of their being, as if they could stand straight for an eternity and not tire.

Ceto let one of her arms drop, the other hugging the first for comfort, her mind drifting to her scarf inside.

"Have you always been friends with the wind?" Khepri asked, swaying forwards.

"I've always been able to sense it. I'd asked mum about it once but she…it didn't seem to be something I was supposed to be able to do." She finished firmly, trying to crush down the memory of her mum's wide eyes when she had asked about it when she was younger. Khepri nodded.

"It's beautiful here. I've always felt most at home surrounded by trees and greenery." She offered to the awkward silence that had started to surround her. Khepri hadn't noticed as they had begun to start a fire in the clearing again. Ceto hoped for breakfast.

"Maybe you are destined to be Folia." Khepri chuckled, more to themselves than anyone else. Their white hair had fallen a little as they bent to care for the flame, they hid their face so Ceto couldn't make out if they were making a joke or not.

"I'm sorry?"

"Well, we do not really know *what* you are." Chuckling, again.

"Excuse me?" This seemed to anger Ceto a little. "I'm human." She offered, feeling a little silly that she had to explain this.

"Oh! You most certainly are *not* human." Still, chuckling. Ceto felt exposed and foolish for being laughed at. This feeling turned to uncertainty and she laughed quietly, a little unsure, along with Khepri. Waiting for them to elaborate their nonsense conversation.

"Adara, she was from Azureus. Aiden, he was from Ignis. I am not sure what you are, but you are not human." Khepri repeated, as if she should already know this.

Ceto had forgotten her frustration and embarrassment, and sank to rest on her knees, sure she was about to pass out from the information she had just gained. A small piece, but powerful.

"Aiden?" She whispered, playing around with the sound coming from her own voice. "My dad?"

"Your father." Khepri reached their hand out and gently placed it on Ceto's knee.

There was a silence again as Khepri went back to preparing

breakfast on the now happily flickering camp fire. It wasn't an awkward silence now, it was a time for Ceto to steady her breathing.

"S-so my dad…Aiden?" It felt strange for her to say this. She had forced herself to become content with never knowing about her dad. But, now she knew, it was as if a flame had reignited inside her and the thirst to know more ran through her body.

"My dad was of Ignis? So surely I'm half Azureus and half Ignis." Ceto shrugged, it seemed that straight forward to her. Khepri looked back at her, their perfectly smooth face blemished by a frustrated wrinkle on their forehead.

"No." They shook their head, feathers rustling on their wings. "I am Sorry." They sighed. "I forget just how little you know."

Another infuriating silence as Ceto watched Khepri push mushrooms and tomatoes around a pan on the fire. She knew they were gathering their thoughts but it was taking every inch of will power to not shout at them until they told her everything from the very beginning.

"It had not been heard of before, we keep to our own kind. It is fate that brought Adara and Aiden together, they should never have even met. But they did, and they had a beautiful baby girl." Khepri smiled up playfully through their white eyelashes. "They came to me for help.

They lived in that house for mere weeks before Azureus and Ignis found out what had happened." Khepri faded out of their story, unable to carry on, the memory of what happened after that, weighing down on their heart.

"I helped Adara escape. I could not help Aiden."

Ceto shook her head a little, for something to do besides staring, open mouthed, at Khepri.

"My main priority was to keep *you* safe. You had to grow up and gain power, to come back here and stop the darkness."

Khepri placed a plate of food in Ceto's numb hands. She used her fingers to eat, not tasting it, not wholly aware that she was eating at all.

"Adara saw the darkness, then she saw you, you were the light."

Ceto nodded, as if she understood. The reality was that she didn't understand at all, but she was starting to feel that it was too much information again. She needed to process.

Another silence as they both sat in the clearing, listening to the rustle of the leaves, the sound of birds grazing the top of the canopy, a caw sounded every now and then, sounding as if it was coming from the meadow. Glancing over at Khepri, they seemed tense.

"Come." They commanded, rising from the tree stump and making their way through the forest. Ceto obeyed.

After a while, they came across the outer tree line and stopped. They were hidden enough so that they couldn't be seen from the outside, but they could see the meadow beyond Folia.

Khepri raised an arm and pointed to the clear blue sky; dotted here and there flew black dots, weaving this way and that.

Khepri moved to point their arm at the meadow; after a few seconds of waiting, Ceto started to notice birds bobbing their heads above the top of the grass as they pecked the ground, then looked around. Ceto knew it was madness but she was sure they looked as if they were *searching* for something.

Khepri waved their hand as if to say 'follow' and disappeared deeper into Folia.

They walked without saying a word. Ceto began with a familiar frustration but it fizzled out the deeper they walked into the sea of trees.

As they walked through Folia, Ceto began to feel a complete sense of ease, as if she belonged here.

The forest changed as they moved and Ceto identified every

tree she could think of. Immense willows drooped over baby fir trees. Great oaks stood tall amongst a sea of silver birch. A coconut tree stood straight and tall, reaching high above the canopy, desperate to soak in the sun. Striking out against the wash of greenery, proudly stood copper beech. Fern, holly, ivy and moss littered the ground and the bottoms of the tree trunks. The deeper they strode, the thicker the foliage grew, the darker the world turned as it blocked out the sun above them. Here in the forest dwelled tiny annoying flies, landing on Ceto's skin and making her itch. They seemed to fly around Khepri but not land on them.

"Are you going to explain what I saw in the meadow?" Ceto grew irritable in the damp, dark and silent forest. Khepri didn't answer, they carried on through the thick undergrowth as it seemed to turn into a jungle, complete with a supressing humid air.

After what seemed like hours of grappling through huge leaves and tangling vines, they finally emerged out into a clearing. Sand dunes surrounding a large clear lake, it sparkled under the watch of the sun.

Ceto took off her boots and jacket, rolled up her jeans to her knees and wiggled her toes in the lake, laying back on her arms. Khepri picked juicy oranges from a nearby tree and brought them over for them both to eat. Ceto had never tasted anything so sweet and she smiled as her taste buds danced at the treat.

"The Raven, they know you are here and they are waiting for you." Khepri gently explained.

"What do they want with me? I'm no threat."

"I am hoping that you are, actually."

Ceto turned her head to glance at Khepri in disbelief, who had a half smile in response.

"Adara believes that you are the key to defeating Krokar." Silence followed whilst Khepri waited patiently for her response. The water seemed to stop rippling, the wind held its breath, the trees stopped rustling. Ceto let out an exhausted high pitched laughter, there was no humour in it. She tried hard to compose a sentence that would let Khepri know how ludicrous their plan was, but all that came out was this laugh.

"I can't do that. I'm completely normal, absolutely unremarkable. What would I stop him with? My amazing super powers?" Ceto exclaimed.

"Well, yes." They replied, oblivious to Ceto's sarcasm. She grew silent, blinked, shook her head and looked out at the lake, unable to think of a better response.

An impatient huff sounded next to Ceto.

"Your lack of confidence in yourself, in *me*, is growing tiresome." Khepri spoke tightly.

Ceto took another bite of her orange.

"I can *teach* you things. I do not expect you to do this on your own, but you have to have a little confidence."

Ceto hugged her knees and lay her head upon them, looking up at Khepri.

"You are already friends with the wind. Ask it to ripple the water." They urged.

Ceto sighed.

"Ask it." Khepri encouraged.

Ceto stood up with an exaggerated sigh, opened her arms wide and glanced at the water ahead of them.

"Magical wind, best friend of mine, pretty please, with a cherry on top, make the lake ripple."

At Ceto's sarcasm, Khepri leaped up from the sand and stood as tall as they could, great wings stretched on either side, anger creasing their once smooth face.

"If you tried for a second, you may just surprise yourself." Khepri enraged.

The truth was, Ceto felt incredibly self-conscious and afraid of failure, but to admit this to an almost stranger felt more terrifying than appearing silly.

"Fine." Ceto nettled back. "What do I ask?"

"You should be able to use your mind. Talk to the wind as you would an old friend."

Ceto instantly thought of Oscar, she spoke to the wind as if she were talking to her old friend. The water rippled just ahead of her. With raised eyebrows, she glanced at Khepri to make sure they had seen.

"Ask the wind to wrap around us."

With a little more confidence, she asked and the wind obliged, playfully billowing their hair and clothes.

Ceto now felt foolish for her childish behaviour moments ago.

"What else can you teach me? I'm sure I can't defeat this Krokar with a gust of wind." Ceto asked excitedly.

Khepri chuckled at this, joy spreading across their face and a little hope, Ceto noticed.

"Come with me." Khepri commanded, placing their long fingers around Ceto's thin wrist.

They walked quickly back through Folia, Khepri's wings carrying them slightly up in the air with every few steps, out of impatience.

Eventually, they made it back to the edge of the forest. Looking out onto the meadow, Ceto noticed it was clear of Raven.

She was about to ask what they wanted her to do, but before she could get the words out, Khepri had hoisted the fabric up to their knee and silently placed their bare foot on the soft grass of the meadow.

Instantly, the screeching of Raven could be heard from the mountains in the distance. Ceto was sure it wasn't a coincidence and a cold panic crept up her spine, her eyes growing wide from realisation.

"You are going to save me." Khepri smiled a dazzling beam down at Ceto.

"No!" Ceto hissed as loudly as she dared.

Before she knew it, Khepri's magnificent form, usually so perfectly held together, was hunched low with their wings pulled tight around their body, as they made their way as far out into the meadow as they dared. Planting their feet firmly, wings pulling in closer with each step. Khepri's piercing eyes met Ceto's petrified ones, willing her to save them.

The world around her grew dull as the vast amount of Raven blocked out the sun's warmth, almost upon Khepri as they stood alone and unprotected.

The Raven circled Khepri now. Fear held Ceto in place, safely inside the tree line.

A few Raven broke off, diving down, faster and faster. What to do? Thoughts, memories, ideas flew through Ceto's mind, each as useless as the last. She searched for a solution, she longed for the strength to save her new friend. Longing turned into anger. Sudden rage at Khepri for putting her in this position, with no guidance other than the wind. The wind!

Please save Khepri? She thought and she felt a gust fly from behind her and towards the Raven. It wasn't strong enough, all it did was slow them down a little but they were still inching closer and closer to Khepri.

Almost upon them now, Ceto was about to give up and run out to see if she could outrun the birds, snatch Khepri by the hand and pull them to safety. Suddenly, each Raven bounced off an invisible dome above Khepri's head, the birds sprang to the floor one by one, unmoving.

When the Raven saw what was happening, more and more came to the aid of their fallen, attacking with strength in numbers. But, like those before them, they rebounded off an invisible force.

Ceto wasn't sure if it was her or Khepri creating the invisible dome, she only knew that she needed Khepri to come back to her.

"Do not doubt yourself!" Khepri shouted from where they stood in the luscious grass and wonderful colour.

The Raven had regrouped and circled above Khepri, teasing their prey. Suddenly, they gathered together and dived in complete unison. A great mass of darkness heading towards Khepri's light, looking helpless and small, completely alone and trusting of her abilities.

Then it all happened quickly.

"Save me!" Khepri shouted from the meadow, a little panic in their voice. Maybe she *was* powerful? Her mum and dad had certain powers, she must have a little of them inside of her? Ceto let the power of her mum flow through her, mixed with the fire from her dad, she clenched up her fists and tensed her body. The Raven were getting closer and closer, she started to doubt herself again and felt the power ebb away.

"DO NOT DOUBT YOURSELF!" Khepri roared in a voice that seemed to ring through the air around her.

Ceto concentrated once more, tensing her body again, the Raven inches away. Closing her eyes, she let out a yell of fear, exhaustion and frustration. Warmth hit the air around her and she opened her eyes wide. The dome she had created wasn't just batting the Raven away now; each bird that hit the invisible barrier caught fire and blew away into the wind as dust, as nothing.

Khepri gently took step after step, making their way back to the safety of the tree line. Ceto held out her hands, as if to hurry them. The Raven admitted defeat and those that were left turned in the air, no longer attacking.

Relief flooded Ceto when Khepri finally reached her, hand in hand, she dragged them the last step. They both stood there, in silence and breathless, watching the black cloud of Raven disappear in to the distance, back to the dark mountains. The smell of burning in the air.

Without a word, Khepri turned on their heel and ambled back towards the hut.

Keeping her fury at bay, Ceto followed.

When they reached the clearing before the hut, Khepri kept themselves busy starting a fire and gathering food, whilst Ceto stood a little way away, silently reeling and astonished at their out of place calm and lack of explanation. As if nothing had happened.

"What were you thinking?" Ceto exploded. Khepri glanced lazily back at her but didn't answer.

"If you have a death wish, please don't involve me in it. I don't need to carry that guilt around with me." She knew she sounded selfish but she was furious with Khepri for their lack of guidance and for making her feel sick with what could have happened. Her chest rising and falling animatedly.

"You are the key." Khepri smiled calmly back. Ceto rolled her eyes and pulled her hands over her face.

"I hate to break it to you, but I have no idea what happened in that meadow." She snapped.

"You saved me." Khepri answered, nonchalantly.

"We don't even know it *was* me!" Ceto was at a loss, she was beginning to realise that nothing she said would sink in. Khepri scoffed.

"I felt your energy, it covered me completely and perfectly." Ceto sighed a great heavy breath and sat on the ground next to the fire.

"I can see your extraordinary magnificence, even if you cannot yet, and I am going to teach you what I can." Khepri reached over and placed a calming hand upon Ceto's.

"I am sorry that this has fallen onto your shoulders, but you are not alone." This sent a calm through Ceto. With the fury gone, she realised how weary she felt and she grew silent, watching the warmth of the fire flicker before her as the sun set slowly in the sky.

Chapter 8

The next few days went by in an exhausted blur as Khepri and Ceto walked side by side, day by day. Ceto asking questions, Khepri explaining and gently building her up. "It is confidence which you lack. The power is already there inside you, you just need assurance." They reminded her time and time again.

As the days passed, Ceto and Khepri grew closer. She would tell them stories of Oscar and Adara.

They were always very attentive when she spoke of Adara, she could tell that Khepri and her mum had a true friendship, much like she'd had with Oscar.

One late evening, they sat huddled around a small camp fire for warmth, the nights growing colder now as summer was drawing to a close.

"The seasons change pretty quickly here?" Ceto asked as she hugged herself, pulling her jumper up to her ears.

"A lot quicker than the season's on Earth; each season will last a month or so here." A frown appeared on Khepri's face. "They are growing unpredictable now, since Krokar began messing with the balance…"

"I know it's not the same, but back on Earth the seasons aren't the same as they used to be either. They seemed to be harsher than I remember them." Ceto mused.

"What happens on Natus, effects Earth directly." Khepri cocked their head at Ceto, "I thought you knew that?"

Ceto was grateful for the darkening night, as she felt her face grow hot.

"I forget what you do not know, forgive me."

Silence grew between them as they each got lost in different thoughts.

"Can you tell me about my dad?" Ceto asked softly.

Khepri smiled into the fire.

"He was a kind man, which is strange for an Ignis. I am afraid he was not well thought of in his home." Khepri took a quick glance at Ceto to see if they had offended her.

"Your mum was extremely fond of him. She was not as narrow minded as the rest of Natus."

Ceto thought this a strange thing to say. How could an entire race be unkind, and think badly of one of their own because they were different? She was sure Khepri was exaggerating. But she let them carry on with their story regardless; she was desperate to learn anything about the mystery that was her dad.

"Ignis can be very unforgiving. It is in their nature to stifle their thoughts and feelings, nothing scares them more than appearing weak."

Khepri picked a long stick up from the forest floor and began to caress the flames as they leapt this way and that.

"He was not weak though, your father." Khepri smiled at a memory.

"He had a strong will. He did not agree with the Ignis way; so unforgiving and unaccepting. They shunned him, cast him out. He took refuge in Folia, he came with me to council meetings he would never have been allowed to go to otherwise." They gave a short laugh and twitched their wing, their smile impish.

"And my mum?"

"Ah, Adara. I had known her for most of her life." Khepri gazed up at the starry sky.

"She was incredibly well thought of in Azureus. They consider their seers their leaders.

It was her duty to confer with the other races regarding the events they had seen. She was an incredible young woman." Khepri grew quiet in thought but after a while, they answered Ceto's unanswered question.

"They met at council meetings. They made sure they did not converse too much, it is against our laws for the races to mix, but I could see there was more between them than that. One snowy day, Aiden offered her warmth from a blizzard that swirled through the trees. He brought her back here," Khepri gestured at the cottage, "and they stayed there for almost a week. That was a bad snow. Right in the middle of spring." Khepri smiled cheekily to themselves and Ceto had an inkling that they may have had something to do with the terrible blizzard.

Calm tears welled in Ceto's icy blue eyes; finally fitting the pieces of herself together was comforting. She ached to be a family with her brilliant mum, full of poise and self-assurance and her dad, full of warmth and kindness. How she longed to have just a single moment of safety and happiness, a single memory to hold on to.

"I have upset you?"

"Not at all." Ceto smiled a tearful grin. "Not all tears are sad."

"For all my connectivity to the universe around me, I fall short on human emotions. I liked to be around your mother and father, their emotions ran so high together; it was intoxicating."

"Do you...do Folia..." Ceto wasn't sure how to ask what she had wondered from the moment she had come across this magnificent being.

"Pairing, children...that kind of thing." She awkwardly blurted out.

"Folia do not procreate. We are not born, we do not die. We live solitary lives." bitterness leaked through Khepri's teeth as they spoke of being alone.

"We do not pair, we do not have children to nurture or love." Ceto nodded uncomfortably, she was afraid she had offended them.

"The wind is our child, the trees are our elders before us. We are everything. Knowledge, nature, we are day and night, summer and winter. We are male and female, we are young and the old. We are born from the ground, and when our time on this land is over, we grow eternally still and enter back into the earth."

As Khepri finished, Ceto gazed at them with new eyes, a sense of insignificance in the company of this ultimate being. But then she felt a wave of sadness for them; she had known solitary in her life. Though Oscar had always beaten away the loneliness the best he could, even he couldn't be with her every minute of every day. She shuffled closer to Khepri, laying her head against their side, a wing wrapping around her.

"My mum, her illness, was that Earthly or something to do with Natus?" She asked sleepily.

"Adara had been placing a barrier through Natus against the darkness. That is why she could not fully be in your world anymore, she had put all of her energy in to protecting us. When the light left Adara, darkness leaked down the mountain and it spreads still. The mountains are far away but the darkness is coming and I am positive you are the key." Khepri replied, but in the protection of their wings, their words didn't scare Ceto, they felt gentle against her ears.

"We're friends, right?" She whispered as exhaustion took over. Khepri's wing hugged Ceto tightly.

"We are friends." Khepri whispered back, and the two fell asleep on the forest floor under the watch of the fire.

The next morning, Ceto and Khepri woke to a blanket of golden leaves; autumn had taken over in the night.
The two didn't take long to wake in the brisk morning and Ceto was glad the fire hadn't died in the night.

"You're burning that, you know?" Ceto gently told Khepri, who had been deep in thought and burnt their breakfast.

"What are we learning today?" Ceto asked enthusiastically. She had become content in her new home in the forest.

Khepri examined the scenery around them.

"The seasons are changing quicker than I had thought. It is time for you to carry on without me. I have taught you all I can, it is time for you to move on to Azureus. They will have answers for you there that are beyond me." Ceto thought she sensed a little sadness in the way Khepri spoke, like a mother would speak to her child leaving the nest; full of stoic logic and anxious concern.

Her breath caught in her throat and a wave of sickness passed through her. She nodded in response.

Ceto guessed she had been walking the forest paths for a few weeks and in that short time, she had become to think of it as home.

With Khepri, she had wandered deep into Folia. Fascinated by the way you could be absentmindedly strolling through a muggy part of the forest, with squishy peat floors and ferns stroking you, and suddenly emerge out onto a landscape you might find on a desert island with sand beneath you and coconut trees swaying high above.

Even though they had walked hundreds of miles in the past weeks, Ceto had a suspicion that she had explored only a fraction of Folia; she longed to spend as long as she needed with Khepri to discover it all.

She knew, deep in her heart, that it was time to leave Folia. She felt stronger and confident, she didn't understand why she had to go on her own though.

"I'd feel better if I had a guide?" She said one afternoon, a little disappointed with herself that it came out as a question, she hadn't intended to come across weak.

Khepri was walking a little ahead, stroking their hands softly against the trees and shrubs as they passed.

"My place is here." They replied.

"No, I know. Of course." Ceto blabbered, looking around her to appear nonchalant, she hadn't realised Khepri had stopped walking and turned to face her.

"I feel you do not understand?"

"No, no, I do. You live here, I need to move on." She didn't understand why her tone was betraying her this way.

I know I've out stayed my welcome and you need to get back to your life. Were the words that ran through her mind, a bitter taste filled her mouth with the thought.

"I am the last defence of Folia." Khepri explained, sorrow in every syllable.

"The *last* defence?" Ceto reached her hand out to touch Khepri, to comfort. Their wings rustled with irritation and Ceto pulled her arm back, a little unsure of the change in emotion.

With a great gust of wind, Khepri had ascended high above the canopy and the screeches of Raven in the distance replied instantly.

"Khepri! Come down!" Ceto yelled but Khepri didn't reply, the caws growing louder. Ceto planted her feet, closed her eyes and concentrated on protecting Khepri. Unable to physically see the danger she wasn't sure if she would be successful. The Raven almost above her now, a cold panic leaked its way through her body.

"KHEPRI!" She screamed, opening her eyes to plead with them. But as she looked up, Khepri had already started to fall slowly back to where Ceto stood, shaking. The Raven passed over the tops of the trees, the force of them almost pulling the trees with them. Loose leaves falling around Khepri and reaching the forest floor.

After what seemed like an eternity to Ceto, Khepri's bare feet lightly reached the golden covered ground, sorrow covering them like a blanket.

"My fellow Folia flew too high. I am the last defence of Folia. I leave and Krokar takes my home for himself, and then there will be no one to stand in his way."

Understanding formed itself in Ceto as her eyes widened and her mouth fell open slightly. She reached her arm out again, to comfort. This time she made contact and wrapped her hand around their arm, a slight tingle running through her palm. She looked up and into their eyes, eyes that had uneased her when they had first met, but had quickly become the reassuring eyes of a friend.

"I wish I could do more." She whispered.

"You have a long travel ahead of you. I wish *I* could do more." Khepri repeated.

The two stood in silence, comforting each other, listening as the wind rattled the leaves from the trees, the remanence of the Raven lingering in the air.

"I'll go in the morning." Ceto whispered, afraid. "You'll show me the way?"

"I will give you everything you need, little Ceto." Khepri wrapped their arm lovingly around Ceto's thin frame and led her back to the cottage.

Khepri busied themselves as they did every evening, cooking and preparing food. This evening, they gathered water and a worn blanket for Ceto to place in her backpack, the way a mother would. Hands on hips, muttering to themselves, trying to not forget anything.

After eating, they sat around the fire, each thinking their own thoughts. Ceto made the fire dance, swirling in on itself and sending out sparks. She chuckled with the wind as it entwined itself through her hair, with gratitude for the fire show. She stopped suddenly when she looked over to see Khepri examining her.

"We Folia know everything, our power is our knowledge but you...you are something completely new." Ceto felt self-conscious at that and let her hair fall around her. Khepri rustled their wings.

"I'm sorry." Ceto whispered.

"Ceto, I am not displeased with you; I am starting to understand you. It is difficult for me; my entire existence I have known everything there is to know about everything…but you, you are very different from anything in this world." Silence followed whilst Khepri shifted their body to sit next to Ceto. "That is not a bad thing." They gently explained.

"How are you doing that to the fire?" They asked. "The same way you commune with the wind?"

"Erm," Ceto was caught off-guard, "No, not the same as the wind. The wind is my friend. The fire…I don't know…I just wanted it to dance and it *danced*." Ceto lamely explained.

"Hmm." Was all Khepri offered in response.

"You can't…" Ceto pointed at the fire.

"Oh no, I do not control the fire. That is the power of Ignis." Khepri replied, hands held up defensively as if they were being accused of a terrible crime.

"Well, my dad was Ignis so maybe that's it?"

"Hmm." Was all she received again.

"Get some rest, and in the morning I will take you to the tree line."

Ceto sighed one last time, turned to Khepri and gave their magnificent body a hug.

"Thank you." She whispered and sleepily stumbled off in to the cottage and to bed.

The next morning, Ceto woke gently to birds singing, leaves eagerly rustling and the smell of cooking.

After washing her face and dressing, she quietly peered out of the front door to see Khepri humming and checking through her backpack. A slight morning mist had gathered behind them.

"Morning." Khepri chimed without looking up.

"Morning." Ceto replied, sleepily. "Do I have everything?"

"I have added a jar of fire, the nights are about to grow

colder." Ceto noticed a little apprehension in Khepri's expression. She put her hand on their arm, as high as she could reach.

"I can do this." She reassured with a new found confidence. Khepri glanced down at Ceto's face, "So much of your mother in you." They said with a warm smile on their perfect features.

"Eat." Khepri commanded, breaking their gaze. Ceto obliged, unsure as to whether she would find comforts like this after she left Folia. As her thoughts went beyond the tree line, an apprehension started in her stomach again. She had to force her food down.

After breakfast, Ceto pulled on her woollen hat, wrapped her tartan scarf around her neck and swung her bag onto her back, nodding firmly at Khepri's questioning glance.

The two unlikely friends ambled silently through the trees as golden, orange and browning leaves fell beautifully around them, dancing to the floor. Autumn was coming fast, the breeze wasn't as soft as it had been days ago. It was sharper now.

At the forests' edge, Ceto began to shiver slightly; partly from the wind that was growing bitter out of the safety and protection of the trees, and partly because she didn't know what to expect over the next week or months…maybe years, who knew how long this would take.

"I have a gift for you." Khepri broke the anxious silence and pulled out a cerulean bundle of fabric from beneath their wing.

"This was your mother's, she would want you to have it. It will keep you warm." Shaking it out, Ceto could see it was a coat of sorts. She gladly took it from Khepri and brushed her arms inside the long wide sleeves, a golden trim running around the cuff. The hem reaching to Ceto's knees. "You are a lot taller than Adara was." Khepri chimed with laughter. "It suits you."

"Thank you." Ceto replied, unable to put in to words the gratitude she felt for her new friend. The coat smelled slightly of her mum, which surprised her as she assumed her mum hadn't seen this coat in a couple of decades. She smiled at the soothing scent.

"Head west." Khepri pointed across the meadow and towards the horizon. "There are seers in the centre that can help you.

Do not stop in the meadow, do not stop until you reach Azureus. The Raven are looking for me at the moment, they thought me dead until the other day; their energy will be on finding me for now. Still, do not stop." Khepri grabbed Ceto by both shoulders and turned her to face them.

"You must reach Azureus before nightfall." Ceto could feel the importance in this last request.

Khepri gave a sad smile and let their arms drop.

"You have exceeded me in many ways. I wish I could come with you, but I have given you everything I can, this is for you to do, Ceto. You were born to save us."

Ceto responded with a forceful hug, wrapping her arms tightly around Khepri's waist, feeling like a child hugging their parent.

She felt great wings wrapping around her, comforting her, and she whispered, "It was nice to make another friend." And with that, Ceto took one step into the dew strewn meadow and in to the unknown.

Chapter 9

Ceto travelled through the morning, the sun rising up behind her and warming her back. She walked as quickly and quietly as she could whilst keeping a constant watch for movement over her shoulder.

She was making good progress through the day and the little huts off in the distance grew slightly larger, whilst the thick foliage behind her grew smaller.

As she made it to early afternoon, when the sun was high in the sky, she began to feel a little tired and thirsty. She glanced around in the skies and grass for any sign of a threat.

I'm sure a second to sit down wouldn't hurt. She persuaded herself, but the wind around her became panicked. She wafted it away, as if shooing away a fly.

"Shush." She demanded.

She lay, hidden in the high grass, watching the white clouds above moving swiftly through the blue sky. Feeling a little chilly, she closed her eyes and concentrated on harnessing the sun's warmth on to her skin.

Ceto fell silent.

The wind raced through the long grass and colourful flowers. It wrapped itself around her, trying to drag her up off the ground. Ceto kept her eyes closed for a moment longer, she could smell the crisp night air and shivered.

Suddenly leaping up, she saw the sun was setting behind the huts out on the sea. Panic set in. She remembered what Khepri had said and glanced nervously to the mountains for any signs of movement.

Ceto ran.

She asked the wind for help, pushing her from behind, making her legs go faster and her inky hair whipped in front of her.

Azureus wasn't too far, if she ran the whole way, she was sure she could make it before the sun set.

She silently cursed herself for allowing sleep in the meadow; but this wasn't the time for self-criticism, this was the time to run.

The sun was minutes away from disappearing now and a low stone wall was coming in to focus.

The border of Azureus.

She wasn't going to make it, she was just too far away.

The world went in to darkness suddenly.

She stopped. Her hair dropped around her. All she could hear was her breathing. Until she heard something else. The gush of thousands of wings in the distance, disturbing the wind.

"No." She gritted her teeth. "I've only just begun, I can't fail yet!" She proclaimed to the world around her.

She focused on the low stone wall ahead of her in the distance.

"Help me." She whispered a plea to the air around her.

The wind came in strong from behind, lifted her completely off the ground for a moment and placed her back down on the soft grass, her feet barely making contact with the ground, the wind doing most of the work.

She could see the low wall ahead of her clearly now, it was quickly growing closer.

Her legs began to burn unbearably and her chest tightened but she was determined not to stop until she reached Azureus.

She was nearly there, she could hear the wings as if they were upon her, she could feel the resistance they made on the air.

"HELP ME!" She yelled at the invisible force all around her and with one last big push, a monstrous gush flung her over the stone wall and landed her on the mushy, short grass on the other side with a painful thud.

The wings didn't seem so urgent now and she could feel that they had changed direction but, without looking back to make sure, she carried on at a run to a steep wooden walkway.

Almost crawling, Ceto reached the walkway that would take her into Azureus. She flopped down at the bottom, the damp wood seeping through her clothes whilst she caught her breath.

"Thank you." She gasped to the wind, clutching at the pain in her chest.

When she had calmed down a little, she glanced up and towards Azureus.

The village seemed tall and daunting, the sea below it crashing angrily against the posts holding the village high above sea level.

She noticed her teeth had been chattering, her body shaking slightly, but not from the cold night that had begun to wrap itself around her small frame.

Fear raced around her body. Anxious and debilitating thoughts making her heart race. She was about to enter her mum's world, the place she was born, the place she had lived most of her life. Had she had friends and family here? Would anyone know her mum? Would they be disappointed with the child Adara had brought into this world? Not a seer, not fully Azureus. Not anything.

Ceto sat there a while, gazing upward, perched on the wet and muddy walkway. It was the cold that moved her on, it had simply become too piercing for here to sit here out in the open, and she knew she had to find shelter.

With heavy feet, she lugged her aching body uphill.

She wasn't sure what she had expected, but when she emerged into the village, she peered through the gloom to be underwhelmed.

Azureus was deserted; the sun had set but it was still early in the night. The large huts on the outskirts seemed empty, there wasn't a single warm glow from any of the windows.

A gust of wind whipped her hair around her and covered her in a salty and cold embrace.

She peered through the window of a nearby hut, there didn't seem to be any signs of life within.

She knocked on the thick wooden door; no answer.

She pushed the door open a crack and waited for a reaction that never came.

Opening the door a little wider and placing her head inside, she spoke, "Hello?" Her voice echoed back to her. There was nobody here.

Ceto made her way inside, closing the door behind her and instantly shutting out the bitter cold, with a long moan from the door hinges.

The hut was perfectly round with no separate rooms. It was completely void of furniture or anything that might make it seem a home. Instead, it had small piles dotted around of wooden crates, fishing nets and crab catchers.

Ceto made her way to the furthest part of the hut from the door, pulled a pile of fishing equipment in front of her, crouched behind it and made herself as comfortable as she could, bringing out her jar of fire for warmth and comfort. Eventually she decided that she wouldn't be able to do much in the darkness and that she was best waiting until morning. She drifted in and out of sleep, startling awake at the smallest noise.

Chapter 10

The next morning, Ceto was woken by the warm orange glow
of the early rising sun coming from a window behind her.
She grumbled to herself about the lack of sleep and her
unwillingness to unfold her body to a standing position.
Eventually she gathered her belongings and made her way out
of the hut, slowly opening the door and carefully examining
outside. She was shocked to find that it was as deserted as the
night before.
Ceto fully emerged now, confident that she wouldn't come
across anyone for the time being.
She turned her attention out to sea and was surprised to find
she could see so much of the village. Azureus seemed to be
built as a slope, the edge closest to land raised higher than the
edge furthest out to sea.
She felt more at ease now that she had a better lay of the
land, a more powerful stance.
Before her, lay an enormous huddle of huts, as far as the eye
could see. At the edge, where Ceto stood, sat large huts,
evenly spaced. Wooden walls and thatched roofs. These
looked down upon the rest of the huts as they dispersed over
the seabed, everything connected by wooden walkways.
As the village angled downwards, the huts seemed to grow
more congested and she could make out hundreds of smoke
streams from the top of the roofs.
So there was life here after all.
Hitching her backpack to a more comfortable position, head
down, nuzzling into her scarf against the sea spray and wind,
she hugged her mum's cloak tightly around her and set off
towards the centre of Azureus. As she walked, the wind gave
an encouraging nudge, Ceto smiled under her cloak.

Through the day, as she travelled further out to sea,
movement grew around her. People going about their daily

business. Sailing out to sea with their fishing equipment, buying and selling from little stalls that would pop up out of nowhere. The smell of salt and fish so strong in the air, it made Ceto's nose crinkle. The wind so cold and wet, it felt as though it was cutting through her skin. She pulled her arms around her middle to keep herself warm. Ceto noticed that the people of Azureus didn't seem to mind the bitter cold. They wore dresses, pants, short sleeves, a few wore shawls or hats. She began to feel self-conscious; those bustling around her had translucent skin like hers, they had blue eyes like hers but her jet black hair stood out in the crowds of blonde. There were variations, ranging from light to dark, but everyone here had blonde hair. Everyone looked strangely similar, and from the odd stares she received, they didn't like outsiders.

Many of the passers-by would stop what they were doing and glare at her, some took it upon themselves to nudge the person next to them, to make sure they had seen this stranger too.

Ceto pulled the large hood of her mum's blue cloak over her hair and hunched her shoulders even more, trying to make herself as invisible as she could. As invisible as she was in her own village.

With her hood up, people seemed to stop gawping and judging and instead, turned to grumbling a low, "Mornin'."

As the midday sun happily perched amongst the clouds high above, Ceto sat atop a turned over crate and delved into her pack to find some food.

As she opened a food parcel, wrapped with a leaf, the smell of cooked fish mixed with herbs and spices hit her senses, her mouth watered at the scent, her stomach lurched with hunger. She hadn't eaten badly in Folia but there had been one thing missing from her diet that she now craved, protein. Turning her head, she used her senses to pick out a cooked food stall amongst the many other stalls selling clothes, fishing nets, the mornings catch and many more delights.

She found it and stood as close as she dared, longingly staring at the food before her, knowing it would warm her shivering body from the inside out.

Ceto's hand slowly went to take the fish, with no thought for the busy scenery around her.

"Ahem." Came a noise from above the food. Ceto snapped her hand back, a little embarrassed. She tucked a stray strand of hair behind her ear that had escaped in the wind. In her hunger, she had forgotten that she could be seen, used to many years of being ignored.

She looked up at the seller, Ceto was taken aback; the seller, a lady, with white blonde hair and shocking blue eyes was looking at her, right at her.

This stranger looked directly in to Ceto's eyes and really saw her. She had never felt seen before, but here this stranger was, *looking* at her.

The stranger's eyes filled with pity and her face changed to a friendly smile.

"You hungry?" The lady asked. Ceto was still processing this blatant interaction with another human, a stranger, and managed a weak nod.

"You got anything to exchange?" The lady continued. Ceto patted down her pockets and shook her head slightly. The promise of hot food slowly ebbing away from her grasp.

The lady sighed and turned her back on Ceto.

Feeling deflated, Ceto turned away from the stall and began to walk away.

"Hey, you! You want this?" The lady called her back.

Ceto lifted her head and ran back to the stall.

The lady had wrapped up a small, warm piece of fish; it smelt divine.

"Thank you." Ceto whispered, taking the slightly greasy

paper.

"'S'alright." She shrugged warmly and carried on with her day as if she hadn't helped a complete stranger.

Ceto ripped open the paper and started pulling bits of steaming hot fish apart, shoving the flakes in to her mouth as quickly as she could.

The warmth filled her stomach and it travelled around her body, not quite reaching her fingers, legs and face but it gave her the energy she needed to carry on a little further.

As the afternoon grew later and the wind grew stronger and colder, Ceto made it to just a few huts from the very edge. Not really knowing what to look for, she browsed at some of the stalls in the busiest part of Azureus.

Here they had fancy stalls, selling clay pots and bright jewellery, intricately woven rugs and cloaks. One stall was selling odd looking ointments and remedies, these reminded her of her mum.

Looking around the stalls, Ceto started to get the feeling she was being followed, but every time she stopped to look around, there was nothing unusual about the dense crowd around her.

After a while of browsing, Ceto looked up to the sky; the sun was setting again, the fish from earlier had well and truly worn off and she had nowhere to sleep once more.

She was starting to think she wasn't cut out for the nomad life.

Just as she felt she was on the verge of giving up, Ceto jumped backwards as a small hand brushed hers.

Looking down, she saw a small girl of about eleven with vibrant yellow plaited hair. Her eyes weren't like the others in the town, they were jet black, just like her mum's had been.

"Come on." The girl squeaked, pulling Ceto by the hand and guiding her through a few side walkways.

Ceto had no issues with trusting the girl, she supposed it had something to do with the astonishing way her eyes reminded her of Adara's, putting her at ease.

Eventually, the pair came to a large round hut. It was the size of those on the outskirts of Azureus, much larger than those around it.

As Ceto grew closer to the front door, she could see the frame was thick, heavy wood and carved into it were shapes of eyes all different shapes and sizes.

The hut had an air of mystery and grandeur about it, although a little rundown. It seemed to be concealed and less open to the elements than the rest of the village. Ceto looked behind to the way they had come and noticed they stood at a lower level to the rest of the village. She wondered if she would be safer to join the hustle and bustle of the market. The sea level rising, the underside of the wooden village visible to her, slimy and green.

Ceto looked down at the young girl; her deep black eyes looking straight up in to Ceto's with an assuring warmth, Ceto's scared silhouette reflecting back in the black pits.

"You can come in." The young girl smiled as if Ceto was afraid of being rude. She pulled on Ceto's hand as if to hurry her along, the way a small child would to their mother. Her hand was icy cold and rough; her mum's hand's had always been that way.

The two girls, hand in hand, stepped over the threshold and in to the large, dark hut.

They left the twilight behind them and descended a dark stairway that felt slippery with wet stone underfoot. At the bottom of the stairway, they entered a dimly lit room.

The hut was similar to the one Ceto had first taken refuge in, only this one had hollows stationed around the outer wall. Each was filled with blankets, pillows, books, melted candles and some had hammocks.

There, in the middle of the large, sparse hut, sat a body of water, no larger than the length of Ceto. An aurora danced across the top, almost touching the water; it reminded Ceto of the Northern Lights.

Around the enchanting water, numerous women sat, stood, hunched, lay, huddled, all staggered around the room, but connected to the water and each other.

The air smelt of musty clothes and damp wood, the atmosphere was stagnant and untouched. Nothing about this place was welcoming in any way. Ceto wanted to run; this was more to handle than the flurry of Raven, at least she was sure of the Raven's intentions, this place was strange and not very welcoming. She found it hard to imagine her mum in this place.

Ceto looked down, but the young girl had disappeared. Feeling as if she'd been led to a trap, she spun around to head back up the stone stairs, but a few steps up stood an elderly woman. She was small and skeletal with silver hair pulled up in to a wispy bun, her eyes the same deep black as her mother's had been, just like the young girl's. She wore a tattered plain nighty and a shawl that had seen better days, her dirty feet bare. Did her mum live like this?

"I'm sorry, I was just leaving." Ceto mumbled to the ground as she tried to make her way up the stairs, her lungs desperate to taste fresh air. But the old woman took Ceto by the elbow and smiled, her black eyes a little watery.

"Come, sit with us, Ceto. We have so much to discuss." The old woman croaked.

Instead of resisting, she let herself be led back towards the centre of the room.

Ceto sat on the cold, wet stone floor, cringing as the damp seeped through her clothes.

She looked around; there was the young girl who had led her here, she beamed, raised her shoulders and gave a tiny but enthusiastic wave from a few places to Ceto's right.

73

Ceto, positioned in the middle of the group, right next to the water, took a quizzical look inside. The water started to ripple a little, as if it were excited to see her. As it did this, one by one, the other ladies started to come out of their meditating states and turned their black eyes to Ceto, excitement showing in their faces too.

Ceto had never been the centre of attention before and she found she didn't care for it.

All the women had a shade of blonde hair, like everyone in Azureus. They all had the same liquid black eyes as each other. The light of the aurora shining in each of them.

"Urm. Hi." Ceto muttered into the echoing silence, giving an awkward hand gesture as if to wave but not quite managing to. The ladies stared at her. She did the wave again.

"Hi, I'm Daylah." Came a little squeak from Ceto's right. The young girl that had led her here had spoken up in the silence.

"Thank you, Daylah." Replied the elderly woman, giving a motherly smile to the young girl.

"My name is Nahlah. Here, drink this, it'll warm you." She handed Ceto a clay cup, full of warm water that smelt of spring flowers and a warm breeze; it smelt like her mum's special tea. Ceto gulped the drink quickly as if it were the first drink she'd had in days.

It tasted as her mum's used to; it felt as though a warm blanket had been draped over her and the cold chill had been sucked from her bones, the floor beneath her felt comfortable and warm now too.

Nahlah gave Ceto a motherly smile and sat, cross legged, facing her, a fraction too close for Ceto's comfort.

"I'm sure you have many questions and I'd like to…" Nahlah began.

"My mother?" Ceto cut off urgently.

Nahlah chuckled, a crackly quiet laugh.

"Very well, you'd like to know everything, I assume?"

"You do know why I'm here, I suppose?" Ceto stuttered, realising that these women had probably seen Ceto coming from a mile away.

"Yes, yes." Nahlah grabbed Ceto's youthful, soft hand in her sand paper, wrinkled one and gave it a few encouraging pats. "You're here to save us all."

Nahlah reminded Ceto of the Grandmother she'd never had. This thought softened her a little and she wiped the grimace from her face and replaced it with a smile.

The ladies began to shuffle along the floor, getting closer to each other and placing a hand on another's shoulder, thigh, hand, foot, whatever they could reach. When this movement began, Daylah shot up and tiptoed through the throng of females to get closer to Ceto. She plonked herself down right next to her, put out her leg for the lady on her right and grasped Ceto's hand in her left, looking up at her and with a big grin she said, "This is going to be fun."

Ceto blinked and when she opened her eyes again, she was back in the meadow. Confusion and a cold panic running through her body. She checked the skies for signs of the Raven but everything seemed peaceful. The sun was warm and high in the cloudless sky, the flowers vibrant and fragrant.

A little ahead of her, she could see a gathering of people. She walked forward but as she did, she noticed the tall grass didn't move out of her way.

"That's weird." Ceto said out loud to herself, but her voice came out echoed as if far away. Her brain working overtime to figure out what had happened. She vaguely remembered being sat in Azureus.

Gaining on the gathered group, her heart stopped as quickly as her body did and her icy blue eyes widened and instantly filled with tears.

"Mum?" She whispered.

This couldn't be real, she had seen her mum on the barn floor, blood spilling from her. She had watched her fade into the air.

What was this? A cruel joke?

She looked young, about Ceto's age, maybe a little younger. Her hair a sharp white blonde and flowing around her like water, like Ceto's did. She looked shy and nervous.

Sat opposite her on a wooden bench, was Khepri, looking exactly the same as the last time they had seen each other.

In between the two, sat a balding man, small and hunched. The man had tanned skin and pointed features, his eyes a piercing yellowish green. His hair a bright white sat in a row from ear to ear, leaving a circle of scalp visible.

Suddenly, Khepri looked up to where Ceto was stood and she gasped.

"Can you see me?" Her voice echoed. But Khepri didn't reply.

"Here he comes." They said instead, a hint of jovial to their tone.

She gave a quick look at her mum. Adara was looking at the ground in front of her, letting her hair flow in front of her face as if to hide it. Khepri seemed to notice this too, it made them smile a cheeky sideways grin.

Ceto had known her mum to stand tall and proud before she had grown ill, it was strange to see her now fidgeting with her nails and her light blue dress, picking at the gold trim at the cuffs.

Turning her head to the right, she saw a giant of a man bounding towards the group. Dark hair that shined beneath the sun. He wore leather trousers and a light linen top which didn't seem to hide much of their physique; their muscles impressive beneath their clothes. He carried a spear in one hand which was covered with carvings and drawings.

"Glad you could join us, Aiden." The man Ceto assumed was

from Ventus drawled.

"Dad?" Ceto took her time analysing the new arrival, knowing that they couldn't see her.

In this stranger, she could see her nose and the shade of her hair, the shape of their eyes were the same. He had a stern look on his face but this melted away when he realised Adara was there and his true nature shone through. Ceto saw kindness in his eyes and a softness to his lips.

He sat on the remaining seat and his head was now the same height as Ceto's.

"Hi, dad." She whispered to him, a tear falling down her cheek. How she would have liked to have known this man. Adara was now busy nervously pushing her hair behind her ear or flicking a glance up at Aiden when she thought he wasn't looking.

Aiden saw every time and replied with half a smile, looking down through his long eyelashes at this beautiful woman.

"Now we are all here and seated, shall we start with the council? As heads, and honorary heads, of our tribes," Khepri gave a quick warning glance at Aiden, "do we have any news on the growing darkness? Adara? Have you seen anything?" Khepri asked gently.

Adara snapped her head up, rolled her shoulders back and sat up straight as if only just realising where she was. She smoothed out her flawless dress over her knees.

Ceto had seen this before; whenever she had asked why she couldn't do something such as going to school or walk down to the village by herself or go to Oscar's house, her mum would smooth down her clothes before giving her an answer, which Ceto now knew, meant she was about to lie.

She was lying now.

"We haven't seen anything. It could just be a shift in the seasons, they speed up and slowdown from time to time, they've done it before."

Khepri narrowed their eyes but didn't push the situation. Instead, replied coolly, "Yes, I suppose."

Did Khepri know she was lying too? They had said they'd been good friends.

"Be sure to keep us informed of anything you might see in the future. If it is something bad, we can stop it if we have enough warning." Khepri said this last bit very slowly, as if trying to give Adara a silent warning.

The four spoke about this and that, wind pressure dropping, avalanches, fires going out in the night, the wind rustling the trees more frantically from time to time, but still, Adara insisted that nothing out of the ordinary was going on in Azureus.

Why was she lying?

Ceto spent the rest of the meeting studying her mum and dad's faces, comparing herself with them both. She had a lot of similarities with both of them.

"I miss you, mum." She whispered to the ghost of Adara, knowing she was unaware of Ceto knelt beside her.

The meeting was now coming to a close and the four members started to go their separate ways, Adara and Aiden both looking back for a last shy glance of each other.

Something was happening, Ceto felt as if she was being suctioned upwards by the head. One minute she was looking at the meadow, the next she was back in the room in the present with the other seer's.

She blinked again and she was stood in Khepri's forest before she could ask any questions about the previous scene.

"We're done with that other bit then?" Ceto echoed sarcastically to herself, finding a little satisfaction in it and hoping they could hear her.

She stood alone in Folia, with nothing but the trees and the wind for company.

There was a rustle in the trees and her mum and dad came

bursting through the foliage to her left.

"Mum! Dad!" She had forgotten her invisibility for a split second, the echo of her voice reminding her. Sadness started in the pit of her stomach and rolled through her body. She had the overwhelming urge to yell how unfair this all felt, but she knew that it would help no one if she lost control of her emotions; she was being shown these memories for a reason. Adara and Aiden stopped, almost hidden by a large tree trunk. Ceto edged closer, unable to hear their hushed tones. Her mum and dad stood hand in hand, Aiden still smiling, Adara's face had turned more serious.

"Aiden, I have something to say and I need to finish talking before you say anything." Adara said, rushing through it and stumbling over her words.

"I'm listening." Aiden spoke with such love and kindness in his voice, brushing a strand of blonde hair behind Adara's ear.

"I haven't been honest in the meetings; I can feel the darkness.

The sea has become more ferocious, the fishermen can hardly get out to fish most days." Adara raced through her confession, adding in quickly, "Then other days its calm again like nothing has happened." As if this bit of information made it okay in her eyes to keep the truth to herself.

"You've had no visions?" Aiden asked, a look of concern now on his face.

"I haven't finished yet, Aiden." Adara whispered. There was a long pause. Adara took her hands away and took a step back. "There have been visions, but they have been changing so often. I didn't want to cause worry before I was sure of what I was seeing." Adara broke off, speaking more slowly now, as if she didn't want to stumble over what she was about to say. "When Khepri married us, and we had our wedding night in the cottage, I went to the stream to fetch us some water and in it…" Adara was trembling now, Aiden tried to grab her hands to steady them but she pulled away, looking down at the ground.

"I had a vision. There were children, a boy and a girl. There is so much darkness around them." Adara closed her eyes, she looked pained.

"Mountains crumble, seas flood, forests burn, flames go out."

"I don't understand, who are the children?" Aiden asked, as if he already knew. Adara placed her hands on her stomach.

"When I think about the child, my visions are sometimes full of darkness, but other times I can see the universe flourishing, it's as if it has conflicting personalities." Adara broke off again. She swallowed hard, as if her words tasted bad.

"And then…I think maybe…maybe I can't risk the child being born…the visions stop altogether then.

Do we risk it? Is it our risk to take? There's a herb I can take…" Fierce tears were now falling down Adara's pale cheeks. Aiden was swiftly at her side, wiping the tears away with the back of his hand, just like Adara used to do to Ceto. Ceto longed for them to turn and look at her, to wipe the tears away from her face too.

"We're having a baby? This is the best news." He said soothingly. Adara looked up at Aiden.

"You're not listening." Adara spat through gritted teeth.

"We could destroy everything through our own selfishness. No one has had a baby from different corners of Natus, we don't know what it could be." Adara was visibly shaking now.

"But I am listening, you're telling me that this baby is a little bit of me, and a little bit of you.

If you're unsure as to whether it will have the dark life you've foreseen or the light, we will guide it together and make sure it's the light." Aiden's absolute certainty that they could do this together seemed to soothe Adara. She was still breathing heavily, her body shaking and tears still streaked her face, but she was nodding now.

Ceto had the sensation of being suctioned again and the forest melted away around her and she was suddenly back sitting on the cold wet floor, with a few dozen pairs of eyes watching her, waiting. They had seen what she had seen and they were waiting for her reaction.

"That was real?" It wasn't really a question, somehow, deep down, she knew that had happened.

"You are everything good in this world." Nahlah patted Ceto's hand reassuringly.

"You seem to have all the elements within you and you can harness the powers of what you need from the four corners of the world." She pulled Ceto's gaze in with her own, to make sure she was listening.

"Everything needs a balance, in nature, your balance is the darkness.

When you left with your mother, the darkness had no balance and it has been steadily growing over the years, unchecked."

"But I didn't want to leave. Why did we leave?" Ceto's eyes narrowed.

"There's something you're not telling me."

The women huddled around her stayed connected to one another but seemed to shuffle a little, restless. Ceto turned her stubborn expression back to Nahlah. She had to know what had happened to her dad, it had been slowly gnawing at her insides like a parasite, cutting a hole inside of her.

Still, silence covered them. She could hear the crashing waves just below where they sat, the howling wind high above them, a continuous drip, drip, drip, off to the side, slapping against the cold harsh ground.

A few of the older ladies had stood up and walked away from the situation and taken refuge in the hollows.

Ceto took to glaring intensely at Nahlah now, unrelenting.

81

"We made a mistake." Nahlah sighed in a whisper. Her ancient body hunching further from shame.

"A mistake? One bad enough so that I never knew my dad? What kind of mistake?" Ceto could feel her overreacting rage as it quivered inside of her. She had always tried to keep her emotions in check, what purpose did they serve? But now, it was impossible. She had let herself go for a moment and now all of her pent up feelings were being thrown at a frail elderly lady.

A wave of shame crashed through her anger, but before she could apologise she was being thrown into another memory.

The wind was strong and angry in the meadow, the night was dark with no light from the moon and Ceto could hear shouting in the distance.

To her right, she could see a huge fire reaching to the sky above, to her left, she could see a huddle of people, carrying fire, struggling trying to drag a heavy bundle from the trees. She ran over to the huddle of people. As she got closer, she could hear a woman's screams, filled with panic and pain, "Let him go! Let him go!"

A baby was screaming a high pitched cry as they gasped for breath; the noise made Ceto's ear prick up painfully.

Getting closer now, Ceto could see it was her dad being dragged across the floor, from the forest and towards the blazing fires of Ignis.

"DAD!" Ceto yelled, her voice echoing again, violent tears spilling out of her eyes.

The vision began to change again, flickering from the excruciating scene unfolding, to Nahlah's ashamed face and then Ceto was back in the forest, facing her mum and Khepri. Adara had a baby Ceto in her arms, bouncing her up and down trying to stop her wails.

"Khepri. Stop it. Stop them! Please do something, is there nothing you can do?!" Adara screeched at Khepri through great heaving breaths.

"They've taken him! They're going to send him to the fire! Please, don't let them take him away from me, from us!" She pleaded with a stoic figure.

Khepri placed a long hand on Adara's shoulder.

They then looked through the trees ahead of where they stood.

Ceto looked to her right to where Khepri was looking.

She saw smoke in the distance, above the tree line

A few sparks of fire dancing in the air and suddenly the fire must have risen a great height as the tops of the flames grew higher than the tree line, dying down as quickly as they grew.

Khepri simply said, "It is done."

They had no emotion in their voice but there was true pain etched in their smooth skin and a single glittering tear, as if a small crystal had been placed in the corner of their eye.

Adara fell to the ground, giving out one last hopeless yell in to the air. It was filled with so much suffering, and then she stopped.

Kneeling on the floor, screaming baby in her arms, she stopped crying, she stopped begging for help, her breathing became shallow, her face became detached from the pain she had felt only moments ago.

"What do we do now?" She asked, determination filling every syllable.

"You have to leave. They are coming for her." Khepri replied, plainly.

Ceto was suctioned out of the heart wrenching scene and back to the present with Nahlah.

"They fed your father to the flame. With the help of Khepri, your mother fled with you." Nahlah concluded. There was silence except for Ceto's fast deep breathing and soft whimpering.

"We became scared when Adara came to us. We told Ignis.

83

We knew they wouldn't be understanding, but we told them anyway." She hung her head. "I'm so sorry."

Ceto processed and became prickly as she began to piece the onslaught of information together.

"So, I was born," Ceto summarised, "My mum came to you for help and you turned both of them to Ignis even though you *knew* they would try to kill us? Have I got that about right?" Ceto hissed. Nahlah nodded slowly, her eyes closed. "Why stop there? Why didn't they kill all of us? I mean, I'm the real threat, right? They let us go without ever trying to find us? That doesn't make sense." Ceto's jaw hurt from clenching it so tightly, she ran her hands along both sides of her cheeks and down her neck, as if she was trying to wipe away the memories she had witnessed.

"From what we can gather," Nahlah explained, "Khepri told them that you had both died whilst trying to transport you to safety."

Ceto nodded to show she had heard but she didn't have the energy to reply with words.

"Since then, the darkness has been growing slightly with every season.

It used to be so peaceful here, bright sun, turquoise sea, a warm breeze, now it's bitter."

There was a pause whilst the other ladies shuffled around, having done their job for the night. Some went back to their own space to meditate like before whilst others retreated to their hollows and lay down for the night.

Daylah stayed by her side.

"Years ago, we would work in harmony, the four corners. We balanced each other, our ancestors became jealous and bitter of each other and slowly, each race began keeping to themselves. Speaking only when they needed to. And then Adara and Aiden broke what little harmony we had left. Now we don't leave our own." Nahlah tried to explain but it was just making Ceto heated again. Had she any energy left, she would have screamed at the frail form before her. But instead she gritted her teeth.

"They loved each other, what does it matter where they are from or who they are. It *shouldn't* matter." She hissed.

"Ceto," Nahlah sounded tired herself now, "It's our most sacred law." She spoke now as if talking to a child.

"There was no knowing what the act would bring.

Each corner brings something to the world and when you start to mix that…we didn't know."

Nahlah raised her hand a little above her head wafted it around.

"We used to be draped in beautiful cotton gowns of sky blue and gold and now we wear these rags." She looked around at her ladies, huddled in corners, unkempt and unwashed.

"No one in Natus wants to hear what we have to say now, each corner looks after their own." She gave a single humourless laugh.

"We now know that we were wrong all those years ago. We should have helped Adara and Aiden, united the four corners, but instead we played a big part in breaking this world.

Now Ventus has suffered, all those that are gone because we are not united." Nahlah grabbed Ceto's hand once more and examined her face, as if she was looking at her for the first time.

"You can unite us now. That's how you beat Krokar. Unity!" The sadness and regret had fallen from Nahlah's face and replaced by excitement and hope.

"I'll help." Chirped Daylah.

Ceto jumped, she'd forgotten little Daylah was there. She was such a small bundle of chipper.

The other women were considerably older, Daylah was the youngest in the group by decades.

It was as if time and circumstance had squashed down these

powerful women and they'd given up, wasting away as they resided in this dingy hole.

Nahlah smiled her grandmotherly smile again, down at the girl.

"I think Daylah will be good company, she certainly knows how to keep everyone's spirits up." Nahlah croaked a little as she chuckled, poking a playful finger at the young girl.

Ceto nodded in agreement, she was still too exhausted to give much more.

"I'm not sure how Ignis will take to you both. You must ask for warriors to help you; they may not be willing. But, Daylah, if you feel ready, I'd be proud to send one of my own out on this important task." Nahlah added.

Daylah beamed, whipping her head from Nahlah to Ceto, almost comically.

The thought crossed her mind that she was probably longing for company other than those her senior. Ceto could relate to that before she'd met Oscar. As a small child, she had always wished for a friend her own age. Ceto also felt desperate for the company on her uncertain adventure.

She peered down at the young girl, it would be nice to have a cheerful presence alongside her. There was something about Daylah that drew Ceto in and made her feel at ease and warm.

"Okay." Ceto smiled.

"Okay." Daylah echoed, but with more enthusiasm.

"Rest a while." Nahlah interjected in to the excitement.

"You'll need the energy and I'll gather some essentials from the market for you."

Daylah took Ceto by the hand, dragged her from their seated positions on the stone floor and brought her over to her hollow.

"Before you rest," Nahlah had followed them, tapping Ceto gently on the shoulder.

"I wasn't going to ask…of course we've seen but…may I see with my own eyes, what happened to Adara? At the end…" She stuttered, trailing off at the end.

Ceto pursed her lips and nodded. Nahlah took Ceto and Daylah's hands so they were stood in a joined circle.

Ceto brought the night of her mum's murder to the forefront of her mind, forcing herself to relive it. Slightly pleased to show Nahlah what had happened, in the hope she would feel a twinge of guilt.

"I see." Nahlah pulled her hands away, dropped her head and shuffled away.

Daylah turned her attention back to her little space, seemingly forgetting what she had witnessed. Ceto followed her lead, unable to relive the worst moment of her life again.

In the hollow, there was a ledge with a melted candle stuck to it, a hammock made from a fishing net and a bundled up blanket under the hammock.

"You take the bed," Daylah excitedly babbled and pointed at the hammock, "I'll sleep below you." Her naïve energy warmed Ceto.

As Ceto looked around, more and more of the women were breaking off and getting in to hammocks of their own or huddling down on the floor and pulling damp blankets over themselves to settle down for the night.

How depressing the sight was. Ceto tried to picture what it would have looked like in here many years ago, when her mum had lived here.

With a sigh, she hopped on to the hammock. It was surprisingly comfortable. She pulled her mum's cloak around herself and up to her chin.

The tea from earlier still inside her body, keeping the chill away for now, Ceto drifted off to sleep, towards dreams filled with angry fire and harsh winds, falling trees and birds flying menacingly around her.

Chapter 11

Ceto woke a few hours later to the sound of dripping water. She didn't open her eyes at first, convinced that she was in a cave as the dripping echoed off the damp walls. Confused, she opened her eyes and blinked as she took in her surroundings, letting her brain catch up for a moment. Realising that everything she'd been through and learnt over the last few weeks wasn't a strange dream she'd had. She sighed and slowly pushed herself up.

She knew she'd had some sleep but how much she couldn't say for sure. With no windows and the hut being set so close to sea level, no natural light seeped into the damp room and her body ached. She felt drained of energy still, she wished she could lay down and close her eyes for a little longer. Just as she started to lay back down, the bitter cold ate through her bones and made her shiver. The distinct scent of cooked fish filled her nostrils and her stomach growled angrily.

With a sigh, Ceto pulled her body up and flopped down with a squish as her boots hit the wet slimy floor.

She made her way to the centre of the room where a few ladies were busy cooking long meaty fish on a grill with smouldering coals beneath. They glanced up at her, smiled an awkward smile and turned back to their task.

Ceto felt extremely self-conscious and out of place in Azureus, her black hair flowing amongst a sea of blonde. She had always been in tune with what those around her were thinking and she had a feeling in her stomach that the people of Azureus felt wary of her. She couldn't help but feel disappointed at this realisation. From the moment she'd learnt that her mum was from a race of people in a strange land, she had assumed she would fit right in with them, having thought herself similar to her mum growing up.

"They're not used to seeing any outsiders." Came a small

voice from Ceto's shoulder.

Daylah's face seemed to fill Ceto with a bright warmth and she smiled sincerely back at the young girl.

"I'm going to have to get you a bell to wear." Ceto joked.

"Err. Okay, I can if you need me to." Daylah replied, a little unsure, the enthusiasm falling from her face.

"I was joking." Ceto chuckled.

Perking back up again at the clarification that she wouldn't have to wear a bell, Daylah grabbed two clay mugs and filled them with the same spring smelling tea that Ceto was given last night.

"I'd wondered where you'd sneaked off too, I looked up and you were gone." Daylah placed her small hand inside Ceto's. "I thought you'd gone without me."

Ceto gave her hand a supportive squeeze and smiled down at her again.

Daylah led Ceto to where the food was being served and they ate and drank in silence, listening to the meal time bustle around them.

As Ceto hungrily ate her food of fish and bread, she was aware of inquisitive eyes examining her.

"That's a little off putting." She commented in relation to the eyes on her, not taking her eyes off her food.

"It's not the best tasting food, so I'm told. The others say that the fish here used to taste sweet but now the water has made it tough and salty. It's all I've ever known and it fills the hole in my stomach." Daylah patted her stomach as she said it, unaware that they were being watched.

Ceto was beginning to suspect it would take a lot to take Daylah's optimism and perky energy away from her.

"A lady in the market gave me a fish yesterday and it was pretty tasty." Ceto told Daylah.

"They put herbs and spices on fish in the market but they're hard to come by. You must be lucky." Daylah looked up at her new friend, a little awe in her round face. Ceto smiled encouragingly.

As the girls were finishing their breakfast, Nahlah shuffled her way over to them, half dragging, half carrying a pack that looked as if was made from an old ragged dress, tied at the top with fishing line and a bit of rope to go over the shoulder. "Your pack, Daylah. Ceto, I've filled yours with supplies." Nahlah said, pointing to just inside the hollow where Ceto's pack rested against the wall, looking very full.
"Thank you." Ceto smiled up at Nahlah.
"It's time to go. You can't waste any more time here, you need to get to Ignis before night falls. You don't want to be-"
"In the meadow at night, I know." She interjected, she wasn't going to make that mistake again.
Standing up and throwing her pack over her shoulder, she looked down at Daylah, "Ready?" She asked.
Daylah beamed up at Ceto, "Ready." And she took the pack from Nahlah, swinging it over her shoulder and grasped on to the rope to keep it from slipping.
Nahlah shuffled over to the stairs that led to the busy market above, the girls followed. She stopped at the bottom of the stairs and turned to them both.
"The best of luck to you both, you should have everything you need in your packs. Daylah," Nahlah turned to the young girl, "If you need any guidance we're with you. All you have to do is ask." She placed a weathered hand on her young shoulder, giving her a knowing look.
Nahlah turned her attention over to Ceto now. "I am very sorry for the part I played in breaking your family. Aiden was a good man and he didn't deserve what happened." The gentle hum of meal time from behind the three of them had suddenly gone silent as the women stopped to listen.
"You didn't deserve what happened, I see that now. I see nothing but light inside you. Your mother and father would

be so proud."

Tears welled up in Ceto's eyes but she fought them back, "Thank you." She sincerely replied.

Daylah scooped up Ceto's hand and the two girls ascended the spongey stone steps, up into the late morning light.

They were greeted by the busy throng of the market, and with Daylah leading the way through the winding walkways, the bustle became quieter and quieter until they had made their way to the outskirts of the village. It was almost silent here apart from the strong crashing of waves below and the harsh gust of icy wind.

The two girls walked side by side down the steep slope that was the walkway between Azureus and the empty meadow. After the walkway, the two dredged through the muddy patch of land, and stepped over the low wall, then Daylah stopped and looked back from where they'd been. The village looked deserted, it seemed strange that in the heart of Azureus was a busy, bustling town full of movement and energy but on the outside, it looked like a ghost town.

Daylah looked up at Ceto and said, "There aren't many that will live on the outskirts now, many find refuge in numbers right out to sea."

She sighed and looked out into the meadow.

"We don't have that advantage, do we?"

Ceto bumped her hip gently on Daylah's arm.

"No, but we're not alone." She reassured.

Looking out in to the distance, the sun low, bright and orange in the sky, warming them as the wind chilled them. The trees in Khepri's forest across the meadow had almost shed all their leaves, the ones that were left danced like flames in the breeze.

Ceto pulled her cloak tightly around her body.

"I swear, it was like summer when I got here a few weeks ago." Ceto mused, more to herself than anything.

"The seasons are turning faster than they're supposed to, it's nearly winter. No one can keep track anymore." Daylah replied, adding, "We'd better move a bit faster if we want to make it to Ignis before nightfall."

There was something about Daylah that reminded Ceto of an adult, she had a logical mind. She felt pity for the young girl who had probably had to grow up too fast.

The girls had some distance to cover, moving through the meadow to the right of Azureus.

Time seemed to pass quickly as Ceto asked Daylah about her childhood, where her parents are, what it's like to live with the other women in the damp room.

As far as Ceto could tell, Daylah had lead a strange life to the one she had known herself.

When she was only a few months old, her eyes turned from blue to black and her parents had no choice but to hand Daylah over to the seers.

She spoke about it so nonchalantly, apparently it was what was done and usually a child's eyes didn't start turning until they were about Daylah's age.

"But I suppose that makes it easier because I've never known another life. It'd be harder if I got to know them and then had to leave." She added.

For someone so young, probably not quite a teenager, Daylah was very old headed, Ceto thought to herself. But for all her wisdom, Ceto could see vulnerability and the kind of fragile frame you would expect from a child. She was beginning to feel fiercely protective of Daylah.

"What was your childhood like?" Daylah went on to ask. This shouldn't have been such a difficult question to answer.

She wanted to say that it was a good childhood, full of laughter and love, but then, as she thought about it, she realised she had more resentment about her childhood than she'd known.

"Sorry, I didn't mean to pry. Obviously I know where you've come from, we all saw, but I just wondered what it was like for you growing up with your mum, on Earth." Daylah spoke quickly and apologetically.

"It fascinates me, I want to go there one day. Watch the sun rise and set as it should, watch the seasons turn as they should, watch the humans blissfully unaware that it all doesn't just happen. I'll go and see for myself one day." Daylah smiled at the far off thought.

There was a pause whilst Ceto deliberated with herself the pros and cons of opening up to a stranger. She felt comfortable around Daylah, as if she were her little sister that she'd always known.

"It's okay. My childhood was great, on paper.

I had a mum that was always there for me, always looking out for me, always fed me, clothed me, knew the right things to say when I was upset or scared.

I had a friend, Oscar, he would always cheer me up no matter what.

But then, I had no interaction outside of my home bubble. The worst part is, my mum let me believe it was because I was different, that it was my fault I couldn't make friends when really…" Ceto looked over her shoulder before her expression had the chance to give her feelings away. Gathering herself, she looked down to Daylah, who was looking up with concern on her face.

"My childhood was great, my mum did everything in her power to keep me safe. I just know now that there could have been more to life. But like you say, I've never known that life so I suppose I can't miss it."

Daylah didn't look convinced, she was looking at Ceto as if she was made of glass, a crack forming in her mask.

"You'd better look after me." Ceto joked as she knocked Daylah slightly with her hip again.

"You didn't know I was completely useless, did you?"
The two girls laughed a little and went on to lighter topics, Ceto felt desperate to change the subject.

The sun grew higher in the sky and their shadows stretched out further before them. They were making progress as the smoke ahead grew closer.

"We've had a surprisingly uneventful journey so far." Daylah mused.

As she said it, Ceto felt a sudden dread fill her stomach, she felt the air shift as it blew strongly against their backs. She had a strange feeling that the sudden gust of wind was coming from the underside of a thousand or so wings taking flight, she could see it in her mind's eye.

The two stopped in the long grass and waited, holding their breaths to better hear the first sound of flapping wings.

After a few moments of nothing but the rustling of breeze rippling through the grass, they let out a sigh of relief and chuckled nervously to each other.

"Come on, it's nearly night, we're not far now." Ceto encouraged.

The tops of huts could be seen off in the distance and smaller pillars of smoke could just about be made out in the twilight haze.

Just as they set off again, at a slightly quicker pace, they heard it before they felt it.

The whoosh of wings' resistance against the air and a great gust of wind at their backs again.

Daylah peered at Ceto with large round, dark eyes and Ceto could see her heart dropping as she was reflected in them.

"They're coming." Ceto whispered, closing her eyes and pleading with the wind to aid her again, but all she could muster was a slightly stronger breeze against her legs.

Looking behind, Ceto could make out what looked like a dark cloud spilling out of the top of the mountain, like an erupting volcano.

"Ceto? What do we do? Will we make it if we run?" Daylah asked, her voice breaking as she tried to keep her fear under control.

"We don't really have a choice. Come on!" Ceto grabbed Daylah's hand and pulled her through the grass, whilst still willing the wind to give them the little push they needed.

As they ran, the long green grass turned to short, yellowing grass. The further they ran toward Ignis, the less green it became, but dry and scorched.

Ignis couldn't be too far away now.

Ceto had one more desperate plan, instead of willing the wind to push her, she willed it to race to Ignis to get help. As she asked, the resistance against her legs lessened.

She could see the dried grass ahead move slightly and then stop, she knew it had worked.

She felt a tiny bit of relief for a split second until her ears tuned back in to the sound of ferocious wings behind her, gaining on them both.

"Ceto, they're here!" Daylah yelled in between gasps for air. Ceto could barely hear her over the noise now, the Raven were too close, almost right above them.

She stopped suddenly, pulling Daylah over onto the burnt grass as she clasped tightly to her hand still, determined not to let go.

"Ceto! Come on! What are you doing?! We have to run! Ceto?! Ceto look!"

Chapter 12

Daylah tilted her head to look above her, still sat on the ground, one arm high in the air as her hand was clamped tightly in Ceto's.

Daylah hurled her other arm above her head and closed her eyes tightly, bracing herself for the inevitable pain.

Nothing came, no pain.

The sound of wounded screeches could be heard amongst the flapping of wings.

Daylah peered up to see Ceto stood above her, straight as a pin, both arms by her side, one hand clasping Daylah's, her eyes shut as tightly, her deep black hair whipping around her face and shoulders as the wind was coming from all directions.

Above them both was an invisible shield that the Raven couldn't penetrate.

As they flew straight as arrows down towards the girls, then bounced off; some rolling to the ground, some flying back to the safety of the mountain.

Daylah slowly stood up, not taking her wary eyes off the Raven but taking Ceto's other hand, encouragingly.

Ceto started to breathe a little harder.

"I can't hold on much longer." Ceto said through gritted teeth. As Daylah peered into Ceto's face, she could see that she was barely with her anymore; all her strength was now focused on the Raven.

A few seconds later, there was a rumbling of thunder added to the sound of the Raven.

Just what we need, a storm. Daylah thought.

But something wasn't right, the thunder was continuous and grew louder by the second.

Spinning around, she could see horses off in the distance racing towards the girls.

"Ceto, they're here, they've come to help." Daylah said with half relief, half fear.

Just as she said it, Ceto crumbled to the ground exhausted and the invisible shield disappeared.

Looking up, Daylah could see the Raven circling and regrouping, ready to try their attack again.

Suddenly, a wall of spears flew into the air and towards the Raven. Some landed, others stood still in the ground behind them. At the sight of the Ignis warriors, the Raven turned in the air and retreated, back to Ventus.

Daylah looked down at Ceto, her eyes were closed, she didn't move.

Daylah rocked her shoulder back and forth, gently.

"Ceto, they've gone, the Ignis are here. Ceto, wake up." Daylah pleaded, struggling to get the words out, her mouth dry and with a taste of ash.

Ceto's breathing was very shallow, but Daylah had naïve hope that she would wake up.

Horses encircled the girls on the ground.

"Who are you?" Demanded a very stern man on the back of a brown horse.

"Please, help us? My friend is exhausted, please? She won't wake up." Daylah pleaded.

"Who are you?!" Demanded the same man, a little more stern this time and not showing any signs of helping.

"M-My name is Daylah, from Azureus…" She dropped the hood on her cloak to reveal her blonde hair.

The men and horses shifted uncomfortably around them. She mustered her courage and pretended not to notice,

"-this…well…this is Ceto." Daylah finished, rather feebly.

Was she supposed to tell them who Ceto was? She wished Ceto would wake up and take the lead. Daylah felt lost without her.

"Ceto from?" The man demanded again.

"Ceto from…Earth?" Daylah shrugged.

Whether it was the right thing to say or not, it was said now. The men began to look at each other. Some grunting disdainfully, some with confused shrugs, most breaking ranks to discuss the news.

The stern man gracefully leapt off his horse and crashed to the ground, sending dust flying over the girls on the ground.

"Ceto from Earth." He said, a little softer. This time it wasn't a question.

He scooped her up, draped her over the top of his horse and leapt up too, sitting behind Ceto's lifeless body.

"Go home, sea-girl." The man jabbed at Daylah.

"You can't take her! I have been picked to accompany her. We are on a mission!" Daylah stomped after the horseman, with an air of importance as she said it, finding confidence in the panic that buzzed through her body.

The man didn't stop, but trotted off towards Ignis, without saying a word, clearly finished with their conversation.

Desperation swelled inside her as the other horsemen followed the stern man and took Ceto away from her.

"You don't know who that is! What are you going to do with her? You need her, more than you know. We all need her!" Daylah yelled after them, as she stood forgotten, alone and tiny on the burnt grass.

The horseman stopped, sighed and turned his horse around to face Daylah, trotting slowly back towards her.

Daylah puffed out her chest, as if she had made a difference to the decisions of this strong man, but also quite afraid of his massive presence; she planted her feet and stood up tall.

"I know exactly who this is." He scoffed

"I'm going to wake her up and she's going to tell me the information I need to know. Information about her father and mother." The man's face turned to disgust.

"You're not welcome here, child. Leave our lands, or wait for the Raven to return. It matters not to me, which course you choose."

The horsemen then turned their backs on Daylah, horses whipping their tails in dismissal, and headed in to Ignis. Feeling deserted and powerless, furious tears ran down Daylah's face, and as she watched the horses grow fainter, carrying her lifeless friend with them. Her tears lost their ferocity and turned to tears of sadness and helplessness.

"I can help you." Came a voice from behind her.

Daylah jumped and fell to the ground again, spinning her body around to see who it was.

She saw a great black horse edging out of the darkness, hidden by the night.

Atop the horse sat a young man, with matted shoulder length hair and broad shoulders.

He reached his arm down for her to hold.

"Come with me." It wasn't a question, Daylah didn't have a choice.

She had heard remarks about the Ignis around the market; how stubborn they were, how blunt and demanding.

Well, so far, she could see that was a correct account of these people.

With an obvious sigh, she grabbed the young man's hand and was pulled through the air. She let out a small "oh" as she suddenly found herself on the back of the horse, sat in front the young man.

"Hold on, we need to catch up with them." He said. Without any indication from the rider, the horse took off through the burnt grass after the horsemen and towards Ignis.

As Daylah and the helpful horseman came closer to the very edge of Ignis, the horse beneath them began to slow down until they were travelling at a very slow saunter. This pace made Daylah very impatient.

"We have to get to Ceto, before they hurt her." She muttered through gritted teeth.

"If we go any faster than this, we will draw attention to ourselves." He shot at her.

"Put your hood up. Your hair stands out like a beacon." He added bluntly.

Daylah didn't feel safe with this man, but she could tell he was a little different to the first rider who had taken Ceto. She sighed, she wasn't going to win a battle of the wills with an Ignis. She chose to trust him instead.

Looking around, the Ignis lived in huts, much like the Azureus but instead of wood they were made from dried mud.

The outer walls had different paintings on them; from what she could make out from the various fire lights all around, some were covered in different patterns in multiple colours. Some showed scenes of war, Ignis on horses spearing down those around them, others had prints of fire on them or symbols Daylah recognised from books she'd read back home meaning protection, strength or warmth.

She'd never seen anywhere other than Azureus before, but she found the scenery around her fascinating. Unable to see the world, she had kept herself sane by reading and learning about it. She was a fountain of knowledge for all of Natus. Her longing to explore was being satisfied but her mind had only one thought; where was Ceto?

Ignis was set up differently from Azureus, aside from the obvious; that is was a heated place with hardly any breeze. Instead of the dwellings being sparse on the outside and growing more compact in the centre, here they were very close together and haphazardly placed as if they had been constructed in a great haste. The closer to the centre they were, the closer to the great fire, the larger and more spaced apart they were.

"Why are the huts so congested on the outskirts?" Daylah asked, curiosity getting the better of her.

"They are for protection. They don't have families in them, they are set up for the warriors to sleep in so they are the first ones to know of any danger.

Closer to the great flame, that's where the families live, under our protection." The horseman answered proudly.

That made perfect sense to her and Daylah found herself wondering why Azureus was constructed as it was, with the families on the outside.

Unlike her elders, Daylah wasn't afraid of change and she could appreciate a good idea when she saw one.

She knew of others from the younger generation that felt this way too. Unfortunately, the older generation, the ones who made all the decisions, did not feel this way.

They were stuck in their habits and saw change as something to fear.

"What's your name?" Daylah softly asked, warming to the man sat rigidly behind her.

"Quidel." He sternly replied. A couple of beats past until he sharply asked, "And you?"

"Daylah." She squeaked. She was sure she felt Quidel's body relax a little.

After a while, the two found themselves in the heart of Ignis. Quidel gracefully leapt from his horse and lifted Daylah back on to solid ground as easily as if he were lifting a feather.

He patted his horse on the nose and began making his way to the nearest hut, whilst his horse meandered away.

"Do you not need to tie your horse up?" Daylah asked, running a little to keep up with Quidel's large strides.

"No. He'll find me when I need him." He bluntly replied, as if Daylah had asked the most stupid question a person could.

As they approached a hut by the great fire, Quidel pulled a piece of material in one of his large hands and pushed it to one side and entered through, what Daylah assumed, was the door.

It didn't seem very safe, anyone could walk in but she supposed if anyone *did* walk in, that meant they would find themselves on the end of a spear.

Daylah nervously edged through the doorway right behind Quidel, making sure she left enough room between them but also close enough so that his great shadow could shield her tiny frame.

"Father?" He grunted into the fire lit hut.

It was, essentially, one very large room, sectioned here and there by an extra piece of material.

Daylah assumed there were beds behind each section, she thought this a good idea and might bring it up when she got home. She'd like a bit of material across her little hollow.

In the middle, there proudly crackled a fire, its smoke funnelled up through a small hole at the top of the hut. There wasn't much else, a few animal skins draped here and there, a few empty glass jars, a saddle that had seen better days.

"Quidel?" An immense bulk of a man walked with purpose to the centre of the room. His hair a dark brown, pulled back at the nape of his neck and tied with red melted wax. His hair reached all the way down his back, jewels and feathers attached to strands at random.

A great leather necklace draped around his thick neck with a large pendant shaped like a flame which sat in the centre of his brawny chest.

Daylah noticed his chest and arms were covered in scars as he pulled a white linen shirt down to cover them; battle wounds. This was an impressive man on all accounts. He held himself with such strength and power, Daylah felt incredibly fragile in his presence but the wisdom she sensed from him made her feel safe. She stepped out from Quidel's shadow a little.

"You're back." The great man stated to his son, but his eyes never left Daylah's.

"The Raven?" He directed at Quidel now.

102

"Fought off." Quidel replied. The two weren't so much as having a conversation but swapping words. There was no warmth between them, the bond between them felt as icy as the winds in Azureus.

"Hm." The great man retorted.

"Fought off by my friend, who is now being kept against her will by your warriors." Daylah blurted with a short burst of confidence, taking off her hood and allowing her hair to fall freely.

That confidence was quickly squashed away by the glare of the great man.

Quidel took one step to his right and covered her, protectively.

"A sea-girl?" The great man rumbled.

As far as Daylah could tell, he wasn't angry but his voice had urgency in it now.

There was silence whilst the two men deliberated with looks and pacing by Quidel's father. Daylah made an inpatient noise and stepped out of Quidel's shadow.

"The Raven, they're being sent from the mount-"

"We know who's sending them, girl. Do not think I don't know what is going on." The large man answered, prickly and offended. He rolled his shoulders with impatience.

"Well, Ce- My friend, she fought them off and is exhausted. She's being held somewhere in Ignis and she needs help."

There was silence, Quidel's blank face wasn't giving away any emotion. Daylah wasn't sure if he wanted to help or not. His father seemed annoyed and put out by the inconvenience of their night time visit.

"She's the only one that can stop all of this fighting." Daylah tried to drive home with vigour.

The room was silent.

She took a couple of steadying breathes and chose a different approach, more pleadingly.

"Please, she fought off the Raven, she saved my life but she was very badly drained from doing so. Your warriors have brought her to Ignis with the intent of torturing her for information, I think, about her mother and father, who I know to be dead." Still, silence.

"I have seen it." She finished softly.

"Who is this *friend* of the sea-girl?" The great man asked his son, curiosity spiking in his mind, his brow furrowed with concentration.

"She is the daughter of Adara and Aiden." Daylah answered instead, hoping that he would know what this meant.

The great man nodded and strode towards Quidel and Daylah, marching past them and through the material door. Quidel quickly followed his father and Daylah, shrugged slightly, and followed Quidel.

On stepping outside the hut, Daylah reached for the hood on her cloak but the great man shouted from a few paces away, "Leave it off." Her body itched to hide away under her hood, she felt exposed but she also feared the great man's temper and she was out numbered in a mass of Ignis.

As the unlikely three marched through the huts, turning left and then right, going straight and then right again, weaving passed hut after hut.

People started to peer their heads from their dwellings and took notice first of the great man, then of Quidel quickly on his heels but their faces changed when they saw the colour of Daylah's hair. She began to bow her head but thought better of it; she was not ashamed of who she was.

There were a few whispers from the people they were passing, some more than a whisper and not at all friendly. Some following with glass jars filled with flames, others carrying spears.

Daylah ran a little to catch up to Quidel and managed to walk beside him almost touching his hand with her arm to feel safe.

Quidel and his father suddenly stopped in front of a hut made completely from clay and stone which was raised a little from the ground and underneath. Daylah could see a great roaring fire placed in the middle, its flames out of sight and she assumed they licked the inside of the hut.

"Amaru." The great man didn't have to shout, his voice had a distinctive quality about it, one that carried and could not be ignored.

Shortly after being summoned, the stern horseman that took Ceto came from around the back of the burning hut.

Daylah hopped from foot to foot.

"You did not inform me of any prisoners." The great man towered over Amaru, even though Amaru was a large man in his own right.

He bent his head and clasped his hands behind his back, but didn't say anything.

Quidel shifted his weight a little. Daylah eyed him from the corner of her eye; this was the first time she had noticed him do anything except resemble a rock.

"Bring her." The great man demanded.

"Yes, Fire Keeper." Amaru obeyed.

Fire Keeper?

Daylah had read about them, it's the name Ignis give to their leader; they forget their childhood names and become Fire Keeper until the day they die.

She felt slightly in awe, she had no idea she was in the company of Fire Keeper, although now she thought about it, maybe she should have guessed.

As they waited, what seemed an eternity, for Ceto to be brought out, Daylah could see Quidel in the corner of her eye again. He was fidgeting with his fists and she could hear him trying to regulate his breathing.

Her own heart was beating in her throat and her body

trembled in anticipation, but she knew why she was so nervous; she was her friend and she felt very connected to her, as if she'd known her for years.

But Quidel, he had seen Ceto for only a few seconds out in the dark meadow, why was he so invested?

His reaction made Daylah feel a little uneasy.

Finally, Amaru came from around the back of the clay hut. Ceto stumbling behind him as he dragged her roughly by one of her limp arms.

She looked awful; her black hair that usually flowed freely around her face, was stuck with sweat to her forehead and neck. She wore a once white sleeveless top that was littered in scorch holes, and her pants the same.

She was bare foot and as she was dragged a few paces in between stumbles, Daylah could see the soles of her feet had fresh burns bubbling on them.

Daylah gave a sharp intake of breath when she noticed a branding mark on her upper right arm, it was in the shape of an upside down flame.

The mark of an Ignis traitor.

Daylah could tell that this strong female that she admired, was holding on to the last of her strength and trying with all her might to stay as standing as she could, but her eyes rolled back in to her head and Ceto finally thumped to the floor.

Amaru made a noise as if she had inconvenienced him by no longer being able to support her weight and he grasped her under one of her arms, flinging her motionless body at the feet of Fire Keeper, defiance dancing on his furious face.

Nothing was said for what felt like an age, why was no one rushing to Ceto's aid?

Daylah willed her body to move to Ceto's side, but the anger that filled the air froze her to the spot.

Amaru glared at Fire Keeper, fury shaking his body and quickening his breathing but he didn't say anything; no matter what their personal opinions were, the Ignis followed the rule of their Fire Keeper with no exceptions.

Fire Keeper was managing to keep his emotions under control and he was giving nothing away, but he was looking back at Amaru, his body like a gigantic lump of stone, not making a single move.

And then he spoke.

"We need this girl. I assume you know who she is, but do you know what she is to do?"

Amaru didn't speak in response, he continued to glare at a spot on the floor.

"The girl is under my protection." Fire Keeper raised his voice a little when he said this, as if to indicate to the gathering crowd that this was an order for them as well.

"Quidel, bring her." Fire Keeper calmly uttered to his son. The second Quidel had the order, he lunged to where Ceto lay and scooped her up in his great arms with hardly any effort at all; it was as though he were picking up a doll. Ceto's head lolled back over Quidel's arm, lifeless, but the relief in his face as he looked down at Ceto was reassuring. He gently carried her off through the crowd and back the way they had come.

Daylah started as if to follow Quidel but Amaru couldn't hold his temper anymore.

"Do you know *what* she is?!" Amaru launched at Fire Keeper.

"Yes." He calmly and with great authority replied.

"She is to defeat Krokar."

This did not sit well with Amaru, it only made him angrier.

"Her father betrayed us. Her mother is one of *them*." He threw his glare at Daylah. The venom in his eyes seemed to pierce through her small frame.

"That thing," he directed at Ceto, "is an abomination. She's hiding her mother somewhere. The sea-witch is hiding, cowering behind her daughter. We must find her and punish her for the crime she committed all those years ago. We can't let this go, Fire Keeper."

Flames burned in the man's eyes, his muscles trembling with adrenaline, his hands curled up in to angry fists. The other horse men behind him moving closer to Amaru as if to fight with him if it came to it.

"The seer is out there. She must pay!" Amaru spat on the ground as if the words he'd spoken tasted rancid.

Fire Keeper, in one fluid motion, flung his great arm from his side and placed his enormous hand on the back of Amaru's neck, effortlessly guiding him down to the floor and on to his knees.

It was then that Daylah found her strength; her tiny feet carried her right to Amaru and even with him on his knees, Daylah only came up to just below his chin.

She mustered all the images the seers had shared with each other of Adara's death, and blended them with the memories Ceto had offered of her mum on the floor of their home. Blood surrounding her, open eyes completely vacant. She reached up her hands and placed them firmly on either side of Amaru's face and transferred the images to him, so that he could see for himself.

Salty tears ran down her face and her body tensed all over as she tried to stop it from shaking, in vain.

When the images had stopped, Daylah pulled her hands away from his face and stood there for a few panting breathes, wishing to herself that she could stop crying.

"She's dead!" Daylah spat through furious tears.

She then turned on her heel and raced after her friend, not caring what happened to the scene she'd left behind.

She made her way through the many huts, aiming towards the great fire in the centre, hoping that was where she would find Ceto.

Finally making it to Fire Keepers hut and sensing her friend inside, she paused for a breath and glanced down at her still shaking hands.

She had felt so much hatred seeping through from Amaru. The amount she felt had scared her a great deal; anybody that can feel that much pure hatred was surely very dangerous. How can someone's mind, filled with an intensity of foul loathing, be changed to think any differently?

Daylah took one last deep breath, ready to face the traumatic sight she knew was behind the cloth door.

As she pulled the fabric gently to one side, she could see Quidel kneeling on the floor next to Ceto who was laying, motionless, on a slightly raised bed, the frame made from a few planks of wood tied together with rope.

The room smelt of sweet and soothing herbs and flowers, the fire in the middle of the hut crackling with smouldering embers. Daylah felt drawn to the remedies, having studied everything there is to know at home. Peering over them, she was surprised to find she didn't know what remedy Quidel had concocted.

Quidel was wiping away the ash from Ceto's skin with a cloth and cool water.

Daylah edged forward and knelt beside the bed, she placed her palm over her friend's skin and wasn't shocked to learn it felt as hot as if it were still on fire.

She grabbed another cloth and helped Quidel cool her skin down.

The two worked in silence. Both wondering the same, but not speaking it aloud. Will she wake up?

Chapter 13

Excruciating pain was the first thing Ceto noticed. All over her body, from the soles of her feet to the top of her head. Keeping her eyes firmly closed, she tried to remember what had happened.

She had used all her energy fighting the Raven and she had a foggy memory of herself letting the shield go.

The next thing she knew she was tied up in a small room, trying her hardest to find cover from the blazing fire in the centre. It was incredibly stifling in the room and the heat filled her lungs until she was unable to breath in anymore fresh air.

Thinking about it now, her chest started to tighten and she found herself gasping for air. Her eyes snapped open and her hands fumbled around, trying to find something that would assist her.

"It's okay, you're okay. You're safe, just breathe." A young voice came from above her and as her eyes began to focus and her breathing became a little easier, Daylah's round face came in to view, and Ceto used the innocent sight to calm her breathing and ground herself.

"You have a little smoke in your lungs and some burns, bruises, cuts. But no broken bones as far as we can tell." Daylah went on, very matter of fact as if to overpower emotion with facts.

Burns, bruises, cuts? Yes, it was coming back to her a little, piece by piece. The feeling of being trapped, of feeling helpless, unable to save herself. Over powered by large men. Burns, bruises, cuts, the superficial evidence; they weren't the worst of it.

Tears welled in her eyes and she threw her arms around her young friend's neck and sobbed silently into her bright hair. Daylah reciprocated with a strong embrace.

The two girls stayed there, neither saying a word, neither

letting go.

After a little while, Ceto released Daylah and lay back down. "I'm so glad you're okay. I tried to stop the Raven but there were so many. More than ever before. I'm so glad you're okay." Tears welled in her eyes again and Daylah smiled her innocent child like grin back at Ceto.

Then something twisted inside her as she realised that whilst she was in the small room with the big fire, she hadn't thought about Daylah. Not even once.

Shame rushed around her body, making her feel heavy with it. "You've gone white. Do you need something? Water? Food?" Daylah fussed around her and the shame only grew stronger. "I'm okay, I just came over all queasy for a second." Ceto replied with an almost smile.

"I'm just going to close my eyes for a little while." She rolled over slightly and closed her eyes, but she didn't sleep. Her brain had so many thoughts in it, as if her head might explode.

She could tell that Daylah was sat beside her, unmoving, for some time, although she was sat so still that Ceto couldn't be too sure.

After a while, Ceto heard her gently lifting herself off the wooden stool and rustle around with one thing or another. After more time had passed, Ceto found herself drifting in and out of sleep, waking up to her body aching and her head pounding, that was, unless she was woken by a dream of sharp Ravens and Daylah's scared face next to Khepri's disappointed one and her mum's lifeless body lay on the floor.

The next few days went by all the same, Ceto would wake up to Daylah wiping her with a cloth that felt cool on her scorched body.

Other times she would wake up gasping for air with her injured lungs.

The worst was when she would have a dream full of dark spaces, and haunting feelings, friends lay strewn on the floor, lifeless.

Dreams of being left in this world alone with nothing but Raven circling around her, screeching and brushing their wings against her skin as they flew closely past, a brush of wing that felt like flames of fire.

She would jump awake at these dreams and the sharp sudden movement would feel like thousands of hot needles piercing every inch of her skin, her skull would throb and the air around her felt as if it was turning to smoke.

This would happen until Daylah would come running to her side.

Sweet, faithful Daylah, always there to look after Ceto when she needed her, never too far away.

And finally, the shame she felt would wash over her again.

This cycle continued for days, Ceto was starting to think she would never feel better.

An extremely overwhelming man would come and check on her burns and her head periodically.

Daylah explained to her that this was Fire Keeper and that he was the leader here, that he saved Ceto and demanded that she be brought back here.

He had spent days doing everything he could to soothe the burns and finally, they felt as though they were improving.

One afternoon, having refused lunch from Daylah and instead insisted that she closed her eyes for a while, Ceto braced herself for the onslaught of dark dreams.

Laying there, waiting for sleep, she caught a little of Daylah and Fire Keepers conversation.

"Her burns are improving well, but mentally, she is quickly growing worse." A man's voice said bluntly.

"There's a herb that we burn at the heart of the fire when we need information from someone...unwilling." Fire Keeper

112

was muttering.

"Torture?" Daylah stubbornly retorted.

Ceto internally smiled at this remark; she liked her frankness, it reminded her that Daylah wasn't simply a little girl. She could look after herself, despite her tiny frame.

"Yes. Ignis have been known to use it for torture if the situation is justified. But I fear that Amaru used it and to remedy Ceto, we need to call for Khepri."

Khepri? Ceto's heart leapt, they could help and these paralysing dreams would finally come to an end.

Then her heart sank. Khepri couldn't leave the forest for that long with the evil that's spreading itself far and wide.

"No." Ceto croaked.

"What do you need?" Daylah breathed, rushing to her side.

"Khepri can't come here, they can't leave the forest. If they do, Folia will die."

"We can't take you there, it's a long way, even with horses. If we meet the Raven along the way…"

"We won't make it." Daylah finished Fire Keeper's sentence.

Ceto was impressed at the leadership Daylah was showing; in the short amount of time they had known each other, Ceto had always felt the young girl needed protecting, but she found herself in awe by the strength Daylah had shown since they had left Azureus.

"Khepri can't leave…the forest." Ceto repeated through gasps of air.

"Shh." Daylah soothed as she lay a cool cloth over Ceto's forehead and forced her back into a horizontal position.

The next few days went by either with a blurry consciousness or hideous nightmares, cold sweats and surges of excruciating pain shooting through her body.

As the days dragged by, Ceto could feel herself becoming worse by the hour and, when she was in control of her thoughts, all she felt was fear.

She could make out flashes of faces. Mainly Daylah's round, kind face, and other times she could make out Fire Keeper's impressive form as he would chant and place herbal medicines on Ceto's burns.

Every now and then, Ceto could make out another face, one she didn't know. Tanned and stern, like Fire Keeper but his eyes were more intense, his features younger.

When this new face was around, she felt watched. Not safely, but uncomfortably.

Just when Ceto didn't think her nightmares and pain could get any worse, so much so that she wished for death, the nightmares grew shorter and the pain subsided a little hour by hour and eventually, she opened her eyes and felt more present than she had in weeks.

There stood Khepri.

Magnificent Khepri. Worry leaking over their perfect angular face.

"Khepri." Ceto breathed.

Tears welled in her eyes, exhausted tears of relief and the overwhelming feeling of safety and comfort.

"You are okay." Khepri replied, stroking the side of her face with the back of their long, thin hand.

It looked like Khepri wanted to say something and Ceto lifted herself up onto her elbows, ready to listen, until suddenly there was a mass of bright hair all around Ceto and arms wrapped around her neck.

"Hi, Daylah." Ceto chuckled even though the laughter hurt her lungs still. It was good to laugh again.

"It's been almost a month!" Daylah accused and pulled back from the hug looking Ceto in the eyes.

Her inky black eyes turned shiny.

"I mean, I knew you'd make it…but you did scare me a little."

The young girl had seemed to revert back to the child Ceto

had met in Azureus; maybe she had dreamt the strength she'd witnessed whilst she was in and out of consciousness. It was difficult to make out what had been real and what had been in her head, was the man she'd seen real? She remembered a feeling of unease when he was around. She felt it thinking back to his face now.

It wasn't an emotional connection, like the one she shared with Oscar, but physical. As if her body was drawing her towards him. She shivered.

Daylah frowned at her and started to fuss once more.

The next few days were spent with small strolls outside of the hut.

She was mainly accompanied by Daylah, but sometimes Khepri would accompany the two girls.

As Ceto become stronger, she and Daylah would explore Ignis deeper.

The huts in the centre of Ignis, where Fire Keeper resided, were spaced apart and larger there.

The further to the outskirts the huts went, the closer together they were and smaller.

Khepri explained to Ceto that they were designed like this so the warriors could patrol the outskirts and also have a place to eat and rest.

Ignis was extremely hot; right in the very centre of the village sat an enormous fire pit which rose high into the air and always roared. It didn't seem like winter here. Khepri explained one afternoon that the Great Fire at the centre gave warmth to this entire land. From that, Ceto made an assumption that the Great Fire wasn't like normal fire.

She liked to stand as close as she possibly could to the heat and watch the flames dance around each other. Mainly colours of orange, red and yellow could be seen but if she looked carefully, Ceto could see sparks of green, blue and purple.

The Ignis people would come to the fire with glass jars of different sizes, Fire Keeper would take their jars and he looked as if he was speaking to the fire. As he did this, a flame would leap away from the rest and place itself inside the jar that was offered.

The ground was crunchy and dry, a mass of desiccated dirt and sand. The only sign of greenery came from the forest in the East and a small pump on the outskirts of the village was the only water the people had.

Daylah explained that the Azureus built the pump and the water comes straight from the West after her people felt it unfair to carry gallons of water to Ignis on a daily basis.

It appeared to be a wasteland to Ceto, but the Ignis made it work and everyone seemed happy as long as the fire was burning. The heart of Ignis.

As Ceto grew stronger, she would see how far she could get to the outskirts before having to turn back.

One day she decided she felt strong enough to make it to the very edge. Khepri asked if they could accompany her this time as they longed to see the green again. They had heard from the warriors that winter had passed from the meadow and spring was here.

The two gathered a small pack with a little lunch in and what little water that could be spared.

Daylah was not best pleased to be left behind but she understood, in a childish grumpy way. This made Ceto chuckle light heartedly.

It amazed her how this small framed girl, could be such a strong and independent force but still act so childish when she wanted to.

Khepri and Ceto set off from Fire Keeper's hut one late morning. Ceto paused as she pushed aside the door and looked around as she did every day, still hoping to catch a glimpse of the young man she'd seen when she was in and out of consciousness, still wondering whether he had been a hallucination.

She had a look around, saw no one, her heart sank for a moment, she then took a deep breath in and exhaled, testing her lungs.

"Let's go." She smiled at Khepri.

Khepri tried their hardest to walk slowly enough for Ceto. She still had some recovery to do, and Khepri's legs already out strode Ceto's.

The two talked of this and that, Khepri asking how Ceto had come along with controlling her powers and Ceto politely asked about the forest and if it would be okay without them. She was skirting around what she had found out about her mum and dad from the seers. She was internally fighting with herself, weighing the pros and cons of bringing it up.

Ceto had gone the entire journey to the edge of Ignis asking polite questions and she sensed that Khepri knew she wasn't asking what she so desperately wanted to.

When they made it to the edge, Ceto felt a little out of breath and with her legs and arms aching, she walked a little to one side where a rock stood and she perched herself onto it in order to catch her breath.

The ground beneath them still dry gravel, but not too far ahead, grass was trying to grow even if it did look a little scorched from the sun. Further on it blossomed into the meadow. A warm spring breeze made its way across Natus. The two looked out at the multi-coloured meadow ahead of them and watched as the various wild flowers danced beautifully in the breeze.

They could hear the Ignis soldiers in the huts behind them, talking in low grunts as they patrolled the outskirts, the gravel under their sandaled feet crunching with their heavy foot falls.

As the sweet spring breeze brushed against Ceto's face, she

117

closed her eyes, smiled and inhaled.

"Spring smells so fresh."

"It is here sooner than I had hoped." There was such a heavy note in their voice, Ceto opened her eyes and glanced into Khepri's.

"Why didn't you tell me about my mum? You knew each other more than you told me, and my…dad." The word "dad" still felt very alien to Ceto.

"You helped them have a life together and then you saved me and my mum. You knew them more than I could ever have imagined."

There was a long pause, Khepri wrapped themselves in their great wings from the coming cold, a little sadness in their droop.

"I could not save your father and I feel shame. In the end I could not even save your mother.

I felt very close to Adara, she was my only true friend. We, caretakers of Folia, we do not have friends. The other races find us strange but your mum was understanding and she could see past my appearance. You remind me of her." Ceto felt pride rise within her and she understood Khepri's withdrawal. The pain was still raw for them.

"You are as kind and understanding as she was and you can see right inside a soul. You see them for what they truly are. That is magic that I will never understand."

Ceto made her way through Khepri's enclosed wings and wrapped herself around their slender muscular body. Khepri wrapped their long arms and comforting wings around Ceto in response.

"Excuse me for interrupting."

Ceto wheeled around, her loose hair flying around behind her.

She recognised that voice, she had been searching for that face since she had come out of her fever.

"Hello." She replied, her guard up.

There was a long pause as the young man shifted his posture, shifted his long dark brown hair. Ceto could feel Khepri gracefully walking away behind her.

"Quidel." He said, folding his strong body slightly in a sort of bow, placing his hand on his tanned chest, which was only slightly covered by a linen shirt that hung loosely on his impressive physique.

"Ceto." She nodded, a defensive glare in her eyes.

Neither said another word and Ceto looked back to where Khepri was trying not to listen.

"I should probably..." She gestured with her thumb behind her towards Khepri.

She was uncomfortable, the boy was glaring at her as if she was a prize he must win.

"It's nice to see you awake." Quidel said in his one levelled voice. Ceto took a step back, unsure of how she felt about the image she had of this man leering over her, watching her sleep.

This young man was beautiful, she couldn't ignore the butterflies she felt in her stomach when he spoke to her. She suddenly felt longing to stand closer to him, to feel his warmth. She felt conflicted.

"You were in the hut? You helped Daylah?"

"And my father." Quidel finished.

"Oh, your father is Fire Keeper? Does that mean you'll be Fire Keeper after him?" She asked, feeling stupid at such a weak question. She was, unskilfully, trying to keep the conversation going to give herself a chance to figure him out, and the strange feelings that were battling inside of her.

"No. That's not how it works. The fire decides who will be next." Quidel answered rather bluntly.

She raised her eyes up to the sky a little, gave him a small sarcastic smile and let the uneasy feeling overtake the butterflies. His closed off and unemotional nature uneased her, this was a quality she didn't find attractive.

"How come I haven't seen you around whilst I've been awake?" She enquired, tilting her head slightly, almost accusingly.

"I've been patrolling the outskirts, staying in these huts to rest." Again, he answered bluntly and with no emotion.

The butterflies were making a return again; it was as if her body was being physically pulled towards him. As if an invisible force had chosen for them to be together, but she found it difficult to hold a conversation with him. She had no connection, no spark, not like she did with...

"Hmm. Well I'll let you get back to it." She awkwardly walked backwards whilst making odd movements with her arms, her mind desperate for her to escape this situation, her body longing to get closer.

Embarrassment flooded her cheeks and she turned her back on the beautifully simple boy before he could see the colour she knew her cheeks were.

The foolish fog lifting from her mind, she turned her attention to Khepri.

She was surprised to find them, not standing tall or majestically gliding as they walked, but knelt on the hard dry floor, their hands grasping the sides of their head, body hunched over and their wings closed around them for comfort.

Their skin, usually a bright complexion, seemed dull and a sickly pale. The sparkle gone from their entire being.

"Khepri?!" Ceto ran over to help her friend. Quidel crunched the ground as he ran behind her.

"The trees. The trees." Khepri rocked back and forth as they breathed these simple words. An immense pain leaking from every syllable.

Ceto dared to take a glance to the East, and instead of rows of green, gold, orange or brown, she was hit with a horrific sight.

They were dead, the trees had been burnt in a flash. A dense section running from the mountain and all the way towards Ignis. All that remained was blackened branch after blackened branch.

The wind around Ceto rushed in all directions, howling in pain. It had no home, no harness to hold it down.

Ceto hushed the wind, calming it into anxious stillness.

"Khepri, what's happened?"

"I have been gone too long," Khepri croaked. They made their way to their feet, painfully and slowly. Khepri's star filled eyes focused on the mountain across the meadow.

"Krokar." There was no emotion in their voice now. No sadness, no fear, no pain, simply the sound of a name.

They turned their desperate eyes to Ceto and spoke as if they knew they didn't have much time left.

"Unity, Ceto. That is how you win. Unity."

The wind twisted around Khepri trying to revive them, trying to help this magnificent creature.

Suddenly, they closed their eyes, placed their hands over their chest, wings raised as if pre-flight, their clothing frantically whipped around them.

The wind heavily dropped to the ground, no sound could be heard. Khepri turned to stone.

Silent tears fell down Ceto's face as her eyes widened in shock and fear.

It was all her fault, Khepri had *told* her that if they left the forest for too long, it would be unprotected and Krokar would make his move.

How selfish she had been, and now she had lost another important person in her life.

She felt great arms wrap around her body and she felt no shame as she sobbed into them.

She was scooped up and carried back to the centre of the village. She let her weak body be carried and wept quietly into Quidel's torso, as he carried her back.

Quidel gently lowered Ceto onto the edge of the bed, but as soon as she was released, she melted to the floor. She thrust her hands between her thighs in an attempt to stop them from shaking.

Daylah, who had been using the day to learn from the Ignis, raced to Ceto's side, kneeling next to her on the floor of the hut.

"What's happened?" She directed at Quidel, somehow knowing that Ceto wouldn't answer.

"Khepri." He replied.

A new wave of grief washed over Ceto at the mention of their name. An image of their body turned to stone flashed to the forefront of her mind. She sobbed into her chest.

Fire Keeper swept into the hut whilst Quidel knelt on the other side of Ceto, explaining what had happened on the outskirts of Ignis.

Ceto listened to the explanation, but there was no feeling to the words. It was an account of what had happened presented in a bullet pointed list. No emotion, no attachment. The way he was speaking of the tragedy of Khepri sparked an angry flame inside Ceto, but no words escaped her.

She knelt, silently, listening. When the account of events was finished, she found her voice.

"My fault." She whispered. Daylah leant closer, asking her to repeat it.

Ceto breathed in, and in, and in. Unable to release her breath.

"My fault." She breathed in.

"My fault." She breathed in. A slow leak in her lungs began and she used the leak to let out sobs.

Daylah, Quidel and Fire Keeper watched as Ceto took the time to calm herself, muttering 'My fault' from time to time.

Dizziness and exhaustion outweighed the need to panic and eventually her breathing turned back to normal.

Ceto still didn't look up from the spot on the floor. She felt foolish for displaying her feelings so openly in front of strangers, but she could feel Fire Keeper's gaze boring into the top of her head. She screwed her face up and closed her eyes, wishing to be the invisible girl at the market once more.

"This is not the girl we were promised. She is broken." He harshly announced, breaking the silence.

Daylah took her hand off Ceto's leg and slowly got up.

"You know nothing of what she's been through." Daylah calmly retorted.

"We've all seen hardship." Fire Keeper didn't raise his voice but he spoke with the importance of a true leader.

"Many of my people have died. Your people have been engulfed in harsh seas." Daylah took half a step back, shocked at the information that this foreigner knew.

"You think I haven't seen the dark cloud that hovers over Azureus?"

Daylah had no answer for this. It was true everyone had seen their fair share of hardship.

She bent down again next to Ceto and took her hand.

"I know you're sad, but we need you now more than ever. We can't do this without you." She placed a strand of Ceto's hair behind her ear.

"Maybe Khepri is still in there, they just need your help." Daylah offered. Ceto turned her head to look at her.

She had nothing left in her, who was she going to lose next? But Daylah was right, this was all bigger than her and no matter how paralyzed with grief she felt, she had to get up off that floor and carry on.

Ceto wiped away the tears from her face, put one foot firmly on the floor and hoisted herself up to stand tall in front of Fire Keeper.

He nodded approvingly at Ceto and addressed his son.
"Quidel, fetch Amaru and Nuri."
Quidel shot a worried look at Ceto and then ran out of the
hut to follow orders.
Daylah fetched Ceto some water and sat her back down on
the edge of the bed.
Ceto pretended to sip at the water, every sip brought up a
little more bile in her raw throat.
The three lingered in the hut in silence, until Quidel rushed
back in, followed by a man and a woman.
Quidel rushed through first, throwing across the material
door, closely followed by a tall woman with a stern face and a
mane of curly golden hair. When Ceto examined her face for
longer, she was shocked to find her strikingly beautiful under
her stern façade, with a rounded face, deep brown round eyes
and the skin colour of chestnut. Her curls held together at the
nape of her neck with melted wax, small curls escaping here
and there.
She wore a piece of leather across her bosom and leather
pants. Her neck looked almost strangled with the amount of
beads she wore across her chest. Her strong arm, proudly
grasping a tall spear, decorated with colourful beads and
feathers of different kinds.
A few beats behind the woman entered Amaru.
The sudden sight of his face crippled Ceto as it brought back
painful memories, but she refused to let the man know how
much he had affected her, and so she leapt up off her perch,
rolling her shoulders back and holding her head high, the
scarred branding on her upper arm tingling slightly. Hiding
the emotions currently electrifying every vain, organ and limb.
Amaru seemed to enter the hut with a little less haste than
Quidel and the woman, it was obvious that he was there
against his better judgment. He wouldn't meet Ceto or
Daylah's eyes.

"Nuri. Amaru." Fire Keeper greeted the two new comers and they each nodded in return.

"We need your skills. Folia has been reduced to ash. Krokar is on the move."

"Khepri? Why is the creature not with the trees?" Amaru asked, a nasty tone coating his words.

"Khepri is no longer with us." Fire Keeper quickly replied. Ceto felt her stomach give a summersault but refused to let it show in her appearance.

"With me." Fire Keeper demanded, and at his word, Quidel, Amaru and Nuri followed their leader to the back corner of the hut and huddled around a small table, leaving Ceto and Daylah. They sat in unison, side by side on the edge of the bed.

The two young girls sat in silence, trying to listen to the plans Fire Keeper was putting together with the help of his finest warriors.

Quidel and Nuri huddled close to Fire Keeper whilst Amaru kept a few steps behind the huddle, close enough to be in the party, far enough away to make it clear he did not agree with anything that was being said.

"I believe Khepri is still in there, they just need a little help." Daylah smiled warmly at Ceto.

"I'm okay." Ceto replied, desperate to not have this conversation.

Daylah gave a wise knowing look, one that Oscar might have used in this situation.

"I'm fine, honestly." Ceto replied to Daylah's gaze.

After a while, the party at the back of the hut broke up. Amaru made his way over to the girls quickly so as to not be over heard by the other Ignis.

"This won't work. Working together will be the death of us, but I have no choice. Just stay out of my way." And he

125

stormed out before Ceto or Daylah could even think to reply. "We must prepare." Fire Keeper told the girls.

Chapter 14

As the Ignis followed Fire Keeper out of the hut to make their preparations, Ceto in her exhausted state couldn't help but feel lost and out of her depth. She found herself longing for Oscar.

A memory of him forced its way to the front of her mind as she stared at the unfamiliar room before her. It was a simple memory.

Adara was at the early stages of her illness and Ceto was deeply buried in the phase of panic and despair. Oscar had spent the whole day with her; helping her look after her mum, making sure Ceto ate and looked after herself, too. He talked her through the options she had, helped her make a plan.

It was incredibly easy to talk to Oscar, she felt as if she was having a conversation with herself, it was one of the reasons she loved him.

As the night went on, Oscar's newest playlist could be heard in the twilight around them. A gentle soothing song began to play and Oscar rose to his feet, offered his hand to Ceto and began to sway side to side in an attempt to dance.

She was barely aware that they were even moving, all her senses were aware of his arms wrapped tightly around her. They weren't strong and protective, like Quidel's had been, and she was sure Oscar wouldn't be able to carry her the same, but she felt safer in Oscar's slender arms than she had in Quidel's powerful ones.

Her heart ached now. It longed for her best friend to be here, to tell her that she was strong enough to do this. To tell her that he would be with her all the way. The same words he spoke to her that day.

She hadn't let herself miss Oscar until now, she hadn't forgotten him, she held him at the back of her mind always.

127

A gentle reminder that she could do this.

Suddenly, a deathly shriek ran through Ignis like a wave, filled with terror and anguish, snapping her out of her peaceful memory.

"What's happened?" Daylah asked, panic in her voice.

"Stay there." Ceto demanded and made her way, cautiously, to the door.

She was surprised to see Quidel running past her and towards the commotion, body positioned like a predator, every muscle on high alert, ready to react when needed.

He looked very impressive; his hair messy and pulled back as best he could in haste, his top half naked.

Ceto comically shook her head to bring her mind back to the danger at hand.

Daylah had quietly joined Ceto, who put her arm around the young girl and together they followed where Quidel had run.

There was panic all around, families stood outside their huts, parents holding their children tightly; others shouting loved one's names as they ran through the streets between the huts.

A woman came running toward Ceto, tears shining on her cheeks, her eyes wide with panic. She assumed this lady must have been the one who had screamed.

"Seraphine! My Seraphine!" The lady screeched. "Have you seen her?! She's gone. She's gone. She's gone." The lady repeated over and over.

"Where is my daughter? Fire Keeper?! Fire Keeper?!" She screeched to the people around her as they stared back, terrified.

From the direction of the Great Fire strode their leader.

He wasn't moving his body quickly, but his legs were so long and powerful that he made it to where the woman knelt on the ground with ease.

He held out his hand to the woman who had collapsed with grief and worry, she didn't take his hand. Instead she continued to hug herself and rock slightly back and forth as she sobbed.

Quidel, with the same stride as his father, made it to the woman's side and somehow he lifted her up with an equal measure of strength and softness. He set her in front of his father, who nodded slightly at his son in acknowledgment of his help.

"What's happened to Seraphine?" Fire Keeper calmly commanded.

Between sobs, the woman tried to explain.

"I woke up and my child was no longer in her bed. She was there and then she wasn't. There's no sign of her. I can't find her. Help me." The woman seemed to calm herself, aware that she wasn't making much sense, knowing she had a better chance of finding her daughter if she could calm herself. "She's young, she could have wondered out of the hut and gotten lost in the streets." The woman relayed this with more conviction than her earlier broken words and uncontrollable sobs. Ceto had a feeling that the woman didn't believe what she was saying. Had something else happened to her daughter? She shivered at the memory of Ravens swirling around her, aiming their sharp beaks towards her.

Fire Keeper put his hand on her shoulder briefly and nodded, suddenly Nuri was by the woman's side and guided her towards the Great Fire with compassion.

Fire Keeper then turned his attention to a group of his warriors.

"The Raven." Ceto breathed.

Quidel was about to join his father and the other warriors but he stopped at what Ceto had said.

"What did you say?" He asked, his golden eyes intensely looking into Ceto's steel blue ones.

He moved his body closer to hers for a little privacy and she could feel the heat coming off him. Her eyes were level with his chest and she could see it rising and falling rapidly with adrenaline.

She moved her eyes up to his. Hers wide with realisation, his steady.

"The Raven. I can sense them. There's a shift in the wind." Quidel didn't move whilst he processed the information.

"I think there have been Raven in Ignis." She whispered rapidly, so nobody could overhear.

"That's impossible. They stay in the meadow, and they wouldn't be able to sneak past our defences." Quidel dismissed, a little hurt in his voice at the thought of the Ignis defence being imperfect.

"Raven haven't been in Azureus either." Daylah spoke up.

Doubt spread through Ceto's mind, maybe she was mistaken, and maybe the little girl had simply wandered out of her hut and had gotten lost in the labyrinth of similar huts.

But wouldn't someone have seen her?

There were warriors patrolling the streets and borders at all times given the outside threat. Something inside her was telling her that the Raven had been here, but she couldn't prove it.

"I don't know, maybe I'm wrong," She shrugged.

She looked at the ground. How was she going to unify the four races, if she couldn't trust her own instincts?

At that, Quidel rushed off to his father, having completely dismissed the Raven theory.

By the time he reached his father, most of the other warriors had disappeared in different directions to follow their orders. Fire Keeper and Quidel both had their backs to Ceto. She could make out the side of both their heads as they had a hushed conversation.

Fire Keeper rapidly spun around and hurried to where Ceto and Daylah stood. The sternness in his face made Ceto tense with fear.

"Come." He simply demanded as he pushed aside the material door to his hut.

Ceto looked back, but Quidel was nowhere to be seen. Her insides squirmed, she had a feeling that something terrible was about to happen.

She took Daylah's hand, which was trembling, and the two followed Fire Keeper into the hut.

When they arrived on the other side of the material, Ceto was surprised to see Fire Keeper sat on a small wooden chair, his head in his hands so she couldn't made out his expression, although she guessed from his posture that it would be one of sadness and exhaustion.

He didn't move for quite some time, enough time to make Ceto feel awkward. She was about to say something or clear her throat, just enough to remind him that he'd summoned them in here and now left them standing there like spare parts.

Before she could make a feeble attempt to make her presence known, his head still in his hands, he spoke.

"What makes you think this was the Raven?" He sounded weary.

"I can sense the wind, it's my friend. I can feel a flutter in it, a disturbance. They've been here." Ceto explained, she sounded sure of herself this time.

Fire Keeper raised his head, his face changed to an expression of respect, however small.

Before she had a chance to say anymore, Quidel launched in to the hut and started throwing things into a leather satchel and strapping weapons to his body. A sword, knives, a bow and arrows and of course his spear.

No one seemed to be paying the slightest bit of attention to the two girls now, still stood by the doorway.

Ceto was about to clear her throat once more, but Amaru entered very closely followed by Nuri, both warriors as prepared as Quidel.

Ceto took a moment to look to Quidel for reassurance, but he was keeping himself busy, unable to give comfort or encouragement.

In the rush of arrivals, Ceto hadn't noticed Fire Keeper's movement. From his crumpled state on the chair, he rose to his greatest height, radiating authority and power. Shoulders firmly back, head held high.

With his hands clasped behind his back, puffing out his chest, he strode to the centre of the room. The commotion in the hut came to a standstill. The other five in the room stood with bated breath, waiting for their next instruction.

"We believe the girl was taken by the Raven." He announced. Amaru made a noise which Ceto didn't catch but she assumed it wasn't a nice word. Nuri dropped her head, eyes closed, and slowly released the breath she was holding.

"We don't know how they got passed our border," He prickled at this, "but we believe this to be true."

"Do you advise through Folia to Ventus? Hide in the shadow of the trees that are left." Quidel asked his father, all business, not meeting his eyes.

"You must go to Azureus first." His body deflated a little at this.

"No." Amaru protested.

Nuri's head snapped to watch Daylah, who shifted uncomfortably under her glare.

Quidel examined his father.

"Daylah, Quidel, may I speak with you outside?" Fire Keeper asked. This was the first time Ceto had heard him ask a question, almost politely, rather than demand and instruct.

Daylah looked up to Ceto for permission. Ceto nodded back with an encouraging smile, when she turned her back, Ceto's brow furrowed.

Amaru and Nuri stood stoic, awaiting their leaders return.

Ceto didn't have the same discipline, she paced up and down, pulled her hair back into a messy bun, took her jacket off, put it on again. She couldn't understand what Fire Keeper could be keeping from her.

It was then that she realised; she wasn't the leader of this group, Fire Keeper didn't trust her to lead his people. She was merely the key to unlocking Krokar's demise.

This thought brought a small spark of anger and the thirst to prove to everyone that she *could* do it.

But there was another part of her, a stronger part, which seemed to relax at the thought of taking orders rather than giving them. She would gladly give the responsibility over to somebody else.

Fire Keeper entered, followed by Daylah who hurried to grab their packs. Quidel entered last, nodded to Amaru and Nuri. The four Ignis exited the hut without so much as an explanation.

"Daylah." Ceto caught her friend's arm. "Is everything okay?"

"We need to go, now. There's a lady we need to go and see. Don't worry, I know the way." She replied with great confidence. One that Ceto didn't feel, she wondered if it was a naïve confidence. But she took her pack from Daylah with a smile and the two girls exited the hut to find the others.

The sun was beginning set on the horizon, it drenched the scene outside with a slight orange haze, as it tried to fight away the darkness.

Off in the distance, Ceto could see restless bodies on the ground around the Great Fire.

Every Ignis had brought a blanket out to sleep on the floor next to the warmth of the flames. Families tried to sleep as close together as they could. Others tossed and turned as close to the person next to them without touching. The woman that had lost her child could be heard in the distance, sobbing and wailing, whimpering her daughter's name.

Ceto had no doubt that one of the reason's the Ignis people couldn't sleep was because they felt the same heart wrenching sadness for the woman and the selfish relief that it wasn't somebody close to them.

Sadness clenched at Ceto's chest, but she knew the best way she could help was to go forward and stop the evil. She took Daylah's hand for support and the two joined the Ignis as they waited for the rest of their company.

The girls caught the end of what Fire Keeper had been saying to his warriors.

"We will stick together by the Great Fire *until* you succeed."

He was so certain in the way he had said 'until you succeed', that it almost sounded like a threat, as if there were no other option but to succeed. Ceto supposed he was right.

Fire Keeper turned his attention to Ceto with his stern face, it softened when he glanced at Daylah.

"You will succeed." And he *smiled* at Daylah. He began to stride away from the group until Daylah wondered out loud.

"Wait? If we're in a hurry, isn't it quicker to take horses?" What she was saying sounded logical to Ceto, but the Ignis faces turned quickly to shock and disgust.

"Horses are for Ignis. Not for *you, sea-girl."* Amaru spat at the two girls.

Quidel and Nuri tried to hide their expressions, whilst Fire Keeper stopped mid-stride.

"No. You will go on foot." He commanded, turned on his heel and made his way back to his people, huddled and scared, by the Great Fire.

Daylah looked up to Ceto, who shrugged back at her friend. The sudden change in mood confusing them and causing them unease.

Quidel, Amaru and Nuri had already begun on their way to the edge of Ignis.

"Come on." Ceto tried to encourage Daylah as she scooped her hand up as they walked side by side trying to catch up to the others.

The group made their way to the border of Ignis with the goal of Azureus in their minds.
Daylah explained to Ceto as they walked a few paces behind the three Ignis, that Fire Keeper had told them of a woman they must find. She lived alone out on the border of Azureus and they were told that if they were to succeed, they were going to need the help of this woman. Apparantly, she had known Krokar.
It shocked Ceto to think that Krokar had *known* people, that he had relationships with people so close that someone *knew* him. Up until now, Ceto had envisioned him as a cluster of dark clouds.

Darkness had begun to cover Natus, and the group had made it to the border of Ignis. Ceto made her way to where Khepri stood, frozen.
Placing her hand on Khepri's stone one, she sighed and looked up into their face.
If I do this, if I succeed, will you come back to me? She thought to them.
A hand gently placed itself on Ceto's shoulder. Turning round, it was Quidel. She jumped from under his warmth.
"We have to go." Was all he said but the look he had in his eyes was one of apology. Ceto felt as if she was beginning to get a better read on him. But that didn't mean she felt any less guarded around him.
Off a little in the distance, she could see Daylah with Amaru and Nuri; Daylah was tiny next to the warriors, she was also so very pale next to their dark features.
"Let's not hold everyone up." Ceto said in an upbeat way that she didn't believe. She smiled a pretend smile which would

135

never have worked on Oscar, and trudged back to the rest of the group.

Chapter 15

It was a warm summer's night as they waded through the meadow. Daylah half jogging behind Nuri and Amaru to keep up. Ceto gave a little chuckle at the sight, and then grew very aware of Quidel watching her from behind.

Ceto could feel his eyes on the back of her and wondered what he saw; she'd never given much thought to how she looked, not really.

She didn't care how other's perceived her because she'd always felt invisible, but now she found herself wondering. In that split moment, even with the weight of what she needed to do and what would happen if she failed grinding her down, she still ached for the towering muscular man behind her to like her. She felt suddenly foolish, so she pulled the hood of her jacket up over her head, regardless of the heat.

Ceto braved a look behind, half looking through her dark hair as if to shield herself from embarrassment but when her eyes met Quidel's, he grinned.

She never thought she would see him grin like that, he'd always seemed so stern and stoic. Something about leaving Ignis had struck a sense of freedom in him and it showed in every angle of his beautiful face.

Ceto flipped her head back to face forward, hoping the ground would swallow her up, she bowed her head. This made Quidel laugh a deep one toned laugh, which in turn made Ceto want to become invisible all the more. Deep down, she knew she did not like this man. So why was she acting so out of character? It was infuriating.

Daylah turned around to see what had happened, an unsure smile on her face. As if she wanted to be in on the joke but also understanding Ceto's hunched shoulders.

Nuri had turned her head now too and had begun an unsure laughter.

Only Amaru didn't join in the jovial scene, he simply shook

his head and carried on through the meadow.

"What are we laughing at?" Daylah asked.

"Not a clue." Ceto said through gritted teeth and swooped up her petite hand into her own and began a conversation with her, in the hope that it would end the awkward scene that had just exploded.

Taking a quick glance behind her, she noticed that Quidel looked just as confused as she felt herself.

She didn't know what was happening to her, but it didn't feel right.

One good thing came from the exchange, Nuri seemed to have broken down a little of her wall and had fallen into step with other girls.

Together they spoke about the sudden explosion of summer, and how long they think it would take them to reach Azureus. Amaru walked ahead of them, alone, as stubborn and difficult to get through as a stone wall.

With the sun firmly set and the moon takings its place, Azureus could be made out ahead. The shadow of the sea town seemed to loom over the group in the moon's light. Tired and aching from their long walk, but seeing their goal in sight, they all quickened their pace, reaching the low stone wall of the town. They each leapt over and made their way up the wooden slope that would take them to the outer border of Azureus.

Standing next to a pile of discarded crab catchers, the group caught their breath, taking gulps from their canteens and breaking off bits of bread.

Quidel took out a folded piece of cloth from a pocket in his satchel and turned to Daylah, bending down to sit on his heels so his height matched hers.

"Could you find this?" Quidel said, a man of few words but it didn't sound like his usual harsh tone.

It would have sounded harsh coming from Amaru, but there

was something soft about Quidel. It was obvious that he was strong and powerful and abrupt like all the Ignis Ceto had met, but there was a gentle side to him that drew Ceto in little by little with every interaction, despite her wary feelings. Ceto caught a little surprise in Daylah's face, she had proved herself before the strongest of Ignis but at her core, she knew she was still from Azureus and no amount of bravery or strength would change that in the eyes of the warriors. Ceto was beginning to understand that there was too much bad history between the tribes to dissolve in a few days.

Daylah took the map; she examined it and then her surroundings. She glanced back down at the map, shifting her body so she was the same way as the map suggested, then back at the map again, her black eyes shone.

"I can get us there. It's just down here." She pointed down the pathway that would take them round to the far right of Azureus.

Her body seemed to tense at the thought of making their way to the right.

"I don't think I've ever met anyone that lives that way." She hesitated.

Ceto tried to adjust her eyes to the growing darkness and all she saw was more of the same huts as she had seen on her first visit.

"*Someone* must live down there?" She pushed.

"Mainly, people live in the centre. Safety in numbers." Daylah nervously chuckled.

"Some of the larger families lived in these," She waved her arm at the larger huts on the left of Azureus, "I've only heard stories of these." She finished, regarding the huts in the impending darkness.

"Stories?" Ceto asked.

"Stories of seers that had gone mad or Azureus that have committed a crime and don't want to be found. We're taught as children to not go down there."

The group grew silent as they imagined the type of character they were about to meet.

"I'll be there." Quidel placed a large hand on Daylah's dainty shoulder. The weight of those simple three words seemed to calm Daylah. But Ceto's more mature mind could sense a fake tone in his words, as if he was just saying them for effect; for the benefit of Ceto. She felt a fire rise in her stomach, which disappeared when he took his hand from Daylah.

The already harsh wind was getting icier, cutting through their clothes and straight to their bones.

"We need to go before we lose the moon's light." Nuri firmly suggested, glancing up at the cloudy sky.

Grabbing their bags, the company set off to the right of Azureus.

Daylah led the way, Ceto and Quidel walked a step behind her on either side like bodyguards. Amaru and Nuri keeping their distance behind, looking around for any followers.

Daylah's little frame seemed to be smaller than usual, her shoulders hunched around her ears.

"Are you okay? Is it the cold?" Ceto asked.

"Er…yes, the cold." Daylah replied with a little hesitation.

Ceto wasn't convinced. She placed her hand on her shoulder.

"We're all here, there's no reason to be afraid." Ceto reassured her friend.

Daylah suddenly stopped in the middle of the walk way, her head looking down at her feet.

"I'm not scared, you know." When she turned her head to look at Ceto, she had defiance in every curve of her expression.

"From a very young age, you're told not to come this way. There are people on this side that shouldn't be interacted with, they're dangerous." Her hands were balled into fists.

"I'm going against everything I've been taught."

"Okay, well…" Ceto tried to say.

"The funny thing is, though, I don't feel that what I'm doing is wrong; I feel that what I've been taught is wrong."

There was silence from Ceto and Quidel as they contemplated this.

They were saved from having to say anything when Amaru shouted from a few paces behind.

"The clouds are settling." He announced with his abrupt disposition.

Daylah spun back around and carried on towards where they were heading, with a little more boldness in each step. Ceto risked a quick look to her right and caught the eye of Quidel, he simply shrugged at Ceto and followed.

A brisk, silent walk later, the moon barely visible behind the grey clouds, Daylah stopped outside a large hut.

It sat on the very edge of Azureus, the angry steel sea thrashing below.

The hut had carvings along the wooden walls that had been worn away over time, the roof had patches of thinning thatch here and there.

It looked as if it had been a grand place to live once upon a time, but it had been left to turn in to disrepair.

Daylah looked up at the daunting hut.

It sat a little back from the others in its row, and it had its own walk way which made the hut a little higher than the others.

The company walked up, keeping close together, stopping at the front door.

"Shall I knock?" Ceto asked, feeling rather stupid. Her body shivering from the cold wind and anticipation.

Quidel lent forward, arm raised and ready to knock on the great wooden door, covered in carvings. But before his knuckles could make contact, the door opened a crack.

It was darker inside the hut than it was outside, and as hard as Ceto tried, she couldn't make out through the crack if there was someone there or not.

"Yes?" Came a hoarse croak from the darkness.

"Maia?" Quidel asked.

"Yes?" Came the voice again, without a change in tone.

"We're here about Krokar." Quidel explained.

After a beat of hesitation, the door opened a little more, just enough for the company to slide through one by one whilst a quick scuffling could be heard, running to the other side of the hut.

One by one, they filed through the heavy wooden door.

As Amaru entered last, the heavy door gently closed behind them, leaving them in complete darkness.

Gasps sounded around Ceto and she reached out for Daylah's hand, linking her little fingers, to reassure and for reassurance.

It wasn't long before a soft yellow glow erupted around them, light coming from a glass jar of fire in the middle of the circular room.

In the half light, Ceto noticed she was a little too close to Quidel than was comfortable for her. She smoothly edged away and placed her arm around Daylah's shoulders. Although, she couldn't deny that his warmth had been soothing and steadied her heart beat.

Looking around, the person that had let them in was nowhere in sight.

The group stood barely inside the hut, facing a large circular room.

It had square indents at intervals in the walls that had once been windows but were now boarded up. Each plank of wood on the windows had the same carving on; an outline of a bird with two horizontal waved lines through it.

There lay a thick layer of dust across everything. Piles of

rubbish lay on the floor and piled high on chairs and tables. Papers, which looked very much like newspapers and scraps of cloth and fish bones, were just a few items making up the mess in the hut. Various clocks covered the wall in between carvings.

In the centre of the room sat a large circular, wooden table, which also had markings carved into it, by each marking sat a chair.

Each chair was different, there sat eight in total; one was a blush pink colour, framed with golden decoration; another was a solid wooden chair with a small heart shape cut out of the back; two were metal garden chairs with intricate leaf designs working together to complete the back rest; one was a chaise lounge chair, green and gold, looking like it had come from an old mansion; one was a black swivel office chair and the final two where plastic burgundy bucket seats.

The jar of fire at the centre of the table, casting a shadow on the mismatch of seating.

Unlike the huts Ceto had seen, there seemed to be other rooms leading away in to the dark, the light from the flame not able to reach that far.

Ceto could hear the tinkling of dishes banging against each other in the darkness of one of the rooms. She assumed the person that they were here to speak with was skulking in the darkness with the sound.

The air smelled strongly of fish and salt, and even though they were safe from the wind in here and the small flame was giving off more heat than it logically should, there was still a chill in the air that cut through the skin and right to the bone. Looking around, Ceto could see she wasn't the only one feeling the chill.

The Ignis had slight trembles to their thick bodies and tried their best to pull what little protection they had in the way of clothing around them.

Daylah was the least affected by the chill, she had moved away from the group and seemed to be examining the symbols etched on the wooden table, the windows and those carved on the walls.

"*Daylah.*" Ceto hissed the way a mother would to her child, and motioned with her hand that she should come and join the rest of them as they stood in a tight group by the door.

Moments went by in silence as they waited. The only sound coming from the waves below as they crashed the wooden foundations, and the wind whipping the outside of the hut, rattling the boards over the windows.

The tinkling from the dark room had stopped and an elderly woman came shuffling from the darkness, and towards the table.

She placed a tray down, which had a large teapot on it, mint green with white polka dots and a rainbow protruding from the top of the teapot lid; six bone china tea cups piled on the tray, each with a gold ring around the top and a floral design.

"Sit. Sit. Sit. Please, sit. Tea for warmth. Time for tea. Drink your tea." The old lady rapidly muttered.

Amaru and Nuri sat first. Daylah followed them, sitting on the opposite side of the table to them. Quidel chose the chair next to Nuri. Ceto, the last to pick a seat, chose to sit next to Daylah, leaving a chair between her and Amaru.

"NO!" The lady yelled, making them jump at the sound.

"Can't you see you should sit *here?*" She directed Ceto to the seat on the other side of the table, placing her next to Quidel and furthest away from Daylah.

The lady seemed happy with the other seating arrangements. The group watched in awkward silence as Ceto scraped her chair out and made her way to sit where she had been directed.

"Better." The lady breathed out, visibly less anxious now. Ceto had been ordered to sit on one of the metal garden

144

chairs, the cold in the metal seeping through her clothes and making its way to her bones.

She was glad she hadn't been forced to sit on the chaise lounge though, that would have been awkward to sit on without laughing.

But the lady poured herself a tea and lounged back on it with ease, not a care in the world, it seemed.

"Drink. Drink." She demanded through gulps of her own. Daylah took it upon herself to poor five more cups of tea and passed them around.

The second the tea hit Ceto's lips, the familiar wave of heat moved from her head right down to her toes.

She knew the others had the same experience, as they each let out a sigh of relief, their arms relaxing a little. Even stern Amaru let out a little defenceless sigh, which he seemed to instantly regret because as soon as he did, he placed the little cup on to the table and grabbed his spear to lean on.

We get it, you're manly. Ceto thought. The old woman laughed in to her tea, making it bubble slightly.

Confusion leaked through Ceto and she looked to Daylah for an answer in her expression, but Daylah looked as confused as Ceto did at the ladies sudden outburst of laughter. Had she been laughing at Ceto?

Everyone turned their attention from their cups of tea, to the strange lady spread across the chair in front of them, laughing into her tea.

She was a squat lady and very round, especially around the mid region.

She wore a long beige skirt which reached the floor when she stood up, hiding what Ceto could now see were pink fluffy bunny slippers.

She also wore a green buttoned blouse which was tucked in to the top of her skirt and a bright blue knitted shawl draped around her shoulder.

Her outfit had seen better days; it had patches of dirt in places that looked like ash.

Her pink bunny slippers were extremely worn too; neither of the bunnies had eyes anymore and one was almost missing an ear.

Her hair, almost completely grey, had streaks of black through it.

So she had once had black hair. Did that mean she was Ignis? Ceto tried to see what colour her eyes were but they moved in a jittery manner, she couldn't make them out.

Her hair hadn't had a brush for quite a few years, her yellow teeth looked like they hadn't been brushed either.

She didn't seem to take much care of herself, Ceto thought, except a splash of bright blue glittery eye shadow which looked as if it had been spread across her eye lids with her finger.

As mad as the lady seemed, Ceto couldn't shake the feeling that deep down, she was a warm person. She didn't feel uneasy around her. Looking to her left at Quidel's body language and expression, she didn't think he had the same feeling about this woman as she did.

"No visitors." She talked into her cup still. "All this way. All this way to talk to me."

By this point, everyone had finished their tea and were beginning to peer around at Quidel to explain why they were here.

Ceto didn't know why they had come to visit this lady and looking at the other faces around the table, nobody else knew but Quidel; he seemed reluctant to begin a conversation.

"A lovely home you have here, very remote, it must be nice to have some peace?" Ceto asked the lady, trying to make small talk to give Quidel a minute to collect his thoughts.

"No peace. Not for me. Night and day. Peck, peck, peck." She replied, her brow furrowed but still not making eye contact with anyone.

Ceto was sure the lady had no idea why they were here or who they were, but she seemed so relieved to have some company. This thought brought a wave of sadness over Ceto; how lonely she must be to welcome complete strangers in to her home without a second thought. Suddenly she felt quite guilty for resenting her mum for keeping her from the world; at least they had had each other. At least her mum allowed her to have Oscar in her life.

"We've travelled from Ignis to see you," Quidel had found his voice. "Fire Keeper, has sent us."

"Nice man, nice man. Keeps me warm." She rattled.

"We're on our way to Ventus." Quidel finished.

There was a pause, no quick response from the lady.

She closed her eyes and her face was completely wiped clean of expression.

She placed her cup gently down on the table and swung her rabbit slippered feet off the chair, setting them onto the damp wooden floor.

"Ah." She replied, out of character. She seemed less jittery, less excitable, and more rational. As if her entire personality had changed with a single word.

"You're here about my son."

There was a collective silent gasp through the group as it dawned on them, one by one, who this lady was.

A tear fell down her leathery cheek, her hands shaking. Ceto reached to her right, placing her ivory hand upon the ladies dark skinned one and gently asked, "What's your name?"

The lady turned her head slightly towards Ceto.

"Maia." She whispered.

"That's a lovely name." Ceto spoke gently as if she were speaking to a scared child.

"Your son, his name is Krokar?"

"Y-yes, I'm sorry." Maia had started to really cry now.

Ceto looked round at the group for more support, and of course Daylah, bright sunny Daylah, came instantly and sat next to Maia on the chaise lounge.

Quidel shifted his chair slightly towards Ceto. Amaru and Nuri shifted uncomfortably in their seats too.

Amaru had chosen the office chair and as he shifted in it, it began to move which confused him as he peered down and grasped his spear tighter, as if he would attack the chair if it came to that.

I'm so glad he chose that chair. Ceto laughed to herself silently. Maia gave a little laugh through her tears.

Can you hear my thoughts? Ceto asked, Maia nodded in reply. Ceto took this opportunity to take her hand away and sit back in her hard chair, and let Daylah comfort Maia for a while.

"I'm sorry. We need your help." Quidel spoke in his deep voice.

Getting better, at least there was an apology in there. Ceto thought, and the corner of Maia's mouth turned up in response, but she didn't reply or make eye contact with him.

"Maia," Daylah tried, "this is obviously difficult for you, but we really do need your help. Without it, I don't think we can help *anyone.*"

Even though Ceto knew that Daylah had no idea what information we needed from Maia, she quietly applauded her for her tact and gentle persuasion.

"I don't know what help I could be. No help at all." Maia muttered, slower than her earlier mutterings.

"Any information on Krokar's background. Who his dad was, who you are, his abilities, his…weaknesses." Quidel said this last bit with a little hesitation.

How likely was it that a mother would divulge her son's weaknesses to a group of people whose goal it was to stop her son. Possibly kill him if it came to that.

"Don't kill him!" Maia snapped her head up and looked

pleadingly into Ceto's eyes.

"Okay," Ceto spoke slowly again, "that's why we need your help. Maybe you could tell us a little about Krokar so that we can stop him destroying Natus, whilst also keeping him safe." Amaru gave a deep chesty noise which she assumed was his version of a sarcastic laugh. She whipped her head around at him, looked him right in the eye and gave him a look that dared him to make another noise.

He stared back at Ceto, defiance etched in every angle of his square face.

A few silent minutes went by before Maia stood up and walked over to the door.

Ceto was sure she was about to open it and ask them all to leave but when she got there, she stood to the right of the door and ran her old hand along an etching by the doorframe.

"I was born on Earth." The etching was of a circle with a flame, a swirl, a waved line and a leaf in the centre.

Ceto held back a gasp. She had assumed that she was from Natus, she never imagined she had come from Earth.

She had to quieten her mind as it guessed at how she had found herself here.

Maia moved on a little more to the right, running her hand along the wall and over a second etching, as if reading a page in a book.

"I wasn't happy there, one winter's night I found my way to Natus. Oh! How my world opened up. I spent endless amounts of time wandering the four corners of Natus."

She moved along further to an etching of a stick figure with wings.

"I settled with the Folia for a long while. The one thing I did learn to do was make bridges from this world to others; I travelled to these other worlds often. Taking a memento here and there," She looked around at the room and chuckled. "I

149

suppose I've taken a lot through the years."

She moved on further around the circular walls and stopped in front of an etching of a great mountain, ringed in tiny flames.

"I travelled to Ventus. The people there weren't as accepting of my visit as the Folia had been." She paused and smiled sweetly of a memory.

"I met a man."

Ah. Ceto thought.

"Ah, indeed." Maia said, with her back still to the group, her head bent a little and she ran her hand, lovingly over the mountain.

"We married in Folia, we had a baby." Maia moved on to the next etching of a man, woman and swaddled baby.

"He never cried." Maia turned to look at the group as she spoke, her cheeks damp with tears, a frown on her forehead. "As he grew up there was something so *off* about him." She shook her head at the confusing memory.

"The Folia grew concerned. They're so accepting of all life but even they could see that my son didn't belong in this world." Maia hunched her shoulders as if all of her memories caused her physical pain.

"We went against nature." Maia clutched her chest and sobbed.

She'd been keeping this in for years, Ceto felt the guilt radiating off her as she finally spoke freely about her past. Daylah began to get to her feet, to comfort Maia, but the old lady waved a hand at her, indicating that she should sit back down. Daylah did as she was indicated, tears welling up in her deep eyes.

Maia sat down herself, on a chair on the opposite side of the table.

"I've been weighed down by this mistake for so long." She shook her head slightly and sat up a little straighter.

"I don't regret what I did. I loved this man and we had a baby together, I love my baby. I love my son, no matter what he's done.

I don't expect you to understand or agree with how I feel, but that's how I feel." Maia took a deep breath as if bracing herself for what came next.

"When Krokar was older…he killed his father." Maia's lip trembled but she didn't submerge herself into fits of tears as Ceto had presumed. The old lady had already cried many tears for her husband over the years.

"One night, he cut his throat in his sleep." Her voice broke. "I woke up to find him stood next to the bed, waiting for me to find him."

There was a pause whilst Maia delved into her memory.

"There was no regret in his eyes." Maia pulled her hands over her face.

"My son never spoke another word to me. He walked out the door as if it were a normal day. I didn't see or hear from him for years after until… the darkness grew over Ventus. An *entire* race of people, gone." She stood up and suddenly threw her torso forward, grabbing her chest again, as if the weight of all the deaths grew physically heavy upon her.

"He's been there ever since, alone. Until the Raven. No one knows where they came from."

Nobody said anything as they processed this.

Reading the wall behind Maia at the next etching of a great mountain, cracked in half. Ceto realised that Maia had etched out her entire adult life on the walls of her home, to remind her daily.

"They come to me. Yes? Peck, peck, peck." She went on, beginning to sound more like the old lady who first let them in, as if something had clicked in her brain.

"Who come to you?" Quidel asked, also feeling the rambling lady starting to come back, taking over the Maia who makes sense.

"Peck, peck, peck."

"The Raven?" Ceto prompted.

Realisation clicked in Quidel.

"Do they harm you?" He asked.

"No, my boy wouldn't hurt me. They speak to me. Tell me things."

"What things?" Ceto asked, shifting to the edge of her seat.

"He knows. A child. Born to destroy. Made to balance. Must make it right." Maia babbled, and even though it sounded incoherent, Ceto knew she was talking about her.

"Maia," Ceto tried to instil in her how important this bit of information was. "What child?"

"Mmmm, another world. Wrong one. Not right. Wrong one, wrong."

Ceto grew cold all over, despite having drank the tea, as the magnitude of her mum's death became clear. Ceto was the one who should have been murdered.

Quidel quickly placed his warm hand around Ceto's arm, his entire palm engulfing her thin wrist, the two different tones of their skin standing out against the other.

"I know what you're thinking. Don't. I think she can hear you." He muttered through the side of his mouth, his eyes boring down into hers as he leaned in closely.

Ceto's mind went blank with the smell of him; burning wood and warmth.

She worked on switching off her mind, certain that Maia had already heard her anyway.

"The birds." Maia leapt up and ran to the window, boarded up with planks of wood, jabbing at the etching of birds.

"Loud, peck, peck, peck. Damn birds." She ran to the door and jabbed at another etching of a bird there too.

"Damn birds." She kept saying.

Ceto knew they had lost her to the madness again.

152

Looking at the etchings on the table, she glanced to her left. Quidel's was an etching of a horse with a man stood upon it, holding a flame above his head; next to him, looking at Amaru's it was an etching of six spears lined neatly beside each other with a flame above each point.

Ceto looked up at Maia, she was losing control, running around the circular room, jabbing at the bird etchings and then going around the room again to count each bird. Daylah went and placed her hands on Maia's upper arms, soothing her gently and guiding her over to the chaise lounge.

Ceto peered at the etching in front of Maia's chair and saw that it was a complicated etching.

There was a woman in the middle, holding the hand of a child, the other hand holding the earth.

The child in the etching held in its other hand the universe, planets surrounded by stars. Below the child's feet were symbols of a flame, a leaf, a mountain and two waved lines.

Ceto glanced down at her own etching, to where Maia had told her to sit.

It was a circular design of a leaf, a mountain, a flame and two waved lines, a human form in the middle.

She already knew.

"We have to go." Ceto muttered to Quidel.

The look of panic in her eyes made him not hesitate. He stood up abruptly, Amaru and Nuri followed suit.

Daylah looked a little confused, completely unaware of the story Ceto had pieced together in her head.

"Thank you so much for the tea, it's been so nice meeting you. I hope to see you again." Ceto reeled off as she stood up and scraped her metal chair under the table.

The group grabbed their things and headed to the door, Ceto and Quidel the last to leave.

As Ceto looked back at Maia, the old lady's aged eyes pleaded to Ceto as she sat calmly all of a sudden.

"Please, don't kill him. It's not his fault."

Ceto looked at the ground, unable to meet the mother's gaze. She grabbed Quidel's hand for comfort and they both exited the heavy wooden front door, covered with a lonely old woman's etchings, and closed it gently behind them.

Chapter 16

Ceto stood on the wooden walkway, arms pinned to her sides, feet unable to move. Her body shivered violently. "We need to go back to my father, tell him what we know." Quidel ordered, his eyes flickering like flames in the dark. "We need a plan. This is bigger than he first thought." Following Quidel sounded appealing to Ceto; she didn't know what to do next and it would be easier to follow orders, rather than to give them. Hopelessness raged inside her, spreading to every inch of her body like a sickness.

She gave an involuntary laugh which came out as a snort. Daylah looked up, first with concern, which turned into a small nervous chuckle of her own.

"What?" Amaru spat, frustrated and enraged.

"I'm starting to piece it all together." Ceto took a few steps away from Maia's house, her arm gestures animated. "It seems to me, that I'm the *key* to saving...everyone." There was silence as the group wondered if she were having a breakdown. She wondered that herself.

"It seems a little ridiculous, don't you think? I feel like I'm in a movie." She laughed from exhaustion and nerves.

"Silly Earth girl, you know nothing." Amaru spat on the ground near Ceto's feet.

"There is more than Natus and Earth; the four points protect what they need to and keep the balance for *all* universes. You did not think your little planet was the only one, did you?" Now Amaru scoffed.

"Silly Earth girl." He commented to Quidel, hitching his thumb at Ceto and turning his back on her, as if it were a private joke between the two.

"Hey!" Ceto shouted after him. "I didn't ask for this. By rights, I should have grown up in Natus, knowing everything. But I didn't and I don't. I was raised on Earth, cut off from everything." Ceto was screaming her words with so much force now, screaming as loudly as the crashing waves around her. She could feel her neck tensing as she tried to get every syllable out.

"I should have been here!"

"Where?" Amaru growled, throwing his arms out in a wide shrug.

"Ignis? Azureus? You don't belong *anywhere*."

This cut through Ceto like a knife. It's one thing to think something about yourself, but to have that same fear thrown back at you, seemed somehow worse.

"It's time to go." He seethed as he flew past Ceto, narrowly missing her shoulder with his own body. Nuri followed, an apologetic sad look on her face.

"Ceto…" Quidel tried to say, but she wrapped her arm around Daylah's shoulders, guiding her towards the centre of Azureus.

"We'll stay here and make our way to Ignis in the morning." She threw at Quidel, asking the wind to carry her voice towards him. She couldn't comprehend spending another second with Amaru right now. How could he be so unwilling to accept anything slightly out of the ordinary? Anybody that narrow minded, wasn't worth her time.

Quidel watched them walk away into the darkness, worry carved into his usually stoic expression.

Once Ceto was sure they were out of Quidel's eyesight, she dropped her arm from Daylah's shoulders and slowed their pace.

"Ceto?" Daylah squeaked, her expression a little wary.

"I don't understand, aren't we better going to Ignis and staying with the others? Under Fire Keeper's protection?"

Ceto cocked her head a little, studying Daylah's dark eyes. How she longed to have her blissful ignorance. She sighed.

"Amaru can't accept what I am." She made sure she looked ahead and held her head high, just in case Daylah felt the same judgment as Amaru. She couldn't stand the thought of Daylah looking at her the same way he had; pure hatred for a creature so out of the ordinary.

"And…what is that?" Daylah prompted. Ceto could feel her inquisitive eyes examining her.

"I'm nature's plan to wipe out a mistake it made." Ceto dared take a quick glance down at Daylah; she had her little face screwed up, trying to make sense of what she was hearing; but there was no hatred. Ceto let out a little of the breath she'd been holding on to.

"I don't…mistake?" Daylah thought out loud.

"Krokar is a mistake. I was made for the sole purpose of correcting that mistake." Ceto could hear her own voice and cringed at the sarcastic way she was explaining to Daylah. It wasn't Daylah's fault that this was happening, she hoped her friend didn't feel alienated by her tone.

She looked ahead, waiting for Daylah to piece it all together now.

"I'm nature's design." She spoke to the bitter cold.

"Maybe Krokar isn't a mistake." Daylah spoke after some time.

"He's done terrible things." She added quickly, afraid Ceto would interrupt her.

"Maybe he needs some guidance. A family, a friend?"

"He had a family. He killed half of his family." Ceto replied in a half whisper, incredulously.

"I'm just saying," Daylah held her hands up, "we could try to talk to him. I don't believe anyone would kill and destroy just because they could."

Ceto smiled down at her innocent friend.

"We could try. I promise." And she meant it. She didn't relish the thought of killing another person either, no matter what they had done. But if there was no reasoning with him…

She wrapped her arm around Daylah again, changing to a

more cheery tone.

"Now, do you think the seers will have some food and a place for us to sleep?"

Daylah nodded joyfully, happy to be helpful to Ceto.

The two made their way to the seers hut, arm in arm, happy to be together, at least.

As Ceto and Daylah walked through the quiet paths of Azureus, a figure could be seen in the distance.

"Is that the hut?" Ceto asked, a little wary.

"Yes, they've foreseen us coming." Daylah nonchalantly replied.

As they grew closer, Daylah whispered rather pleased, "Nahlah." A grin on her round face.

"Come." Nahlah uttered, as she held out her arm.

A withered pale hand protruding out of her plain beige cover, held together with a length of fishing rope.

Her wrinkled face had a smile on it, but there was sadness etched in every line. Ceto could feel the lack of hope as if it were being emitted, like a bad smell.

Nahlah turned her slightly hunched back and led Ceto and Daylah down the slippery wet stairs.

"I've put on some tea." She said in a weary voice.

Ceto sighed a breath that she didn't know she'd been holding on to, and let her exhausted legs carry her down the stairs.

When they reached the bottom, the girls gasped in unison at the sight before them.

The candle light cast a glow on a handful of seers. The lights had been gathered into the centre of the room and, what was left of the seers, huddled around them.

"Nahlah?" Daylah asked, shock and confusion spread across her young face.

"Drink your tea." She replied in a grandmotherly way, handing them each a shallow bowl of warm liquid.

Ceto took hers but Daylah didn't move.

Nahlah admitted defeat and sighed, it wasn't an impatient or exasperated sigh; it was filled with sadness, fear and a little defeat.

"They've been taken." She didn't meet Daylah's eyes. Instead she set the bowl down on the floor and sat cross legged next to it, a little way out of the huddle of scared and sleep deprived women.

Daylah knelt next to Nahlah, tears filling up in her black eyes as she silently pleaded to know more.

"Every night they come and they take more and more." She took a shaky sip of tea.

"Raven." She replied to their disbelieving stares.

"A child was taken in Ignis." Ceto told Nahlah, who's forehead wrinkled.

"Yes, I've seen this. Masses huddled around a great flame. I'd assumed I was foreseeing this," She gestured to the six or so seers before them.

"I suppose I was seeing Ignis too." She ran her bony hand across her face.

"I'm getting old and the darkness is blocking my vision. It's getting harder to see. We are blind." She raised her eyes to meet Daylah's, true terror leaking from them.

Ceto placed her hand upon Nahlah's and smiled reassuringly. Nahlah sighed deeply and loudly.

"Sleep with the group," She whispered. "I don't know how much safety we can give you but I will stay up and watch over you." Nahlah said.

Ceto began to protest but the old seer spoke over her, "Sleep."

Ceto and Daylah finished their tea and joined the other seers. Daylah curled up into Ceto's body, the same hopelessness surrounding them both, it was infectious.

Chapter 17

The next morning, Ceto woke up to a cloud of relief from the seers.

The sadness was still there, but there was an underlying hope that they'd all made it through another night.

Ceto stretched and made her way over to where Daylah and Nahlah sat, drinking tea and eating fish.

A cup and a plate was handed to her as she sat, cross legged. "Thank you for last night." Ceto said to Nahlah, who smiled in response.

"Nahlah says the more experienced seers have been taken." Daylah told Ceto, a strange excitement in her tone.

"To blind us." Nahlah added.

"She was also saying that the loss of an Ignis child would devastate them, which it did." She spoke erratically whilst shovelling fish into her mouth.

"To weaken their defences." Nahlah added again. There was silence between the three as Ceto tried to catch up.

"I'm sorry, I'm still a little sleepy," She shook her head, heavy hair flying around her face.

She took a bobble off her wrist and scooped up her mass of hair.

"What have I missed?"

"It's a plan. His plan." Daylah replied with the same strange excitement.

When Ceto looked back at her with a blank face, she glanced to Nahlah for reassurance.

Nahlah nodded back at Daylah, urging her to go on with what she was saying.

"Krokar is weakening the tribes to draw us out…or thin us out, I'm not too sure," She shivered, "but that's his plan, it's already begun!"

"He's ready." Nahlah added, again.

"Well…that's bad, right? We're not ready." Ceto asked,

furrowing her brow, unable to grasp Daylah's enthused demeanour.

"We need to go…now!" Daylah shovelled more fish into her mouth, barely chewing.

The urgency scared Ceto. She had known what must be done for a while now, she just wished she had more time. The crush of impending doom rested heavily on her shoulders.

"You need to find your warriors, you can't do this without them." Nahlah chided the young seer a little.

"Whether we're ready or not, he's ready. The decision has been made for us." Nahlah directed at Ceto.

It felt as if these words had been physically thrown at Ceto, she could feel the blood running from her face.

Daylah and Nahlah were right, they had no choice. There was no more stalling, no more collecting information or recruiting more members. Their hand had been forced.

Even though Ceto now understood Daylah's excitement, she didn't share in it.

What she wouldn't do to be back in her safe and comfortable cocoon at the back of her home. One of Oscar's uplifting playlists filling her brain, with him lay next to her, emitting his warmth like he did. Like he used to.

The rims of her eyes stung, from the cold or exhaustion, or more tears, she didn't know. But she ran her finger tips back and forth across her eyelids.

"Let's go." She muttered, the true weight of what she was yet to do weighing down on her every limb, every inch of skin.

"You're angry." Daylah accused up at Ceto as she dragged her aching body up from the cold floor.

"Not angry, no." Ceto held out her hand and pulled her friend up. She felt a twinge of guilt at the thought of dulling Daylah's energy.

"I want to finish this and go home." She rephrased, trying to give an encouraging smile but she was too tired to make it

161

look convincing.

"Oh...Okay." Daylah examined Ceto's expression.

"Thank you." Ceto said again to Nahlah, who nodded in response, and the two girls made their way up the steps and out into Azureus and the salty wind.

Silently, Ceto and Daylah made their way to the edge of Azureus, over the little stone wall and through the meadow towards Ignis.

It had started to rain, great heavy drops of rain that smelt of warm summer rain.

Ceto was in no mood to get wet this morning, she tilted her head up towards the clouds, gave them a stern look, and suddenly they parted for her.

It was as if a large invisible umbrella had opened above them.

"Wow!" Daylah exclaimed. Ceto looked down and gave her a weak smile, her mind taken over by her foul mood.

After walking a while, Quidel came in to view, hunched against the rain.

Soaking wet, he stomped to meet them. Water making his linen shirt stick to his body beneath. His dark hair, made even darker from the rain, stuck to his forehead and cheekbones. A strand was caught in his long eyelashes. His face full of stubborn anger.

With Ceto's mind suddenly preoccupied, the rain crashed down around them.

 Daylah gave a small giggle, and Ceto glared down at her.

"Let's go." Quidel said, after he recovered himself, his expression softening.

"Still no horses?" Daylah crossed her arms.

Quidel chuckled uncomfortably. "Not for you." He half joked back.

Instead, they trudged through the soft soil and pouring rain.

As they strode towards Folia, the rain relented, leaving their clothes sodden as it coldly clung to their skin.

"Aren't we going to Ignis?" Ceto asked as the rain was slowing.

Quidel turned his head to one side a little.

"We're meeting the others in Folia. We decided last night that we need to push ahead. We couldn't wait any longer." He wasn't asking for her opinion, he was telling her what had been decided in her absence. A slight disappointed air to his voice.

She couldn't shake the feeling that he was upset with her for not coming back to Ignis. This made her feel strangely prickly and she fell a step behind.

"Stop!" Daylah screamed from behind Ceto. As she did, Quidel reacted by herding the girls together and covering them with his stance, spear held at the ready.

Daylah had one hand grasping her chest as it raced up and down, the other hand covered her forehead.

It scared Ceto.

"What's happening?" She asked.

"There's..." She looked as if she were trying to figure out a puzzle. "A boy?"

Ceto realised that Daylah was seeing something that she and Quidel couldn't.

"I think there's a boy, but like nothing I've ever seen." There was a little disgust on Daylah's usually innocent and accepting face.

"Hair of flames?" Her face contorted with concentration.

"Where?" Ceto urged.

"An archway of branches?"

Ceto pushed her body as tall as she could, trying desperately to peer into the distance. She knew the archway wasn't far away. She could just about see it, small in the distance.

"He's hurt." Daylah whispered.

"Oscar." Ceto quietly announced and made off at a sprint through the meadow.

She was vaguely aware of Quidel and Daylah shouting after her but she didn't give it a second thought.

Arms swinging fluidly at her side, Ceto could recall running this fast only once before; up the steep hill to her home, one dark night.

"No. Please, no." She uttered whilst sprinting, her deep exhales forming the words. Despair infected her mind as she tried to push her body to go faster, faster than was physically possible.

She knew from Daylah's face that what she would find in the meadow wouldn't be pleasant.

She knew in her bones that it was Oscar, the bond they had pulled her to him.

A sickness started as it became harder to breath, her legs became numb. Sweat mixed with the rain on her clothes. She didn't stop, she couldn't stop. She needed to push harder, she needed to be with Oscar.

Finally, the archway was only a few paces before her, but she still couldn't see Oscar, the meadow was too tall.

As she stood in front of the archway as still as she could, she gasped for air whilst listening intently for any signs of movement.

Then she saw it, a familiar boot.

She leapt forward, throwing herself on the floor beside Oscar's still body.

Painfully still.

Leaning her body over his, she checked for breathing, for a pulse.

It was there, but it was weak.

Ceto checked for damage with shaking hands.

His clothes had scorch marks in places and she gasped when she pulled his collar aside and found angry burns.

His hands and lower arms were burnt too, cuts slashed across his exposed skin as if he had been whipped.

She could see Quidel and Daylah pounding to where she was positioned, crumpled, on the ground.

"Hold on, Oscar." She pleaded, whilst feebly waving her arm in the air to signal where she was.

"Oh." Daylah flinched at the sight of Oscar's mangled, burnt, dirty body on the muddy ground.

"Is…is he alive?" She asked. Ceto didn't have time for, what she thought, was a silly question.

"Quidel, can you lift him?" She was all business now, blocking off her emotions.

"There's a cottage in Folia, if we can get him there…" She couldn't finish her sentence for fear of her wall falling.

Quidel didn't move, he glared down with disdain on his face.

"Quidel?" Ceto growled, trying to force him into action. When he still made no attempt to help, Ceto began to try placing her arms under her friend and lift, but it was impossible.

She used every muscle she had, firstly trying to not jostle Oscar but as desperation set it, she became less careful.

"Move." Quidel demanded and took Oscar from Ceto, making his way for the scorched tree line, Oscar's limp body bobbing with every footstep.

Ceto picked herself up off the ground and jogged to catch up, assuming Daylah would follow.

The group made their way to the cottage, with Ceto leading the way.

Amaru and Nuri had been waiting for them in the tree line and followed. Quidel thundered past them.

On arriving at the cottage, Ceto flung the door open and silently directed Quidel to the dusty bed, who roughly flopped Oscar down and flew back out into the trees.

Ceto then looked to Daylah.

"I can heal him." She answered to Ceto's desperately silent question.

She instantly got to work, gently pulling Oscar's clothes from him.

"Ceto," She was speaking calmly, trying to keep her mind focused so she could help, "I need you to boil me some water and pass me my pack."

Ceto did as she was told, on autopilot. She struggled to look at Oscar, barely breathing, inches from death.

After watching the water boil, painfully slowly, she made her way over from the kitchen and to where Daylah was caring for Oscar.

She had already laid herbs across his burns, and covered them with a fabric she had found, and ripped to smaller pieces.

Ceto watched with bated breath as she soaked the fabric in the, now cooled, water.

Lifting his head, she dripped water into his parted mouth. Ceto thought he looked quite peaceful, no longer in pain.

"All we can do is wait. He should wake up soon, we can give him a little food and water and change the dressings." Daylah spoke professionally and matter-of-factly, as if they were in the middle of a busy hospital and Oscar had just had some routine surgery.

Ceto couldn't help feeling wildly impressed with her small friend. So young, so wise, so knowledgeable.

Ceto wanted to tell her thank you, tell her how grateful she was and how remarkable she found her, but the words wouldn't come without a gush of emotion, which she wasn't ready to release just yet.

Instead, she nodded and sunk down to the floor next to the bed, placing her hand closely to Oscar's, afraid to touch him.

"I'll be in the kitchen." Daylah whispered and busied herself with brewing warming tea and different tonics they might need.

Ceto sat on the dusty wooden floor, her knees brought up to her chest, her shoulder leaning on the bed where Oscar lay, barely alive.

"Ceto!" Came a growl from outside the cottage.

She buried her face into her scarf and ignored the shouting through the closed door.

"CETO!" The voice growled again.

She let out a frustrated growl of her own under her breath and reluctantly made her way outside.

Quidel was pacing up and down the clearing. Amaru stood with his arms crossed behind him.

"Yes?" She hissed, harsher than she'd meant to.

"We cannot stay here! We must go!" Quidel demanded, unrest in every aspect of his being.

"I'm not leaving until I fix him! You do what you want, but he's my first priority." She mimicked Amaru's crossed arms.

"You would risk the lives of everyone in Natus, for a boy from *Earth?*" Amaru spat at her.

"I would." She calmly retorted, defiance in her expression.

Suddenly, in one fluid motion, Amaru launched himself from his stoic position and made his way to where Ceto stood.

She rocked back on her foot, her reactions not as quick as Amaru's. Luckily, Quidel held his arm out and firmly placed it on Amaru's chest, stopping him in his tracks.

Ceto didn't let her fear show at what she thought was about to happen, she wouldn't give them the satisfaction.

"You heard Fire Keeper. She's in charge." Quidel calmly said, not taking his eyes off Ceto.

He let his arm drop from Amaru and took a single step forward.

"When the worlds turn to darkness, Earth too. Remember this moment. The moment you chose a *boy* over everyone else." And he stalked into the trees and out of sight, leaving Amaru and Nuri glaring right through her.

She turned on her heel, closed the door behind her and leant on it for a moment.

They were right, she didn't have time to help Oscar. But there was no scenario that Ceto could think of, where she would leave Oscar to die. To her, a world without Oscar wasn't a world worth saving.

She made her way back to the bed and sank onto the floor, careful not to make eye contact with Daylah.

She knew she was being selfish, but she had no other choice.

Hours passed, Ceto refused food and water, and she refused fresh air. She was determined to stay by Oscar's side until he woke or...

She couldn't finish that thought, she couldn't lose anybody else, and she wasn't going to.

The sun set and rose again, still Oscar didn't wake.

Daylah flitted around every now and then, changing the herbs that lay gently on his raw skin, and dripping water into his mouth. She assured Ceto that his pulse was growing steadily stronger, but Ceto wouldn't let her hopes rise.

Sometime the day after, the sun not long from setting outside, Oscar groaned.

Ceto sat up from the foetal position she had adopted on the floor next the bed.

"Oscar?" She whispered, not daring to speak too loudly in case she missed something he was trying to tell her.

"Ceto." Her name escaped his lips and the wall she had built to keep her emotions behind came crashing down and she released everything.

She sobbed uncontrollably, noiselessly.

Daylah rushed over, checking Oscar's pulse, asking him gentle questions whilst she checked his wounds.

In a matter of minutes, he was being fed soup Daylah had been busy working on. A little at first, but he regained his hunger quickly as the night drew in.

Ceto and Daylah helped to prop him up gently, he was beginning to look like her Oscar again.

"What happened?" Ceto blurted, an anxious tone to her voice.

"I went looking for you, I saw you disappear in front of me. I needed to know you were okay." He said through a raspy voice.

"I don't mean why are you here, I mean, what hurt you?" She wasn't impatient to know why he was here, she was elated that he was with her.

"I was trying to figure out how to follow you, with the mirror you'd left behind. Then I noticed the forest in your back garden was on fire. It was huge, raging! It started so quickly." His face contorted a little as he thought back to the flames.

"I went out to unlock the animals, they were minutes away from being in the flames." The memory was painful to relive for him, it showed in his pale complexion, usually beautifully golden.

"The fire grew faster than I'd thought it would, it was all around and I couldn't see a way out.

I could just about make out your house through the smoke. But then…" He trailed.

"What?" Ceto edged forward, eager to know what had come next.

"The barn was gone, replaced by a meadow. I could see a gap out of the fire and I ran."

Ceto barely made a sound as she breathed, not wanting to disrupt the story.

"I made it out of the trees. But there was a row of these great black birds, they looked like they were…waiting for me?" He gave a humourless laugh.

"It doesn't sound silly, go on." Ceto reassured him, placing a hand on his shoulder.

"Well, they were *waiting* for me and then they attacked me."
Ceto closed her eyes and inhaled sharply through her nose.
How could she not have known to help Oscar? She berated
herself for not thinking to bring him with her in the first
place, at least then she could keep him close and out of
danger.

"How did you escape?"

"The fire died down and they just…stopped. Turned around
and flew off." He shook his head as quickly as his injuries
allowed. "It was weird."

"You're safe now, I can protect you."

"I came here to protect *you*." He seemed disappointed in
himself. Ceto was surprised that he didn't have more
questions, he seemed completely fine with being in a different
world, where oversized birds attacked you for no good
reason.

"You don't have any questions about where we are?" She
asked sheepishly. Part of her wanted to share her whole
experience with her best friend, but there was a more
insecure part of her that wanted him to never know. She
didn't know how he would feel about this new Ceto.

He looked equally as sheepish back at Ceto. She asked 'what'
with her eyes.

"Adara, she…I've known everything. Her story, your story."
Oscar shifted uncomfortably.

Ceto stood up and away from the bed as this sunk in. Betrayal
washed over like a tsunami.

"Now, just let me explain." He tried to stand up too but his
injuries wouldn't let him.

"Your mum knew she was getting sick, she didn't know how
much longer she would be able to hold on for. Before it was
too late, she told me everything."

"But, that makes no sense." Ceto scoffed. "Why wouldn't she
tell *me*?" She crossed her arms tightly in front of herself.

"If I'm being honest? I was just *there*. You were feeding the animals, I was making dinner for us. I think she thought, it's now or never."

This made Ceto feel even worse. If a stranger had been there in place of Oscar, would she have told them before Ceto too? "She didn't last much longer after that, the next morning, she'd turned in to her shadow." He finished softly.

Ceto had no words, only tears. She began to build her emotional wall again, brick by brick.

"She told me because she trusted me. She knew I loved you and that I would tell you in the way that you needed to be told."

She stopped building her wall. She was too exhausted, she had felt relief only moments ago and she didn't want to turn it into bitterness.

"Give me some credit." He joked. "The small flame in that jar that gave off enough heat to warm your house? Adara's black eyes? Those odd remedies? I started to suspect something early on."

Ceto felt a twist in her stomach. She hadn't realised that none of those were normal on Earth. She'd led a half-life so far, and that thought brought a wave of sadness with it.

She nodded and took a step closer to Oscar.

The two sat in silence, listening to the gentle rustle of trees and the crackle of the fire, a sweet breeze brushing through the cracks in the window.

Daylah lay curled up in an armchair in the corner of the cottage, its leather old and worn.

Oscar labouredly shifted to the side of the bed, making room for Ceto, who willingly lay herself next to him.

Together, they slipped into a peaceful sleep for the first time in a long time.

Chapter 18

Ceto was woken the next day by the sun's gentle rays as they crept through the cottage window.

Oscar was still soundly asleep, she watched him breathing steadily and took pleasure in its rhythmic rise and fall.

There came muffled voices from the clearing outside, the sound burst Ceto's contented bubble.

Peering through the window, she saw Quidel, Amaru and Nuri sat around a camp fire. She could just about hear them talking through the wooden front door, picking up a word or two.

As she pushed open the door, the conversation stopped abruptly and awkwardly.

"Morning." She prickled. There was no reply from Quidel and Amaru, Nuri smiled in response.

"What are we discussing?" She moved her way around the close circle so that she was visible to all three of them.

When nobody answered, Nuri took pity on her and spoke. This surprised Ceto a little, she knew she was an extremely strong and powerful female, but was yet to see her speak up for herself.

"We were worried about the progress we'd made." She said. "Whilst you've been healing that *human,* the summer has gone. It'll soon be winter."

Ceto expected the words to have come from Amaru, in his usual venomous way, but she was shocked to see that these words had come from Quidel.

She felt a little sad at first, but that quickly turned to irritation. "No, you're right. We should have left Oscar in the meadow. He would have died and we could have gone on with our journey. Would that have been better?" Ceto was on her feet again and was shocked at her volume. Her words seemed to echo through the forest and bounce back in her ears.

"I didn't mean to hold things up for you." Oscar leaned on

the door frame as it held most of his weight, the shouting must have woken him.

Quidel, who had his back to the cottage, turned in his seat and stood up, spear ready in hand, at the sight of Oscar. His thick auburn hair stood out at odd angles from his bed rest, his torso exposed as most of his burns and cuts were on his top half. Ceto was unaware of how defined his thin body had become over the years, the sight now made her stomach flicker.

She was staggered at the expression he held firm, up against Quidel's mass of body and skill with the spear he held tightly, his face was defiant and a little cocky.

Surely he knew that Quidel would win if it came to a fight, which the atmosphere felt as if it would.

Ceto made her way to stand in front of Oscar, facing Quidel. "What's your problem?" She spat.

"It doesn't belong here." He spat back.

Ceto took a quick glance at Amaru, she was still so shocked that it wasn't him staring her down.

"No, Oscar probably shouldn't be here. I'd be happier knowing he was safe on Earth." She peered over her shoulder a little whilst she said this, before turning back to Quidel. "But he's here to help me, and I'm glad of that."

"You have Ignis help, you don't need Earth boy help."

Amaru piped up from the camp fire, but still not taking the time to stand or even look in their direction.

"*I* need Oscar's help, and there is no universe or world where I would have left him to die in a meadow, cold and alone." At that, Ceto turned quickly, pushed Oscar back into the cottage by spreading her hand on his torso and gently applying pressure.

Closing the door with a slam behind her, she still had her hand on Oscar's chest. She tilted her head towards his face, feeling slightly dizzy to find his head was tilted down towards

173

hers.

"Good morning." Daylah cheered from the back of the room, stretching and making her way over to the kitchen to start on breakfast.

Ceto broke their eye contact and went to sit next to her friend.

"You look better this morning, Oscar." Daylah made conversation.

"Yeah, I'm feeling okay, still a little sore, but those dressings and tonics you used worked really well.

I just wish I could have a shower." He raised his arms, examining himself. He was still covered in ground in dirt from days of lying in the meadow.

"After breakfast, I can take you to a river." Ceto said, rubbing her eyes and pulling her hands down her cheeks.

Midmorning, Ceto and Oscar made their way slowly to a thin trickling river.

Early autumn had suddenly crept upon them in the night. Ceto had to admit to herself that she did have the same worries as the Ignis, this warm weather wouldn't last for very long. It would be harder to make the toughest part of this journey in winter. Autumn was almost here now, but it could last a day, a month. With the season's past record, there really was no knowing.

"What are you thinking so hard about?" Oscar asked as they sat on a large rock, looking out over the flowing river. It trickled musically over rocks and pebbles; somewhere in the distance, a crashing waterfall could be heard.

Little birds flitted from branch to branch, a warm breeze wrapped around Ceto, smelling of flowers.

"Oh, you know, everything." Ceto tried to joke, but Oscar gave her one of his knowing looks.

"We need to make our way up the mountain. I'm grateful that you're here and I don't want this to come out wrong, but we're already days behind." Ceto gave Oscar an apologetic look. He examined her intensely.

"When did 'we' stop meaning you and me?" Sadness brushed across his face. "I'm sorry I followed you, I thought you needed me."

"I do! Oscar, I do. From the moment I got here, I've needed you with me. But it's selfish for me to want that, you're not safe here."

"I'm safest with you, and you're safest with me." He took her hand and placed it in his burn scarred one.

"We belong together." His sadness turned to a cheeky smile.

"Maybe you should stay in the cottage while we go on?" Ceto suggested but as it was coming out of her mouth, she wished that she could say the complete opposite.

Oscar tilted her dropped head upwards with his index finger. "You're not leaving me again." And he gave her a swift kiss. This took Ceto by surprise and she pulled away slightly. Oscar gave his musical laugh and eased off his shoes, made his way to a standing position, with a pained grunt, and began to take the rest of his clothes off.

"Oh. Er." Ceto flushed.

"I'm here to wash, remember?" Oscar gave a long laugh this time. It infected Ceto who began to laugh, reserved at first, but it became more sincere as she allowed relief to wash over her. She began to process that Oscar was willing to stick with her on this task, no matter what.

She lay back on the rock and placed one of her arms over her eyes to give Oscar a little privacy. She basked in the sun and let the heat seep into her skin.

Unable to see anymore, her ears tuned in to Oscar's whereabouts as he soaked his skin in the water and let it take away the dirt. She noticed he gasped quite a lot, she wasn't sure if it was from the cold water or if he was still in pain. After a while, she could hear wet feet slapping against the rocky ground towards her, a rustle of material and Oscar achingly lying on the warm rock next to Ceto.

"You can look now." He announced. Ceto took her arm away from her face but kept her eyes closed. She let her hands fall lazily to her sides and let her mind forget her sadness, insecurities and fears.

Oscar intertwined his fingers with hers and they lay there whilst he let the sun dry his skin.

"What are the angry vibes I'm feeling from that guy?" He muttered.

"Amaru? He's an angry guy. I'm surprised that he didn't speak up more when he saw you this morning though."

"Oh, no. Not the one sat down, the one that threatened me with his spear." Oscar scoffed at the memory.

"Quidel? He's not usually that angry. Amaru, he's the outspoken angry one. Quidel is usually…understanding."

"Hmm." Oscar gave back.

She lifted herself onto her arm, resting the side of her head on her hand to get a better look at Oscar, who lay in the sun in his underwear. The sight made Ceto's stomach flip but she quickly regained her composure.

"What's your opinion? I know you have one." She poked his arm, playfully.

"There was a lot of aggressive testosterone there." He replied, nodding slowly.

"See, I haven't got that from Quidel until today; that usually comes from Amaru." Ceto was surprised to find herself defending Quidel's out of character behaviour, but she couldn't stop herself.

"He likes you." Oscar said flatly. Ceto didn't reply.

She couldn't deny she'd had a similar thought, she didn't find him repulsive. But she knew she could never be with him, his personality was all wrong for her. She then quickly felt guilty, she had grown silently lost in her thoughts, when she should

176

have brushed off Oscar's fear immediately.

"You've been gone for months, I didn't expect you to be in exactly the same position you'd left me in." He peered at her through one of his eyes, but didn't move his body to face hers. She didn't know if this was because it would cause him too much pain to move or if he was displeased with her.

"Months?" Ceto screwed up her face.

"Yeah, almost a year."

There was silence as she tried to comprehend this, it had only been a few months here. She supposed time didn't matter in Natus as it did on Earth.

"I told myself," Oscar gave a nervous laugh, "that if I ever saw you again. I wouldn't hesitate. I'd kiss you."

Ceto flushed again.

She'd wanted him to do just that for so long before she found her way here, but now she was filled with a twisting confusion.

Her feelings hadn't changed towards Oscar but she had different feelings for Quidel. Very different. She felt at ease with Oscar, she could be herself, he made her laugh, and he made her feel safe, physically and mentally. Even though she chose not to, she knew she could tell Oscar anything and there would be no judgment. He would listen and maybe offer some gentle advice. If she needed it, a warm hug. That's what she needed.

Her feelings towards Quidel were completely physical. She couldn't confide in him, they didn't have the same way of looking at the world, he didn't have a humorous bone in his body. She felt safe in the way you would feel safe inside a tank, but he was volatile, as he had proved this morning. She didn't know him and she felt as if she would never be able to get to know him, he had a guard up that she didn't think she would ever be able to break.

She placed her hand on Oscar's shoulder, leaned close and

kissed the corner of his mouth. It pulled up into a beautiful smile.

"We'd better go." She stood up and held her hand out to Oscar, who stood more slowly.

"You're sure you're ready for this? We can wait a few more days. Daylah's medical expertise seems to be healing you quickly."

"Her tonics and dressings remind me of your mum's." He smiled warmly at the memory.

"Daylah and my mum are from the same village. I see a lot of similarities in them, to be honest."

Oscar cupped the sides of Ceto's face with both of his hands. "You can't wait anymore, and I'm fine. You worry too much." He kissed her forehead and slowly pulled the rest of his clothes over his still raw skin.

"Hey, what's that?" Oscar glanced down and moved his arm to hover over the Ignis branding on her upper arm.

"Did you join a gang without me?" He joked, but his face turned quickly to one of concern when Ceto's body began to shake violently.

She was suddenly plunged back into the memory of the intense fire in the small room. The feeling of being trapped with no way out. Her lungs grew tight as she tried to fill them with air.

Oscar quickly draped her scarf loosely around her. He sat beside her and rubbed her shoulders until the shaking stopped. Adara's scent and Oscar's embrace slowly calmed Ceto. They stayed in their embrace for some time, not wanting to leave this perfect spot as the water trickled lazily at their side. The low sun finding gaps in the canopy and shooting beams of sunlight onto the ground.

Neither of them wanted to face what would come next, but they knew they had no choice.

The two walked hand in hand back to the cottage, Ceto broke away from Oscar's grasp before they reached the clearing. Oscar made a slightly disappointed exhale next to her, she didn't look at him to check.

Ceto found Daylah and Quidel having a hushed conversation around the camp fire. Nuri and Amaru where nowhere to be seen.

She swiftly made her way past Quidel, and with a quick smile for Daylah, she swung open the cottage door and stepped back in surprise.

Amaru and Nuri were sat on the dusty bed. At the opening door, they sprung apart as if an electric shock had parted them.

Nuri sprang from her seated position and flew past Ceto and off in to the trees, embarrassment painted on her flawless face.

Amaru didn't have the same reservations that Nuri did. He stood slowly and adjusted his dishevelled clothes. Only when he was satisfied with his outfit, did he exit the cottage, head held high.

Ceto scowled up at him as he swanned past her, knocking Oscar intimidatingly with his shoulder.

The knock seemed to cause Oscar some pain and her scowl turned to a look of concern. She put her arm under his elbow and guided him to the arm chair in the corner. She felt eyes boring into her shoulder blades from the clearing.

She clenched her teeth and ignored it.

"You need to rest." She fussed, bringing him water and a little something to eat.

Oscar admitted defeat and closed his eyes as he hunched in the arm chair.

Ceto made her way into the forest without looking at those sat around the campfire, not even to smile at Daylah. She needed to be invisible again, just for a little while.

The wind was already beginning to feel fresher, a distinct change from the autumn sun that morning.

The leaves fell beautifully around her and a gust of wind raced through them.

Autumn usually brought Ceto immense comfort, but it was a cruel reminder that winter was waiting around the corner.

After a while, she'd wandered to the scorched edge of Folia. Taking refuge behind a large fern, she examined the sight before her. The ground blackened in a perfect line through Folia, mixed with white ash. Tree stumps stood in rows, like gravestones. Some lay on the dead earth, like fallen soldiers. She turned her head left and right, there was no sign of the Raven.

She placed a foot across the line. The hard ground crunched under her boot. She took another wary step and turned her body to the left, to where she knew Khepri stood. Frozen in a woeful terror.

A rustle came from the mix of greens and oranges, Ceto's heart slowed a little when she saw it was Nuri.

"Stay this side of Folia." She said. It didn't sound like a command, as it would have if any male Ignis had been in her place; it was laced in concern.

Ceto did as she was told and joined Nuri.

The two walked a while. Ceto didn't feel any animosity towards Nuri. She was strong and skilled, Ceto was sure that if she wanted to, Nuri could win a fight with a single move. But there was a gentle side to her, a control. As if she resented the aggression that came with being Ignis, but she respected the skills she possessed.

"I was surprised." Ceto awkwardly tried to bring up the scene she'd witnessed earlier. "I wasn't mad."

Nuri smiled, but continued in her silence. Her eyes glistened with the words she wasn't supposed to express.

Ceto guided them to a fallen tree, where they sat side by side, listening to the cold wind, the scent of autumn filling their lungs.

"I know you don't know me, but you can talk to me." Ceto shuffled her foot into the forest floor. She had an overwhelming need for this almost stranger to confide in her. She knew there was something Nuri needed help with and she had a strange necessity to fix her.

Nuri rubbed her palms over her knees.

"Are you and Amaru…together?" Ceto didn't know how to phrase it, she assumed the customs here would be different to what they were on Earth.

"He's of Ignis." Nuri shrugged.

This didn't answer Ceto's question, and she felt a little confused at her reply.

"Do you like him?" She pressed.

"He's…of Ignis." Nuri rubbed her palms across her knees faster now.

"Does he treat you well?" Ceto placed her hand gently on one of Nuri's arms. There was no reply.

"Nuri, I'm a good listener."

She turned to look at Ceto now, eyes wide as they pleaded with her to help.

"Nuri, you don't have to do what he says because he's of Ignis." Ceto felt wildly unsettled at her guessing of where the conversation was leading.

"He says if I don't do as he says, I'll be a disgrace to Ignis. That it's my duty to do as he says."

Ceto gave a gasp that stuck at the nape of her neck.

"Does he…hurt you?"

Nuri began rubbing her palms on her knees again, but didn't reply. A tear fell down her smooth cheek, her palms not stopping.

"You don't understand. He's not cruel. I don't want to Fix with him." Nuri stopped still and looked down at Ceto again.

181

"But he still demands that of you?" Ceto cut in.

"It is expected of the Ignis women to please the men, I thought by becoming a warrior it would exempt me from this lifelong task but…"

"You don't have to be alone with Amaru as long as I'm around, okay?" Ceto finished. She wasn't sure what 'Fix' meant, but it was clear that Nuri didn't want it.

Nuri nodded once, her chin quivering.

Ceto stood up to give Nuri a hug, wrapping her arms around her shoulders. She felt them as they moved up and down. If she was crying, it was a controlled and silent.

Ceto broke from the embrace and rubbed her shoulders, giving her a kind smile.

Nuri's chest raised and she exhaled a breath of relief, as if she'd been holding on to this burden for a while now.

The two walked back to the cottage, each feeling stronger for the bond they had found in the other.

The scent of sweet salty fish hit them, Daylah was preparing their evening meal.

Nuri chose to sit next to Daylah. Amaru gave her a warning glance but didn't appose to the seating arrangements.

Ceto discretely took Nuri's pack into the cottage and gently woke Oscar for food.

That night, everyone sat around the campfire. Now the sun had set, the dark brought a crisp cold with it.

After eating, Quidel spoke.

"Winter will be here soon." He wouldn't look Ceto in the eye.

"We'll leave tomorrow." She responded. No one disagreed but there was an obvious amount of people shifting in seats.

Daylah, Oscar, Ceto and Nuri made their way into the cottage, leaving Quidel and Amaru with the campfire.

"Nuri." Amaru spoke coldly.

"She wanted to stay in the cottage tonight, that's okay, isn't it?" Ceto shot back, a false question in her words. He simple sunk back down to his seated position. She saw him subtly notice Nuri's pack was missing too. She gave him a sickly sweet smile, closing the cottage door at his dangerous glare.

After a chilly restless sleep, everyone rose early with the uncertainty of what lay ahead.
They spent the morning filling their stomachs with a warm breakfast and checking their packs.
As late morning was upon them, an orange sun above, Ceto found Quidel helping her with her cloak and pack.
Not wanting to carry on the cold atmosphere, she thanked him as if nothing had changed. He gave her a smile in response.
Those dimples. She unexpectedly swooned. Feeling embarrassed, she turned away quickly and joined Daylah and Nuri.
Since last night, the two had become quite close. Ceto caught the last of their conversation as she approached them; they were discussing each other's customs and questioning each other on their way of life.
The warmth between the two brought an amiability to her heart.
Making their way through Folia, towards Ventus, Quidel and Amaru at the head of the troop, Quidel spoke over his shoulder.
"It's a long walk to the foot of Ventus, much longer than a day. We will have to take refuge for a night in the trees."
Nobody replied. If they were each thinking the same as Ceto, she knew the thought of trying to sleep, propped up against a tree, with the autumn wind enveloping them, didn't sound all that appealing.
Mostly, they marched through the day in a comfortable silence, listening to the birds above singing sweetly.
Amaru turned every now and then, seeming to try talking to Nuri. When he did, Ceto made a point to involve her in

conversation. This seemed to make him bristle; Ceto took pleasure in this.

They didn't stop for food in the day, but walked until the sun was an hour or so away from setting so they could prepare an evening meal.

This time, everyone helped Daylah; some more than others, but even Amaru took to poking the camp fire around, claiming to keep it alight by doing so.

They didn't stray far from each other. Nuri and Daylah huddled in a great oak, its branches seeming to enclose them in an embrace; Ceto made herself comfortable, resting on Oscar's side; Quidel positioned himself so that his back was to Ceto and Amaru planted himself against a particularly uncomfortable looking branch, but it was directly opposite Nuri. He spent most of the night shooting disapproving glances at her.

The wind howled, as if in pain. Ceto tried to tune it out, its sorrow unbearable.

She had been sensing for a few days, that the darkness had embedded itself into the seasons. There was so much sadness in the wind and a malice in the sun's rays. She glanced around at the roots and foliage, a layer of frost already forming there. She had a feeling that winter was here to stay, unless they succeeded.

Ceto tilted her head towards the canopy and smiled up at the bright moon, unburdened by clouds.

There was silence around her, she was sure the others had drifted off into a sleep. Unable to drift off herself, she broke away from the others in search of solace.

She found a reasonably comfortable tree stump and slowly eased herself to perch on top of it, bringing her knees to her chin and dipping her head as far back as it would go, to silently converse with the moon. As she dazzled at its beauty, she was aware of the curvature of the sky. She wondered how similar Natus was to Earth.

A rustle in the semi-dark foliage made her jump and then stiffen as she waited with bated breath for the culprit to show themselves.

It was Quidel. She quickly buried her chin in her tartan scarf. He knelt on the cold ground beside the tree stump, making him only slightly taller than Ceto.

She took to looking up at the moon again, finding it difficult to look at him, her body growing tense in anticipation.

They sat in silence together.

Quidel called the fire to a tree branch that had fallen from above.

"We'll….." They began to say at the same time. Quidel swept his hand to indicate that Ceto should finish.

"We need to make our way through Ventus. I think the others are hoping for winter to move on as quickly as the other seasons have but I know, I've felt for some time now, that winter isn't going anywhere until Krokar does. At this point, all we can hope for, is a day that isn't harsh.

We may have to enter Ventus tomorrow."

There was silence for a while.

"What do you think?" Ceto asked.

She knew she was right, but she felt better knowing that Quidel felt the same. Despite their difficulty since they had found Oscar, she felt in her bones that they made a good team.

Quidel glanced at her for a moment and quickly glanced back at the beautiful scene before them; moonlight kissing every branch and leaf.

"Ceto…" Quidel began.

"Don't compare me to the moon." Ceto laughed and then instantly regretted it. She had never imagined that he actually *was* about to do that. She felt an immense mixture of pity and foolishness.

More silence followed.

She wished, with every aching bone in her body, that she could take back those words. She longed for him to recoil with disgust, as the people in her village used to.

She glanced down at her clasped hands as they grew white around her knees.

"I don't know what to say." Quidel spoke into the emptiness. It sounded lame as it fell flat on the air but she appreciated the sincerity.

Ceto looked to her left, brushing a fallen strand of hair behind her ear. She smiled at Quidel and when he smiled back, dimples prominent, her stomach made an involuntary flip. She buried her face once more.

Her feelings confused her; she knew, now, how she felt about Oscar. She loved him, she was comfortable with being herself around him. She felt as though they had an invisible line, tying them together.

When she wasn't with Quidel, she could honestly say that she didn't feel anything towards him but friendship and respect, but as soon as she found herself near him, as soon as he smiled at her, acknowledged her, her body betrayed her. She had no control over it.

"I feel...weird...when I'm near you." It wasn't a proclamation of her feelings, but rather a stuttering way of asking if he felt the same.

"I'm drawn to you." He replied, but he seemed as confused as Ceto felt.

Ceto couldn't help but wonder if it was her genes that were telling her that Quidel was a good match.

Whereas, she *knew* it was her heart that was telling her that she needed to be with Oscar.

She turned her head back to the moon.

"We begin in the morning?" She asked so quietly it was barely audible.

"In the morning." Quidel replied and she could hear that he smiled when he said it.

He began to shift his body as he stood up from the freezing forest floor. But before he reached his full towering height, he lightly brushed his hand on top of Ceto's.

Still unable to look him in the eye, she settled with feeling the air to her left shift as he walked away. Ceto placed her right hand over where Quidel had touched hers and smiled.

The next morning, they woke to a blanket of frost. In the night, winter had crept upon them.

They sat around the morning camp fire, hunger and anxiety fastening their mouths shut.

Daylah broke the silence mid-meal. "If the seasons carry on changing the way they have, it might be spring by the time we get to Ventus, anyway." The others agreed in mumbles and nods, their spirits marginally raised.

Deep in Ceto's core, she sensed a different reality. She shared a knowing look with Quidel.

The company walked in silence through the trees; Amaru, head down and ploughing through the forest, headed for the foot of the mountain, with Quidel a step behind, head held high and his strong muscular shoulders pushed back.

Ceto felt her face burning across her prominent cheekbones. She shook her head and pushed her hair behind her ear slowly so her arm would hide her face.

Daylah's blonde head suddenly popped up from her elbow. "Is everything okay?" Daylah asked, looking up slightly at Ceto.

"Yeah, I'm fine." Ceto flushed brighter, internally cursing herself and willing her heart rate to calm.

She shot a quick look towards Oscar, worried that he could over hear their conversation. But he was walking a distance away, awkwardly not knowing how to compose himself amongst these strangers, having had Ceto to himself all these years.

Daylah didn't take her inquisitive eyes from Ceto, who dropped her arm from a second hair brush and turned her head. "I'm fine. Honestly." Ceto tried to convey to Daylah that she should stop asking questions, by widening her eyes a little.

Nuri had seen and heard the whole conversation and it wasn't until it was too late that Ceto realised Nuri had probably pieced it together.

Ceto smiled at Nuri who walked a little behind, using her spear as a walking stick, and turned to face forward again.

"Do you miss Azureus?" Ceto asked Daylah, trying to change the subject.

"Not really." She replied, looking at her surroundings and then back at Ceto. "I'm grateful that you let me join your journey."

Ceto made a little noise, a nasal laugh, almost a scoff. Daylah had hurt all over her face at Ceto's awkward response, she had always found sincerity exposing.

"I mean, you must have had a good life back home. You don't miss it at all?" She pushed.

Daylah screwed up her little face, trying to piece together her feelings.

"I don't have any friends. The other seers will say the odd word but they're all a lot older than me. I talk to people my own age in the market, but that's my job. They ask me questions." She paused. "No, I don't miss Azureus." She finished firmly.

The two walked silently again for a couple of beats whilst Ceto examined the side of Daylah's face.

Her white blonde hair falling over her cheek. Ceto called the wind and a breeze stroked her cheeks, blowing Daylah's hair behind her shoulders.

"I'll always talk to you." Ceto said, bumping Daylah's side with her hip.

"I hope you'll always talk to me too?" She asked, bending slightly so their faces were almost on the same level.

Daylah didn't reply but her face lit up at Ceto's playful manner and she let out a little laugh, breathing relief as she did.

Ceto looked back to Nuri, offering a warm smile. Aware that she might feel a little left out, she offered the same question up to her newest friend.

"How about you?" She said to the air, but falling behind to come in to step with Nuri. "Do you miss Ignis?"

Nuri looked relieved to be a part of the conversation again. This sent guilt through Ceto's stomach. Ceto looked over at the tall, golden goddess striding beside her. Her hair different streaks of browns, blacks and gold. Parts of her hair, plaited tightly to her scalp, brought together at the back of her head and bound together with the same wax that seemed to be fashionable in Ignis. The rest of her hair falling down her back to below her shoulder blades in tight curls.

Her eyes reflected the late morning sun, the light brown seemed to become translucent, flecks of gold in the iris shone out clearly. Her face was perfectly symmetrical, her teeth bright white and impeccably straight. Ceto couldn't help but feel struck by a blow every time she really examined Nuri. An ache of sadness as she realised she would never look like her.

"I miss the warmth, but I suppose I do not miss it as much as I'd first thought." She laughed pleasantly. Ceto felt infected with beautiful laughter and joined in. Daylah, not one to be left out, began to laugh too.

The ruckus warranted Amaru to spin his head around and to scowl unattractively.

Nuri stopped laughing instantly.

"What's funny?" Oscar interrupted, noticing Ceto observing

Amaru.

Ceto answered with a smile and linked his arm to placate him.

As midday quickly caught up with them, Quidel lightly commanded, "We'll stop here for a quick rest. Drink water, we set off again soon."

Everyone took out their water, the girls and Oscar sat on a fallen tree a little off the path, whilst Quidel leant on a tree a few over. Amaru paced up and down slowly, throwing looks at Nuri, who didn't seem too bothered but his glares bothered Ceto.

"What's with *him*?" Ceto asked, jerking her head at Amaru.

Nuri glanced at his pacing and then quickly down at the floor, but she still held her head high above her shoulders, although Ceto saw a little pink in her golden cheeks.

"He doesn't think we should get too close to you. Or you," She added, nodding sadly at Daylah. "He believes we should *even it out.*" Nuri shifted uncomfortably, not taking her eyes off the ground.

"We should even...everything out." She tried explaining again.

Ceto furrowed her brow in confusion; she sensed that she was trying to explain something without saying the words. She shook her head a little and then her eyes widened and her mouth came open as she realised what Nuri meant.

"You mean me?" She replied bluntly.

Daylah flitted her head from Nuri to Ceto, as she waited for an answer.

Ceto, for some time now, had come to terms with the fact that she was the answer to correcting the "mistake" that was Krokar, but she hadn't put much thought into what would happen after she'd met him.

"He believes that Krokar is a crime against nature and since you were created to correct a mistake...you are also a mistake and...*you* should be corrected." Nuri explained, she said the

190

last part very uncomfortably. "He also doesn't believe that we should talk to Azureus." She continued to Daylah.

There was a silence.

"I can't deny that I had similar thoughts when we were in Ignis. But seeing your connection with Daylah, your love for Oscar," Ceto flushed and tensed every muscle in her body to restrain herself from turning to look at Oscar, "The way you've helped me. I don't believe anyone with that much heart could be a mistake."

Ceto placed her hand on the back of Nuri's.

"Don't worry, I can tell you're not like Amaru." Ceto glanced over at the stern man, still pacing, in hearing distance.

"As a girl, I'd always thought I'd Fix with a *humorous* male. Amaru is so serious, I see that now, and I thank you for breaking me of that bond." Nuri glimmered her eyes down into Ceto's and a sticky negative thought latched onto her brain like tar.

Oscar is funny, he's attractive, as far as Nuri knows, they were just friends. If this woman decided she wanted to 'Fix' with *her* Oscar, there was no stopping her.

Ceto shivered, not from the cold, but she wrapped herself in her mum's cloak all the same, offering a small smile and nod as a reply and hiding in her scarf.

Two large feet crunched the freezing earth before Ceto.

"We must go on." It was Quidel. She quickly busied herself with gathering her belongings, happy for the distraction from her thoughts.

The four joined Quidel and Amaru on the path.

"We're about half a day's walk from the foot of Ventus." Quidel let the group know.

"I think the best way to do this is to rest at the foot of the mountain and make our way up as soon as the sun sets." Quidel looked at Ceto and raised his eyebrows as an enquiry. Ceto nodded once and smiled warmly up at him and she saw a little pink in his cheeks, which made butterflies dance around in her stomach. The butterflies blew up in a painful explosion and the dust floated to the bottom of her stomach when she realised Oscar was examining their exchange.

She wished that she could stop, but she was slowly beginning to realise that she didn't have a say in the way her body reacted to Quidel, and that uneased her, she didn't like to feel out of control.

The group made their way along a path through the thick forest, with the mountain ahead of them growing closer and closer.

Chapter 19

As they made their way through the changing trees towards Ventus, Ceto enjoying the others' amazement as they made their way from dense tropical terrain to robust evergreens, and everything in between.

Most of the group spent the time getting to know each other a little better, Quidel walking ahead of them so he was in ear shot. He would turn and add to their conversation if it suited him. He was a man of few words.

Ceto made a conscious effort to not look in his direction, this proved extremely difficult.

His dreadlocked hair, now swirled into a large bun at the back of his head, merged together with the wax substance.

Amaru marched a fair distance ahead of the group; but Ceto was sure that the more the group laughed, the closer Amaru marched to them. The crunch of his heavy feet on the gravel ground grew louder as the day went on.

The path carved out below them, littered with ivy as it crawled its way across the path unchecked. Weeds growing tall at the edges of the unused path.

As winter's day grew darker, conversation died and everyone felt exhaustion wash over their body. The path they had been walking on opened wide, wide enough for the six to walk side by side easily.

Ahead, there stood an archway made of stone. Intricate carvings wound around it; carvings of swirls, mountains, birds and unrecognisable symbols.

The air was deathly quiet and Ceto suddenly felt unease in the pit of her stomach. The cold wind picked up and became menacing.

There was no sound from the group, it was clear that it wasn't just Ceto and Oscar that hadn't been here before. The six stood like stone, gazing up at the great structure, intimidation settling around them.

"Ventus." It was Amaru who broke the silence, his deep voice hung in the air as the wind lulled for a moment, his breath leaving a fog before him.

"We'll go deeper into the forest, as soon as the sun goes down, we make our way up there." Quidel instructed, nodding through the archway and towards a gravel path and a steep incline.

A small makeshift camp was set up. Finding a boulder to rest their backs against, the group sat in silence whilst trying to keep warm.

Daylah wrapped herself in a sky blue woollen blanket which made her blonde hair stand out strikingly; Ceto pulled her own sky blue cloak around her, buried the bottom half of her face into her tartan scarf, and pulled out a bottle green blanket she'd found in the cottage. It was more hole than blanket and it smelled musty, but it brought a little comfort to her.

She closed her eyes and asked the wind to blow around them rather than into them, she felt the chill lift a little from her skin. She jumped at the feeling of a large warm hand on her shoulder. She threw open her eyes and lost concentration, soon the wind was dancing around her again.

"Don't use your energy yet. Here." Quidel said as he passed her a glass jar with a strong flame inside. As she grasped it in both hands, he flourished a light brown woollen cloak around his broad shoulders. It was decorated beautifully with small flames around its edges.

"Thank you." Ceto smiled up at Quidel, expecting him to walk away, but he sat with his back up against the rock next to Ceto.

He sat close, extremely close. Ceto could feel his warmth radiating from him. She found herself wondering if she could edge her body away from his without being noticed.

She felt a little awkward at first, automatically scanning

around for Oscar. Her stomach gave a lurch when she saw him deep in conversation with Nuri. Stubbornly, she decided to commit to this moment with Quidel.

She racked her brain to think of something to say, just to fill the silence. But when she searched and searched her brain and came up with nothing, she noticed Quidel wasn't trying either. So they sat in an uncomfortable silence.

Ceto noticed Daylah looking miserable and sat shivering by herself. As much as Ceto wanted to go over and comfort her, she longed to sit here next to Quidel, leeching off his warmth.

"You okay, Daylah?" Ceto said, loudly enough for her to hear. It was, honestly, the least she could do for her friend.

Daylah bobbed her little blonde head in response.

Her eyes then landed on something in the trees up ahead. She stood up, blanket still pulled tightly around her, her body hunched over in an effort to keep some warmth in. She reached out her hand and pulled up a handful of flowers. All of them; flower, leaves, stem and root. When she turned around, her eyes were bright with excitement and she scurried over to where her pack lay, and rummaged.

When she turned around, she had a black pot in her hand, it looked like a mini cauldron with a long thin handle.

She carried it over to the fire Quidel had made, it had started to really burn by now, the wood within crackling happily and emitting a beautiful aroma.

"May I borrow your knife, Quidel?" Daylah asked, holding her shaking white hand out to him. Quidel obliged without a word.

She then dug a little hole at the edge of the fire and stuck a tall branch in it. It had forked branches at the top and daylah wedged her black pot in the middle and filled it with the remains of her water bottle.

She then grabbed the bunch of flowers and began to expertly dismantle them.

She snapped the flower heads off and placed them on the ground around her, she then separated the stem from the roots and the leaves. She lay them all out on a large piece of slate she had found.

First, she took the thin stem and, very carefully, sliced them in half; she then took the edge of the knife and scraped along the length of the stem until she had a yellow-green sticky substance on the edge of the blade. She tapped it firmly once on the edge of the pot and the substance plopped into the now boiling water. She disregarded the used stems and threw them with the flowers on the floor.

She then gently placed the slate with the leaves and roots over the top of the fire to heat and dry them.

Ceto, curiosity getting the better of her, came to crouch next to Daylah.

"What are you doing?" She didn't feel stupid in asking, looking around she could tell that the Ignis didn't know either.

"Making tea." She replied, bluntly but still in her usual upbeat tone.

She then happily busied herself with flipping the leaves and roots over on the slate.

Ceto hadn't ever wondered how the tea magically warmed her, she had just accepted it; as she had learnt to accept the way of life here very quickly. Self-preservation.

"Ventus grow the flowers, usually up in the rocks of the mountain. They dry them and send them to Azureus for us to brew, and then we send the tea to the different corners ready to drink.

I never dreamed I'd be so lucky as to find some amongst the trees. Just when I thought I might freeze to death." She said, oddly brightly.

"So you can eat the whole thing?" Ceto asked, taking one of the intact flowers from the floor that Daylah hadn't used.

"Almost, the roots, the leaves and the inside of the stem are fine. The casing on the stem and the flowers are actually really poisonous and will definitely kill you." Daylah finished, with a little chuckle.

Ceto pulled off one of the leaves and sniffed it; it smelled of burning tar. She pulled off a nails worth of the leaf and put it on her tongue, chewed and finally swallowed.

"Yuergh! Tastes like tar." Ceto announced and threw the rest of the leaf down.

Everything around her had gone very still, the wind felt as if it was holding its breath.

Daylah had stopped stirring and flipping.

Quidel was on high alert; probably because of Daylah's reaction. Her black eyes were perfectly round, her already white face had paled even more. Her mouth had parted a little to form an "Oh!" and her arms were held up, palms facing Ceto, as if to ward off an evil spirit.

"What?" Ceto asked, her voice a little pitchy in anticipation. Then she felt it.

An ice cold pain stabbing through her body, starting in the base of her throat and then it travelled slowly down towards her stomach. It almost felt as if her insides were freezing solidly as she began to struggle to move her torso.

She was vaguely aware of Oscar calling her name, but he sounded far away.

Quidel put one of his hands under the back of her neck, sweeping her dark hair out of the way, and his other hand behind the back of her knees and he guided her body down gently so that she lay on the cold ground.

She was certain she was about to die.

Not now. Not like this. A panicked voice screeched in her mind. The sounds around her became muffled.

Daylah was shouting instructions to the Ignis who towered around her.

197

Quidel, fierce panic in his golden eyes, pushed Ceto's hair from her clammy face. In that moment, she wished Oscar was by her side.

She could taste and smell burning tar. The inside of her nose felt as if it was burning with every ragged breath that she grasped for.

Amaru and Nuri crouched down at her feet. Their palms outstretched on the ground by her lower body.

Quidel knelt by her head, hovering over Ceto, both his palms placed side by side, starting at the base of her throat with his little finger, ending with his other little finger just above her belly button.

Daylah stood above everyone, looking like the most important person in the world. Little Daylah, shouting orders to three giant warriors.

Ceto began to calm as she accepted the end and she searched the faces around her, rifling for the most important. She needed to see Oscar one last time but he was nowhere to be seen.

After a while, Ceto could feel heat starting at her feet and travelling up towards the top of her thighs, as if the ground beneath her had been heated.

Her torso underneath Quidel's hands began to warm too, and she could feel the inside of her body begin to thaw.

Some time passed and Ceto regained feeling in her chest, she began to wriggle it stiffly.

The four around her breathed out a sigh of relief in unison, even Amaru. She didn't know he cared.

Quidel gently placed his strong arm behind her shoulder blades and lifted her to a sitting position.

Daylah threw herself into a crouch and searched Ceto's face. Ceto wasn't sure what she was looking for but when she seemed confident enough, Daylah turned to her slate over the fire again and began to chop the dried leaves and roots into miniscule pieces and brushed them into the vigorously boiling water. She stirred and stirred until she was happy, poured some into her empty water bottle and handed it to Ceto.

"It's hot, just sip it." She instructed.

As soon as the warm tea made its way down Ceto's throat, down her chest and towards her stomach, Ceto began to feel much better.

Amaru and Nuri had moved away from the crowd to sit on the other side of the fire, still close and on alert.

Quidel stayed by Ceto's side, she leaned on him for support and comfort; he didn't seem to mind.

"Oscar." She weakly pleaded.

Quidel stiffened at the name, straightened up and made his way out of her vision.

Oscar was sat on his heels just behind where Quidel had been kneeling. His face a tinged grey, noticeable pain painted across his features. His hands in a prayer position as they pressed against his lips.

He lunged forward to catch Ceto's drained body as she started to fall after Quidel's hasty exit.

They didn't say a word to each other, but their looks said more than words ever could.

Daylah busied herself with the rest of the leaves and roots, making more tea.

"You're lucky we had Ignis with us. If it was just you and me, I wouldn't have been able to make the tea quick enough to save you." Daylah explained.

Ceto could only see the side of her face, it remained stern.

"I'm sorry, Daylah." Ceto replied, getting up to kneel next to her friend.

"I just assumed, because you were putting them in the tea, that they were okay to eat. I just wanted to try one.

At home, we ate everything we grew. I didn't think. I'm sorry." She finished rather lamely.

"When we dry and then boil the leaves, they lose their poisonous property. To eat them without preparing them first, they're just as poisonous as the flowers." Daylah explained as a concerned mother would. She expected Ceto to know just how poisonous the flowers were. Of course she had no idea, but she already felt foolish enough. So instead, she glanced down at her hands and nodded sadly. As a lectured child would.

Feeling ridiculous and with a warm stomach, Ceto scurried back to her spot with her back pressed firmly to the rock, arms crossed against her chest.

She was pleased when Oscar came to sit next to her.

He placed her petite pale hand in his large one. She smiled up at him, a wave of contentment that he had followed her all this way to sit with her now.

She rested her head on his arm and slowly drifted off to sleep, the world and worries melting around them.

Ceto hadn't realised that she'd drifted off into an awkward sleep; her head fit perfectly onto Oscar's torso, his solid arm curled around her body.

Her body, however, sat rigid at an odd angle with her legs pulled right up to her body, almost in an upright foetal position.

"The sun is setting." Quidel rumbled to the group, Ceto felt the words quake through her.

She stiffly and reluctantly began to untangle herself from her warm sleep.

She glanced at Quidel through her lashes, he glared back with a fierce heat that made her uncomfortable. She took refuge behind Oscar's form as they gathered their belongings.

The group packed up the camp silently. Ceto felt a cloud of apprehension surrounding them.

This was it, the beginning of the end.

Whose end, secretly, no one was certain of.

Through the growing dark, they made their way under the stone archway and along the gravel path that led up the mountain.

The road beneath began to change to cobbles which glittered beneath their feet. Ceto bent down to wipe her finger along one, wondering if it was glittering from being wet.

"The stones are made from the ore they mine from inside the mountain. Most are stone, but some are precious metals or jewels." Quidel explained as he crouched down next to her. "Come on." He nudged her playfully with his shoulder and a smile reached his dimples.

This out of character display took her by surprise. It took her half a second to react.

When her brain caught up, she nudged him back and gave him a bright smile. The two stood up together and Quidel brushed the inside of her palm quickly before heading off up the now cobbled path.

As Quidel walked ahead before them, she noticed that Oscar had seen their interaction. She wondered if Quidel had done that for Oscar's benefit.

She suddenly tasted bile as Oscar followed the rest of the group up the mountain.

She breathed deep and vowed that she would come back and see Ventus in the bright summer sunshine, unburdened by anything or anyone else.

In her quiet contemplation, Ceto didn't notice where she was going, and her foot collided with something metal, kicking whatever it was ahead of her with a clattering and clanging that seemed to go on forever.

Clang. Clink. Clash. Clang. Clink.

The clamour echoed into the still, cold, dark night around them.

When the racket finally stopped, everyone stood statue still, scared to breathe.

They listened to see if the commotion had disturbed anyone or anything lurking in the mountain.

After a few seconds, which seemed like a lifetime, had passed and the sound of flapping or cawing couldn't be heard, Ceto felt the others relaxing a little around her. Clouds of fog escaping their mouths.

Ceto grabbed the edge of her tartan scarf and wrapped it tightly around her chin; partly to hide her face and partly to give her hands something to do, rather than standing there like a naughty child. She fiddled with the tassels, furious with herself.

In the last few hours, she had nearly killed herself and now she had nearly gotten them all killed.

She was painfully aware that she had possibly given their position away to Krokar, who still sat high above them at the top of Ventus.

For all she knew, krokar *had* heard the clatter and now their element of surprise had been kicked away.

She let out a steadying breath, expelling her negative thoughts.

Amaru silently but rapidly flew down the path to where Ceto stood, heart hammering, fury on both of their faces.

He didn't say a word, he didn't make a sound. He stopped suddenly, as close to Ceto as he dared.

Quidel followed more slowly.

Even his breathing was silent, but she could still feel the ferocity in the way his broad shoulders rose and fell. She could feel the heat of his anger pushing away from him and settling on her.

His reaction sparked something inside Ceto and she forgot about feeling sorry for herself; she mimicked Amaru's anger back at him.

Oscar led Daylah away from the danger; Amaru's eventual explosion.

In the back of her mind, she was grateful for this, but the majority of her brain was caught up in the adrenaline that raced around her body.

Nuri took Amaru's hand and guided him away from the situation. Quidel pinned Ceto's arms to her side with his large hands.

She waited for the panic from not being able to move set in, but when it didn't, she took another calming breath and let herself be led to sit on a low stone wall, Quidel sitting stoically by her side.

Across the way, she could see Nuri trying to talk quietly to Amaru, assumingly trying to calm him down.

He did seem to be calming, his shoulders were a little more relaxed but the fury he held in his face was directed towards Ceto.

She glanced over to Oscar, hoping he wasn't angry that she was sitting so close to Quidel. But she saw nothing in his face but love and support.

It was nice to know that, no matter what she did, he was on her side.

Turning her attention back to Amaru, his face had smoothed, and Nuri had stopped whispering to him.

The world seemed quiet; no sound of birds or insects, even the wind was still, uncomfortably still.

She let her eyes adjust to the almost moonless night and took in her surroundings.

Standing, she took a few steps to take a better look.

Surrounding the mountain path, stood Ventus homes.

Caves had been skilfully carved into the mountain. Each cave had a wooden door and a window, some had their wooden shutters closed, and others had their shutters wide open.

Ceto turned to look where the moon should be. She could make out a glow behind the thick clouds.

Taking a deep breath in, she closed her eyes and asked the

wind to shift the clouds.

The wind obliged and Ceto opened her eyes as the moon illuminated their surroundings, the path's colours glowing under the moon's watch.

She peered inside one of the cave's windows and took in a small sharp breath.

Inside the cave, it was set out as if the family were sat down for dinner, but the family was missing. It looked as if they'd been missing for a while.

Mouldy remnants of food lay on the kitchen table, plates and cups still set out as if they were being used.

A wooden structure sat around where a fire had once crackled, still with clothes hanging on it to dry.

At the back of the cave, two rooms stood, each with beds eerily unmade.

Ceto made it to another cave and peered through the window; it was much like the first.

She went to a third cave, its shutter closed. She creaked open the door and let in the moonlight. As she did, a swirl of dust glided into the air and settled back down on a scene like the other caves.

She turned around. Oscar, Daylah, Quidel, Nuri and Amaru had all seen what Ceto had witnessed. Their faces showed shock and a sad disgust as they came to the same conclusion.

"They had no warning." Nuri whispered.

The clouds covered the moon once more, the path below them grew dull and the wind gave a threatening howl.

They edged closer together at the edge of the path, in the shadow of a home.

Nobody answered, it wasn't a question, they all knew it now.

"Ceto's mum knew." Daylah's little voice came from the darkness. This was also met with silence from the group.

Ceto braved a look in Amaru's direction. She was surprised and also pleased to see the look of shame on his face. He shook his head a little, his dark hair falling slightly into his face.

"She knew and people like you," Ceto prodded a finger at Amaru's chest, "ignored her and chased her away.

People who can't feel anything but hatred for anyone who is different from themselves."

She couldn't shout; she didn't know who was listening. She didn't have any anger left inside her anyway.

She had nothing but sadness for the families who once lived in these caves, and pity for those that only know how to hate first and try to understand second.

She tried to hold back tears of frustration as they pricked at her eyes.

Ceto's words hung in the still air.

Amaru looked genuinely remorseful, although she knew he was too proud to admit it.

There came a clatter from a cave a little way up the mountain path.

The group spun in unison to where the noise had come from.

Quidel, Amaru and Nuri jumped in front of the others; Ceto tried to get her emotions in check in case she had to call on the wind for help.

Nothing came after the sound for a while and the group began to relax a little, edging forwards as a unit to where the noise had come from.

A shadow shot out from a cave nearby, running, almost gliding, up the path.

Krokar!

Quidel, Amaru and Nuri ran after the shadow and Ceto called the wind.

The wind lifted the shadow from the ground and tried to hold it there but the shadow effortlessly ran along the gusts. Ceto asked the wind to enfold the shadow and carry it closer, the wind obliged. After some resistance from the shadow, the

205

wind finally managed to bring them to the ground, just ahead of the Ignis. They pointed a spear each at the shadow.

Ceto, Daylah and Oscar ran to catch up.

Ceto stood above the shadow and glared down, asking the wind to stay near, just in case; giving her a sense of control.

"Krokar?!" Ceto shouted, not afraid to make a noise anymore, they had found what they had come here for.

Ceto asked the wind for a little moonlight again.

Below them, sprawled on the cobbles, lay a man.

He was older than Ceto but by no means old. His hair was a silver grey but his face had no signs of age.

His jaw line was square, his eyelashes long and dark, his eyes an emerald green, his torso lean. He was a beautiful man.

She hadn't imagined Krokar to look like this.

"No. No, please. My name is Samir." He spoke, a little over a whisper. Loud enough for them to hear but soft enough to not draw attention.

Hands held up to his face, palms upward. His knees pulled up for protection.

Amaru and Nuri looked to Quidel and Quidel looked to Ceto. She nodded and the Ignis lifted their spears, stepping back half a step.

Samir sat up, "Thank you." He whispered. His throat was hoarse. "I've been alone for so long, alone in the quiet."

Sadness etched in every corner and angle of his face, in the rounding of his shoulders.

His clothes were dirty, there was a deep hollow in his cheeks from hunger.

"Here." Ceto whispered. She took Samir's elbow and pulled him from the ground. He peered at the skies all around, fear visible on his face.

The group walked slowly to the nearest cave, closed the window shutter and the wooden door. Sudden darkness closed in around them for a couple of seconds until Quidel started a fire in the kitchen's stone oven and they were covered in an amber glow.

Ceto sat down with Samir at the kitchen table, Quidel took a seat too.

Daylah jumped up on the kitchen top.

Amaru and Nuri stood guard by the front door, whilst Oscar shuffled around the cave, making sure they were alone.

A small clay pot sat at the centre of the table, filled with dry soil and a brown twig, a sign of past life.

Daylah searched the kitchen for signs of something to eat, there was nothing but rotted fruit, meat that gave off an unbearable stench, a clay pot filled with flour, some questionable butter on a lidded dish and a hard cheese that may or may not have been intended to be hard.

She got to work, combining the flour, butter and a little water from her pack, handing what was left of the water to Samir who sat quietly, eagerly watching her nimble hands work.

Quidel placed the sticky substance into the stone oven and joined them at the table again.

The room was silent but for the crackling of the fire and the wind howling menacingly outside. It sounded far away as it grazed the sides of the thick walls.

Nobody spoke.

Samir looked nervously down at his thin and dirty hands, nervous at the intimidating group who had threatened and then kidnapped him.

Quidel, Amaru and Nuri watched Samir. Quidel rested one hand on his firm thigh and the other leaned on his spear, which stood proudly next to him.

Daylah happily watched her bread bake in the fire and busied herself making a fresh brew of warming tea.

Oscar watched Ceto as she bent her head, fixating on the wooden table, soaking in the different emotions that ran high around her.

Daylah jumped up, startling Samir and Ceto, as she made her way over to the stone oven and peering in as close as she dared.

"I think that's cooked." She announced happily to the room. Quidel placed his hands around the flat bread, seemingly not bothered by the heat of the fire, and placed it on the table. Daylah crumbled some cheese on a plate next to it and poured tea into chipped cups.

More silence followed whilst everyone ate and drank. Samir started by taking a few nibbles of bread and then a few crumbs of cheese.

After a couple of these timid mouthfuls, he then began to rip at the bread and shovel the cheese into his mouth, finishing with gulping the cooled tea.

His body froze for a second. He slowly placed his cup back on the table, and clasped his hands on his lap as if he'd just realised the situation he was in.

"I'm sorry." He said, barely above a hoarse whisper.

"I can make more." Daylah replied, cheerily. Samir seemed to flinch a little at her high voice.

Ceto reached over the table, stopping before her hand reached Samir's.

"Eat as much as you need." She soothed, and then she subtly changed her tone to a more a business-like one.

"We do have a few questions for you and time isn't really on our side." She brought her hand back to sit under the table.

"I'll tell you everything I know." Samir whispered, his eyes wide, willing his captors to believe he will comply.

Daylah went about making more flat bread and brewing more tea.

"How is it everyone is gone, except you?" Quidel probed. Ceto cringed at his intimidating style. She wanted Samir to feel at ease, to be an ally, not a vessel for information.

"I work in the mines. I'd gotten stuck in there but managed

to get myself free." Samir motioned to his left leg.

Ceto could see that his tough trousers had a large rip in them, and underneath, dried blood matted in his leg hair.

"When I finally made it to the entrance of the mines, near the top of Ventus," His arm barely moving as he tried to motion to the top of the mountain. "The first thing I noticed was the eerie silence. No children playing on the mountain path. No mothers calling in their families for dinner. No clang and clatter of dishes. There was no sound." His thin body shivered. "Even the wind stood still as if it had been stolen away too. The sun was setting but there was just enough light to make my way down the mountain to my family home…" Samir stopped, he swallowed.

"They were gone?" Ceto asked, injecting compassion in to her words, whilst her head spun with more and more questions.

Samir nodded, his head bent so low that his chin touched his chest. His shoulders shook with tired, silent sobs.

Ceto reached across the table again, this time, placing her slender pale hand on his arm.

Quidel stiffened at this, but Ceto ignored him.

"I'm sorry about your family." She pulled her arm back and shifted impatiently in her chair.

"I don't mean to sound insensitive, but we *really* need to know what happened. We need to find who did this and stop them." Ceto spoke softly as not to scare Samir into his quiet shell again.

"I don't know what more I can tell you? In a matter of seconds, it seems they had all been taken, all at once, all of Ventus. No warning. No reason." He began to shake noticeably. Ceto made the conscious decision to ignore this, she needed to get every morsel of knowledge from him before it was too late.

"Go on." She nodded.

"That was months ago, maybe longer. The seasons don't make sense, it's difficult to keep track." He scratched his matted hair. "I've been following the stream down the mountain. Some days it dries up, other days it flows fast. Its dry now and it has been for days." Samir smacked his lips together and looked longingly into his cup.

Daylah quickly filled it, smiling brightly at him.

Ceto felt a wash of gladness for Daylah having come along on this journey.

She had never been very good at hospitality and accommodating other's needs. It had been her and her mum all her life, Oscar had always treated their home as his own and had never needed waiting on.

This skill seemed to come naturally to Daylah. Ceto wondered if her gift of foresight helped her to anticipate people's needs.

She nodded appreciatively at her friend who smiled as she stepped back into the shadows.

Samir took a long drink of his tea and looked up at Ceto. His eyes boring into her own. Her icy blue connecting with his emerald green.

"I want to help. I don't believe my family are simply gone. I know they are somewhere, waiting for me." His eyes lost some of their fire. "I don't know how much I can help."

"Tell us your story from the night they disappeared." Ceto encouraged.

"I've been making my way down the mountain, checking in every home, taking what I need. At the start, there was much food to be eaten, but as the weeks went on the food became stale and rancid.

Before tonight, I couldn't tell you the last time I've eaten." He tilted his head to smile at Daylah with gratitude, but he didn't quite meet her eyes.

"I've spent these months in complete silence. In fear of the

Raven." At the mention of the birds, he voice grew even more quiet.

"It's okay." Ceto reassured again, hoping she didn't sound too eager.

"They fly overhead and hop down the mountain. They peer in open doors as if they're looking for something but I know I'm the only one left, I haven't seen a soul.

My progress has been slow. I've been growing weaker as the food became scarce. Only moving at night and even then, only the nights when the clouds cover the moon's light."

A tear rolled down his tanned, hollow cheek and he spoke in a quiet, almost ashamed whisper. "I've been alone. I've been alone in the silent darkness for so long. I've almost forgotten what came before." His shoulders showed silent sobs again. Ceto knew they had almost lost him, but she sensed he had more to tell them.

"We've all known loneliness at one point or another." Ceto tried to sound caring, but she came across pushy instead.

"If I didn't have Ceto, I would have been alone." Oscar interjected, stepping forward and placing his sturdy hand on her shoulder.

"I've spent my whole life living in a group of old women." Daylah added, coming round the table to wrap her arms around Ceto's neck in a warm hug, a little laughter at her own misery.

Nuri pulled up a low stool next to Ceto and sat next to her in solidarity. A knowing expression on her beautiful face. Her long toned legs pulled up to her body as she tried to squeeze as close to the table as she could.

Samir seemed to pull strength from the show of unity before him.

"The Raven come from the top of the mountain. As far as I can tell, there is only one way in and out." As he spoke to the group around the table, his hunched shoulders grew straighter as his hunger, thirst, sadness and fear lessened.

"I watched them, I don't know how long ago," He jittered, "fly almost all the way to Ignis until a great dome filled the air, disintegrating some of them. The rest flew back to the top of the mountain.

Before that, I saw them fly together to the outskirts of Folia, only to be brought down by an invisible shield." Satisfaction crossed his broad face.

Ceto felt her cheeks burning at the memories and found she was glad of the gloom around them.

She didn't find pride in hurting and killing living creatures, but she couldn't say that to Samir. These creatures had taken everything from him. This starving, hunched and quivering display before her, a ghost of the former Ventus she guessed he had been.

"We now know that there are fewer Raven. We know where they come and go. We know where the fight will be, we need to get there." Quidel, all business, brought them back to reality, turning his shoulder to partly block Samir from their conversation.

They were brought back to the present with the immensity of what lay ahead of them now.

They simply had to make it to the top of a very steep, eye wateringly tall mountain, without being detected by the Raven, silently and in the dark.

Silence filled the hut again as everyone had the same fears. It was Quidel who broke the silence once more.

"We rest today. The sun goes down and we make our way up." He commanded.

Amaru was the first to move, Ceto had forgotten he was there; he was so silent and still.

"Come, Nuri." He grunted to the room, not making eye contact.

Nuri looked at Ceto and stuttered a few sounds and Ceto

212

knew that Nuri didn't want to go with Amaru.

"A-actually, I thought the girls could stay together and the boys could sleep in the next house." Ceto suggested.

Amaru stopped as he reached out to open the door.

"Nuri. Come." He repeated. Ceto flinched at the anger and sharpness in his words.

"Stop this." Quidel stood up and strode easily to where Amaru stood, seething.

"Amaru, Samir, with me. Ceto, Daylah, *Nuri*," he said the last name with a hidden warning, "stay here. Rest." Quidel organised.

"Er...I'd...I...I'd like to stay on my own," Samir spoke up, "If that's okay?" He hastily added.

Quidel glanced at Ceto, "I don't know if that's a good idea." He said but Ceto knew he was leaving the final decision to her.

"I think that's okay." She turned to look Samir in the eye.

"We can trust you, can't we?" She warned with her eyes.

Samir smiled back and nodded politely.

"I've been on my own for so long, it would feel strange to sleep with company. You can trust me." He bent his head low, in submission.

At that, Quidel nodded, opened the thick wooden door a crack and slowly peered outside.

The sun was beginning to rise and the wind had eased off a little.

Soundlessly, Quidel and Amaru made their way to the hut at the other end of the mountain path.

Samir followed the two Ignis men and turned around to those left in the hut.

"Make sure the door is closed tight and don't make a sound." He whispered almost inaudibly and pushed the door closed slowly.

A strange feeling crept up the back of Ceto's spine and it

spread across her scalp, leaving it tingling. Her stomach somersaulted and she felt queasy.

She was suddenly very aware that they were not alone on this mountain. That there were creatures here that wanted to find them and cause them harm.

"So glad I'm not considered male." Oscar joked. Ceto snorted a little through her nose, feeling the tension break. The sensation of laughter lifted her worry and anxiety for a moment.

Daylah took her hand, "Let's sleep." She softly suggested. Ceto glanced down to see exhaustion on her little face.

Ceto and Daylah took the double bed, whilst Nuri and Oscar took the single beds.

Exhaustion took over their bodies and minds, and within a matter of seconds, even with their thoughts of the night unfolding in their minds, they were all fast asleep.

Chapter 20

Tap. Tap. T-t-t-t-tap tap.

Ceto gasped as her body flung itself into a seated position. She felt as though she'd been submerged in water and suddenly found the surface.

She had been so soundly asleep that she'd forgotten where she was.

She peered around in the darkness, a small orange glow coming from the kitchen where Quidel's fire was just about burning.

As Ceto's eyes began to adjust to the darkness, she spotted Nuri, spear in hand, her long legs bent and ready to pounce, her muscular shoulder leaning against the bedroom wall.

Tap. Tap. TAPTAPTAPTAP.

Ceto looked next to her in the bed where she knew Daylah was. She was still lying down, she hadn't moved an inch but her eyes were large and round, full of fear.

Ceto squeezed Daylah's hand to reassure her and, with her other hand, pressed her finger to her lips, suggesting that Daylah should be silent.

Oscar was in the other room, she felt panic at not knowing if he was still there or if he was about to come out of the room making a noise.

They waited.

After a couple of minutes, they started to relax a little as they grew more sure that the danger had passed, for now.

Suddenly, the dying fire in the stone oven cracked as a piece of wood broke from the heat.

Tap. T-t-t-tap. TAPTAPTAP. TAPTAPTAP. T-t-t-tap.

The three girls held their breath and Nuri, as quietly as a cat stalking a mouse, made her way over to the fire and seemed to suck in the remaining embers with her arms held wide.

They were plunged into darkness.

Daylah grabbed Ceto's hand. She could tell that Daylah was

trying to stifle her body's shakes.

They stayed as statues in the endless darkness, only breathing as much as they dared. Unable to see even their noses in front of them.

After a while, Ceto closed her eyes, coming to terms with the fact that no matter how long she waited, her eyes would not adjust to the dark world around her.

With her eyes closed, her mind leaned on her other senses to keep her safe, and her ears pricked up when they heard multiple wings on the roof and outside the door as they skimmed the air, landing all around.

Hearts hammering, they waited in silence.

Ceto now came to appreciate Samir's hoarse voice and fear of noise. She couldn't imagine someone living like this. Without the support of others around, completely alone and petrified to simply breathe too loudly.

As her ears grew more sensitive, Ceto heard the Raven take flight, one by one until there could only be a few left.

Next, a single Raven squawked loudly and the rest pushed down on the air and flew away.

They girls didn't move immediately, they daren't.

After, what could have been further hours of silence, Nuri quietly blew the embers back into the stone oven and peered into the bedroom at Ceto, shaking her head in disbelief.

She was still soundless, not that Ceto needed any confirmation of how Nuri was feeling.

It's one thing to be afraid, it's another to sit in absolute darkness, waiting for what you fear to find you, with no obvious escape. Relying on luck and fate.

Daylah jumped into Ceto as Oscar appeared, leaning on the doorframe. His copper hair pointing this way and that, his disbelief at what they had just survived mimicked Nuri's.

Ceto rubbed Daylah's arm subconsciously as she responded to Oscar's expression with her own of relief.

Nuri motioned for the rest to stay where they were, and she headed to the door.

Ceto wanted to shout out to stop her from opening the door but she knew, if she moved quickly enough to achieve that, the bed would creak and attract any Raven left.

So she sat still and silent, powerless to what could be waiting on the other side of the door for Nuri.

A slither of daylight leaked into the hut.

Ceto held her breath.

A little more light now, it almost reached the bedroom. Nuri, crouched slightly, her body and mind alert, her spear pointed forwards. She slowly stepped one foot in front of the other, not making a sound.

A lioness stalking her prey.

A Raven screeched and Ceto's heart stopped.

Then, there was silence.

Ceto glanced down at her young friend, still lying next to her. Her eyes and cheeks wet with tears. Daylah was petrified and couldn't move.

Ceto put her lip next to Daylah's exposed ear and told her, "I'll be right back. Stay here. Be silent." She didn't speak the words, merely moved her lips to form the words and let out a breath of air.

Ceto pulled her hand from Daylah's grasp and slid off the bed.

She stalked as quietly as she could, whilst asking the wind to stay close but undetected, just in case.

She held her hand up to Oscar as she moved past him, telling him to stay where he was.

Ceto peered one eye around the wooden door, holding her breath.

Relief washed over her, she closed her eyes and released the wind, thankfully.

Quidel, Amaru, and Nuri stood huddled on the path.

The fierce female warrior, proudly stood with a Raven skewered onto her spear. Its neck dangled backwards and its wings were splayed out at either side of its body.

Ceto couldn't help but feel a little sadness for the creature. Samir could be seen a distance away from the Ignis. His body turning in on itself as he hugged his arms, his head bent low. Quidel turned his head when he sensed Ceto stood in the doorway, and made his way over to her.

The others followed him without a word.

Ceto examined his effortless leadership and tried to imitate it. She pulled her shoulders back and changed to an intense expression.

She then noticed Oscar trying to pat down his untamed hair as he stood in the kitchen, awaiting the group, and her expression softened as her stomach flipped.

Quidel brushed past her in the doorway. He stopped, glanced down at her and one side of his mouth pulled up into a smile. The dimple in his cheek made her stomach flip once more, until she began to feel uneasy under his gaze.

"Good morning." Quidel playfully whispered.

Ceto closed her eyes and tried to keep a calm demeanour.

"Good *evening*." She replied impishly.

A sickness ran through her as she felt regret as she caught sight of Oscar again, and she dropped her head, moving to the side to let the others in.

The door shut firmly after Samir, the last one in, shutting out the late afternoon's light.

A fire had been lit in the stone oven again, everyone took a few seconds to adjust their eyes to the flame's light once more.

The seating arrangements felt less formal than the previous night.

Oscar milled about with his hands in his pockets, looking through the kitchen cupboards and the bedrooms.

Amaru and Quidel sat on the edge of the double bed, deep in a quiet conversation.

Daylah sat on the kitchen top, her hands pressed under her thighs and staring at the ground.

Ceto, at the kitchen table with Nuri and Samir, laced her fingers together and circled her thumbs in quiet contemplation and internal chiding. Why couldn't she control herself around Quidel? She felt no connection to him. He was simply a pretty face.

She noticed that Samir had his hands clasped together in between his thighs and his shoulders and head hunched over. His face had turned ashen.

Ceto examined the room, she quickly realised what was the matter.

"Nuri, do you mind putting that outside? Or at least down?" She asked as Nuri still had the dead Raven on top of her spear, raised high as if she were showing off her kill. Ceto had to admit, it made her a little queasy too.

Nuri shrugged, pulled the Raven off the end of her spear with a sickening wet, snap and hurled the bird to a dark corner of the room.

Ceto, Oscar, Daylah and Samir flinched at the show but the Ignis didn't seem the slightest bit bothered by it.

Ceto was beginning to form a clear picture of the different races she'd met here.

Ignis, the warriors; Azureus, the healers; Folia, the wise mind; Ventus, the watchful eyes. The different races seemed to be designed to work together in harmony, but they were too busy keeping themselves in their corner and despising each other.

She was fond of Samir; she could tell Quidel was wary of him, and she couldn't make herself understand that.

She felt he had a natural warmth to him, if she could just bring him out of his anxious shell that he'd cocooned himself

219

into in his solitude, then she could show Quidel that Samir wasn't another problem he had to worry about.

"Daylah? Shall we make some breakfast?" Ceto suggested. Daylah didn't need much persuasion, looking after others came naturally to her, which was one of the reasons why Ceto often forgot how young she really was. But not now, Ceto could see blank fear on her small face.

Ceto came to stand next to Daylah, their eyes level as Daylah sat on the kitchen top.

"You'll have to show me how to brew the tea and make the flat bread so you don't have to do it all yourself." Ceto, still in hushed tones, tried to sound cheerful for her friend. Daylah eased herself to stand on the ground, but didn't respond. Ceto bumped her gently with the side of her hip to try to get a smile, but there was still no response.

"Are you okay?" Ceto asked as quietly as she could, so as not to draw attention to their conversation.

Daylah's head bobbed slightly up and down in response as her hands busied with boiling water and mixing flour, butter and water.

Becoming aware that she wasn't going to get anything from her, Ceto gave Daylah a hug, wrapping her arms completely around her and folding her body over so Daylah was hidden from the world. Ceto could feel Daylah's body stuttering slightly as she let out a few quiet sobs.

Daylah pulled away slightly and lifted her blonde head upwards to bring her black eyes to Ceto's blue ones.

"Are they going to get me?" She asked in a voice that might have belonged to a mouse, and when Ceto realised that she was asking about the Raven, her heart gave a painful jolt. How could she have led a child down this dangerous, possibly life threatening, path?

How selfish she had been for needing the company and letting Daylah do what she naïvely wanted, because it suited her own needs.

The gravity of where she had brought Daylah, an innocent child, hit her suddenly and swiftly.

"No." Ceto answered firmly, pulling her into their embrace harder, so that Daylah had to turn her head back into it. "No. I will not let them get you." Ceto emptily promised.

The sun set outside as they hid in the darkness, filling their stomachs and resting as much as they could; mentally preparing for the night's trek uphill.

Ceto made her way to sit at the kitchen table next to Samir, with the hope of bringing him out of his shell. She needed to prove to herself that what she felt in her gut was right; she felt he wasn't a threat and that he could help them.

"Samir, I've only explored Ventus at night, but it looks like a beautiful place to live?" She prompted.

He looked up and gave a small smile, a flash of something behind his eyes, but he didn't respond.

"Have you explored the rest of Natus yourself?" Ceto prompted further, making sure to end each sentence with a definite question.

There was a long pause, she shifted in her seat. She hadn't had much practise in conversation starting. She hadn't had much use for that particular skill on Earth, having only Oscar and her mum for company. But she was saved the trouble when Samir cleared his throat.

"We take trips down the mountain and to the edge of Folia as young adults. We collect flowers for brewing.

There is an old family whose responsibility it has always been to get the flowers to Azureus for brewing but, no, we have not been welcome in Ignis for a long time now." Samir explained, finishing with a stern tone as he glanced at the Ignis.

Nuri had a passive look across her face but there was a small hint of shame hidden in there in the way her eyes wouldn't

221

meet Samir's. Amaru actually growled from the next room and if the situation hadn't been so tense, Ceto might have laughed at the response.

Quidel seemed defensive. "We have never kept anyone from Ignis. You hide in your caves with our fire for warmth…" He began but was cut off by Samir, his voice growing uncomfortably louder.

"We haven't had your flames for years, we make our own fire. It is all we need." He closed his eyes and held a defensive hand up towards Quidel.

"Ignis haven't accepted our help for a long time. We used to work together, Ventus and Ignis. We were once warriors like yourselves but we took to the mines when you no longer needed our help."

Regret instantly rushed its way through Ceto, but before she could break up their fight, a small voice stuttered it's way between the grown men.

"Sh-shouldn't we still be quiet? Just in case…the Raven?" Daylah squeaked.

Samir was on his feet now and looked down his pointed nose at Daylah. His green eyes turned to a liquid fire.

"We are not welcome in Azureus either." His voice quiet now, but still with an underlying fury of many generations. Daylah shrunk back into the shadows.

"Folia are the most accepting race but they are few." He went on.

Ceto's stomach lurched at the mention of the Folia.

"If the races hadn't spoken in so long, then why were you making your way down the mountain? I assumed it was for help?" Ceto asked, her voice shaking. The way he had treated Daylah turned a protective switch on inside her.

Oscar made his way over to where Ceto stood, placing his arm around her as he would have done at home when she needed comfort. But she shrugged him off now, not needing him, she needed to feel her anger in this moment.

With a quick glance at his forlorn expression, she felt shame at her reaction, but she didn't show it. There was much more at stake here.

"I needed help." Samir's glance turned back to the table top, but he remained standing.

"Help for my people...for my family. My daughter." His voice caught in his throat and he seemed to crumble back into the kitchen chair.

"But if the other races are so unwilling to help each other, what makes you think they would help now?" Ceto goaded. She had felt a shift inside herself and she wasn't too sure that Samir wasn't a threat now.

Samir lifted his head proudly and stared intensely into Quidel's.

"I had no other choice."

Another silence fell around them, they had exhausted their anger.

"I haven't been in Natus for very long, and I assume there is a lot that I don't know." She remained standing whilst the others took seated positions. Nods of agreement bobbed around the room at her.

"But it seems to me that you need help from each other. That you're struggling to get by on your own? Afraid to ask for help." Ceto then turned to Quidel. "If Samir turned up in Ignis, looking the way he did when we found him last night," She turned to Samir with an apologetic expression, "Would you have helped, or would you have turned him away because he is Ventus? Or worse, would you have hurt him because he is Ventus?" Quidel's expression turned to shock at the last part.

"If he wanders into Ignis, we would do what we needed to. For Ignis." Amaru cut in.

"Quidel?" Ceto implored, not taking her eyes away from his

golden ones.

"We would help, we would not turn him away." Quidel calmly replied. Samir looked at Quidel and Nuri as if he was seeing them for the first time.

"We would help too!" Daylah piped up, looking as if her mood had lifted. "We helped Ceto when she walked into Azureus, looking lost and afraid." She giggled at this.

"I *was* lost and afraid." Ceto giggled too. "Khepri had sent me with no explanation, to Azureus, and Daylah found me. She helped me; a complete stranger with black hair and strange clothes." Ceto smiled warmly across the room where Daylah sat high on the kitchen side, her bare legs swinging from side to side, her dress riding up as she did, showing her pale calves.

"You know Khepri?" Samir asked.

"Yes, Khepri was my first friend." A jolt ran through Ceto's chest as she remembered the magnificent creature. "Everything I know came from Khepri; I can ask the wind for help and I can keep the Raven at bay, for a while anyway." She explained, a pink tinge hinted on her cheeks.

"That was you?" Samir whispered in awe. Ceto knew he was talking about the "dome" as he had put it before.

"That was me." Ceto replied, not as enthusiastically as Samir. She still didn't feel right about killing creatures, even if they were trying to kill first.

"I killed one with my spear." Nuri's words fell flat in the air. She liked Nuri, but Ceto felt they had different views in life. Ceto's was to preserve life; Nuri's, like most Ignis, wasn't. She rearranged her face quickly, unfurrowing her brow and changing it to an encouraging smile.

"Listen, I don't want to overstep. I don't know your customs, your history, but I do have an outsider's perspective. It seems that the majority of Natus are willing to work together, but there are a select few that aren't willing to be inclusive." She threw a look at Amaru, sat alone in the bedroom. A flickering orange running across his face as he glared up at Ceto. His body thrust forward, resting his forearms on the tops of his thighs, his head facing the ground, his eyes seething up at every word Ceto uttered. She carried on without a care for his anger.

"They are stuck in their ways. They are angry and I think they have forgotten why. They are filled with a hatred." Everyone, even Oscar, had their heads dipped low as a wave of shame spread through them.

"Unfortunately, that hatred has been allowed to overpower the good. But there's more good in this group than bad." Amaru finally dropped his gaze, the back of his neck visible as he rested his forehead on his clasped hands.

The others glanced up at Ceto and each responded with their own version of a smile. Daylah's the brightest. Oscar's filled with awe.

"Can we work together? Can we stop bickering like children and actually do some *good* together?"

The heads around her bobbed up and down in agreement. A wave of intense emotion flowed through her when she realised Amaru was nodding along with the rest.

Chapter 21

Samir, his body clock tuned perfectly to the setting sun on the other side of the door, quietly and without warning, made his way over to the heavy wooden door.

He asked the Ignis to lower the flame's glow, Quidel obliged. Samir opened the door a crack. Daylight didn't flood the room as Ceto's mind had assumed it would, but moonlight, bright silvery moonlight.

Samir, his shoulders hunched again, turned to the group. "There are no clouds tonight and the moon is almost full. If I had more energy, I could shift the clouds to give us some coverage…I don't think we will be making much progress tonight." He shuffled back over to the kitchen table and slumped back into his seat, utterly defeated.

Ceto went to take a look outside and kindly asked the wind if they could move the clouds to block the moon's light a little. Almost instantly, great thick clouds came flying in from skies far away and settled naturally in front of the moon.

"Let's go." Ceto spun around and announced to the group in an excited whisper.

Samir lifted his head to her with a strange expression, half impressed, half disgusted.

She ignored him, grabbed her pack and quietly made her way outside. She put it to the back of her mind for now, but frowned behind him.

The group made slow progress, following the winding mountain path. Always careful not to make a sound. Always watching and listening for a rustle of wing or an ear piercing squawk.

Ceto noticed that the mountain dwellings grew grander the higher they climbed. They had changed from the simple design they had first taken refuge in; now, most had intricate etchings around the door frames and great wooden doors with impressive ironmongery. Some had elaborate door knockers in the shapes of animals, birds mainly. She also noticed that outside the houses higher on the mountain, there seemed to be less clutter. No upturned wooden crates, no empty troughs, no dusty flower pots.

They walked through the night, not stopping for rest or water.

Ceto assumed that Samir would be at the back of the group due to his lack of energy, but he was leading the way and he never faltered. Growing up in this landscape probably helped, spending his life walking up and down the steep path.

She found herself watching Samir as he climbed, looking through the Ignis as they had positioned themselves in the centre of the group.

Samir was a couple of inches taller than Quidel and Amaru but, where they were broader in the shoulder, Samir was incredibly thin as if he'd been stretched.

The three men were equally as muscular, but the thinness of Samir seemed to make him seem taller than the others. His appearance reminded her of Oscar. She glanced over her shoulder at Oscar and gave him a grateful smile, which he responded to with one of his own.

When she turned to face forward, she was surprised to find Nuri was now glaring at her, anger on her face.

More confusion spread through her mind at another strange encounter.

First Samir, and now Nuri. She couldn't understand what she had done to warrant these glares. Her stomach made a painful twist and she fell into step with Oscar and Daylah, taking Oscar's hand for support.

She smiled down at Daylah but found her friend was lost in her own thoughts.

"Hey." Ceto whispered so quietly, she barely made a sound, so she coupled it with a gentle hip nudge. Daylah looked up and gave an unconvincing smile.

Unexplainable despair leaked through Ceto as the mood of the group seemed to consume her and her steps became sullen.

Tired and a little damp from the sleet that had begun, the group huddled into a large house near the top of the mountain.

If they hadn't been worn down by the night, they would have noticed its grandeur.

The wooden door was at least 8 feet tall and each panel of the door, reinforced with steel strips.

A large dense door knocker sat bolted to the centre of the door, an eagle with its wings thrust out proudly at either side of its streamline body, the detail almost life like.

Swirls and waved lines masterfully carved into the stone door frame.

Unlike the smaller rustic homes down the mountain, this house had been expertly smoothed and shaped into the mountain.

As soon as the last of the group had entered, the door was firmly closed behind them and the moon's light cut off as if someone had flicked a switch.

The only sound the settling dust around them.

Ceto let the darkness cover her eyes, happy to feel as if she were on her own for a moment. Longing to have solitude for a breath as she let exhaustion roll over her. She let the burn in her legs grow loud and prominent in her mind.

An amber glow came from the back of the house and Ceto realised that the group had lazily made their way to the kitchen at the far end of the stone house, as Ceto stood by herself in the half light.

Daylah's childlike face in the distance softened Ceto's fatigued one, and she tentatively made her way to the warm kitchen.

The kitchen table, long and thing, was big enough for everyone to sit at with chairs to spare.

Daylah made a batch of warming tea which everyone gulped gratefully. There was a little flat bread baking in the stone oven that Daylah had made with the last of the ingredients. Everyone had the same thought; this was the last of the food. Ceto knew that the lack of food was a much more pressing matter, but the worry at the forefront of her mind was the morale surrounding her. Two of the group seemed angry with her and Daylah was distant. She knew it was her fault, somehow, but she didn't have the skills to do anything about it.

The only person she knew she could count on to lift her mood was Oscar. She quickly scanned the room for him. Her stomach squirmed painfully when she found him sat at the other end of the kitchen table, in a quiet discussion with Nuri. Ceto let her eyes drop to the kitchen table.

Ceto's drained mind was vaguely aware that Daylah had wandered off into another room. Her subconscious ear hearing tin gently hitting tin and a small voice saying her name as loudly as it dared.

Without knowing it, Ceto had gotten up from her chair and made her way to the small room off the kitchen.

Ceto's weary mind took a couple of seconds to piece together what she was seeing.

Without saying a word, she staggered back into the kitchen to where her pack lay discarded on the floor. Reaching in, she pulled out a glass jar and scooped out a flame from the stone oven where the last of the flat bread lay forgotten and blackening.

She made her way back to Daylah, casting an amber glow on what she had found.

Shelves upon shelves of tinned food; soup, beans, fruit, meat, olives, fish, spices, dried pasta and in the corner of the room sat large containers of water, stacked up high and half covered with a heavy cloth. Ceto's eyes widened as hope grew from her navel up to her throat.

She firmly grabbed Daylah's thin arm and breathed, "Food." Daylah's dark eyes widened in realisation. She hadn't known exactly what she was seeing at first, the tins had been brought from Ceto's world.

Ceto and Daylah enthusiastically grabbed various pots and pans and brought them to sit, covering the kitchen counters, a little more loudly than they should have. Samir openly flinched at the high pitched clangs.

"Sorry." Ceto whispered to the group with a large grin, the smile felt strange on her face but the rest of the group smiled back in their various different degrees.

Even Amaru gave a slight smirk with one side of his mouth. She disappeared into the back room again, grabbing different foods and filling the pots and pans with almost everything they had found.

Samir inquisitively joined the girls and offered help. Between them, they eventually created a large and exotic feast.

Daylah handed out plates and bowls to the Ignis as they looked on with mystified expressions.

Ceto glanced over the wide range of food in front of them and her body relaxed at the promise of a warm substantial meal, the mood in the room lifted too.

Three different soups, slices of canned meat, a large bowl of tomato pasta, plain noodles, sardines, olives, scrambled eggs, crisps, peach slices, custard, jelly and a large warm chocolate cake, drenched in warm chocolate sauce, plus pots of coffee and all the water and warming tea they could ever need.

If they weren't on the brink of starving, the different smells would have made them nauseous, but each of them grabbed a spoon, ladle or fork and filled their plates with as much as they could.

They had spent days in silent fear but this was a joyous silence, everyone was completely consumed in ecstasy as they shovelled food into their mouths.

After some time, the soft clang of cutlery halted, half empty bowls and plates lay in the centre of the table. Each leaning back in their chairs, some holding their full stomachs, others closing their eyes as the feeling of contentment washed over them.

"What's this?" Amaru asked, poking the coffee pot, quickly pulling his finger away. "It's warm." He glared at the pot as if challenging it to shock him again.

"It's coffee, try some." Ceto encouraged whilst stifling a chuckle, handing him a mug.

Amaru didn't take it, instead he glared back at her, mistrust across his dark face.

Ceto rolled her eyes, poured herself some coffee, drank it and shrugged her shoulders at him as if to say, "See?" and handed him another mug.

After examining the liquid, he tried a little sip and jumped back, holding the mug at arm's length as if it would attack him at any minute. Brow furrowed and the corners of his mouth tilted downward.

"Bitter." He announced.

Ceto couldn't help but give a little throaty laugh, her stomach shaking up and down.

"It's better with milk and sugar," She explained, "but we couldn't find any." She sighed.

Looking around at the content, warm faces of her companions, she voiced something she'd had on her mind through the night.

"I've been thinking." She began. "We should probably stay here through the day and stay through the night too. There's enough beds for everyone and more than enough food to keep us fed for weeks. It seems a good place to regain our strength. We can reach the top of the mountain the following night."

"Impossible." Amaru bluntly threw back at her.

"We don't have much time left. You've seen Folia, and Ignis and Azureus are being taken through the night. We don't even know what happened to Ventus." Quidel tried to explain Amaru's feelings.

"I know, I know." Ceto waved away. "But as far as we know, Krokar still has no idea that we're even on this mountain, and I'd rather have what little advantage we can manage. We're risking the element of surprise if I spend another night covering the moonlight with thick cloud. I'd rather not give him even a slight nagging feeling that we might be somewhere near." She looked round at the group, pleading them with her eyes. She ignored Samir as he narrowed his eyes at her speech. What had she done to offend him so? Part of the reason she wanted them to wait another night was that keeping the clouds around to cover the moon was leeching the strength out of her and she knew she would need all the strength she could gather if she had even the slightest chance of winning this fight; she couldn't tell the others this. She didn't want to look weak.

"It's not a bad idea." Samir was the first to agree, though he wasn't offering support.

"It's for myself and Ceto to decide." Quidel fired at Samir. Samir looked Quidel straight in the eye, emerald against amber.

"Before tonight, I can't remember the last time I ate more than a mouthful. I think Ceto makes a good argument." There was silence for a few beats whilst the tension built up in the room. Amaru tensed for a fight, an excited blaze in his eyes.

"The doors and windows in these houses are thicker. Nothing will get in and, as long as we try to keep quiet, we shouldn't be heard from outside." Samir used his knowledge of Ventus to persuade Quidel.

"See, it's the best idea we have." Ceto added on to the argument, whilst also trying to fill the angry silence with empty noise.

"It's a good idea." Oscar muttered into his mug of coffee. Ceto's heart lightened at the sound of his musical voice.

"I think it's a great idea, too!" Daylah happily chimed in. The tension seemed to break down with Daylah's infectiously happy nature.

"I get the best room!" She childishly ran out of the kitchen in search of a bed.

At the sight of her juvenile enthusiasm, Samir and Quidel seemed to forget about their anger and they all had a small laugh, except Amaru who seemed disappointed at the tension easing.

Ceto was starting to grow tired of his behaviour but at the risk of starting a new argument, she let it go.

Realising how achingly tired her body felt she announced with a smile, "I'm going to find the second best room."

Daylah was right, she had certainly found the best room. It wasn't the biggest and was sparse except in the centre of the room lay a large bed. It was low to the ground and a navy blue quilt lay on the top.

Daylah lay curled up in the middle of the bed, already fast asleep. A gentle smile visible on her soft face. The luxuriously thick quilt almost swallowing her up.

Happy in the knowledge that her small friend was content, for a few hours at least, she placed a jar of Ignis fire on a small glass table at the edge of the room.

She then made her way across the large house to a room that stood on its own, the majority of the rooms being on the side Daylah was sleeping.

She had chosen a room across the hall because she longed for the chance to be on her own for a while, for a chance to get lost in thought without being asked what she was thinking. She needed some quiet contemplation as to what she could have done to offend Nuri and Samir. She racked her brain, thinking back to the last few hours. Had she said something? Done something to offend them? After a while of mentally retracing her steps, she was stumped. She concluded that it could be anything she'd said or done, after all, she wasn't very knowledgeable on Natus and the customs of the people that lived here.

She then finally turned her attention to the information she'd pushed to the back of her mind regarding what she now knew about Krokar; she was starting to piece together a little about him.

Then there was the story of who she was and where she had come from. The story of her mum and dad. She felt as if it was just a story she had been told, but she now needed to pick every piece apart. She wouldn't be able to do any of this with others around, she couldn't guarantee her facial expression wouldn't betray her.

She examined the room, taking in its beauty.

On each of the three walls stood great tapestries of a forest, the fourth wall had a large picture of a footpath lined with lavender. The ceiling was scattered with hundreds of bright tiny dots, they seemed to twinkle with the light of her Ignis fire. The floor was covered in a thick carpet.

Ceto took off her dirty boots and flexed her toes into the soft fabric.

Ahead, lay her bed for the next couple of days. A large canopy bed proudly stood, towering up to the ceiling. It looked as if it was made with trees from Folia, unshapen but they held together perfectly. Soft, thin curtains hung from the top of the bed and draped across the floor.

Ceto walked over to the bed, stroking her hand across the

curtains and placing her pack in the corner of the room. When she turned back around, she jumped at the sight of a silent figure leaning on the doorway.

It was Nuri, her arms crossed defensively across her chest. "Oh, hi. Did you find a good room?" Ceto asked. Nuri was giving off a stubborn vibe, her face almost passive.

"How do you feel about Samir?" Nuri pried. This caught Ceto a little off guard and her brow furrowed.

"I think he can be trusted." She began, assuming this is what Nuri meant, but when she didn't answer, Ceto prompted further. "Don't you?"

"I'm angry with you." Nuri replied, in an oddly calm manner, still not moving from the doorway, her arms still crossed.

"I-I'm sorry. What did I do?" Ceto asked, tears prickling in her eyes. She wished she'd had more time to assess the cause of Nuri's anger.

She quickly racked her memories now, but nothing jumped out at her.

"I'm sorry if I've offended you, Nuri. I would never..." Ceto began to try explaining.

"And Quidel? Oscar? How do you feel about them?" Nuri interjected.

"Oh. Well. You see-I..." Ceto was at a loss of what to say. This seemed to have come out of the blue. Was she angry because she was jealous? This concept seemed ludicrous to Ceto.

What did Nuri want her to say? What was the safest way to navigate a situation so alien to her? She thought it safer to keep silent. Her face growing hot, her heart hammering at the base of her throat at the glare of a young woman who was becoming her friend in the not so distant past.

"You can't have Quidel, Samir *and* Oscar. That's not fair." Nuri explained, her voice careful to be void of any emotion. Ceto let out a short sharp laugh of relief. If that was all it was, she could navigate her way out of this.

But Nuri took her relief as an insult, her eyes narrowed.

"Nuri, I don't feel...anything for Samir. I don't know where that's come from, I'm sorry." Ceto spoke quickly, like ripping off a plaster. Quickly and painless.

"I hardly know Quidel. I don't think we get on in that way, he's very...stiff." She inched her spine upwards to express how she felt about him. She risked a glance at Nuri to see if she had softened, hoping that she had defused the situation. But she hadn't moved. So, she hadn't said what Nuri had come to hear yet. "If...you like Quidel...I won't stand in your way?" Ceto spoke as a question, she felt very uncomfortable.

"He's our leader. I follow him." Nuri cut in.

"Oh, I'm sorry." Ceto felt like she couldn't stop offending Nuri, she wasn't saying the right things.

"I just thought...I'm really sorry for making you angry. I'm still learning your customs. I'd hate to think you were upset with me, Nuri."

At that, Nuri dropped her arms and let out a deep sigh.

"I don't know what I'm feeling." Nuri said, making her way into the bedroom. "It's frustrating."

"Would you like to talk to me?" Ceto warily suggested, hoping that this wouldn't offend her again.

"Samir is thin, he's weak, he's...strong," It seemed to cause Nuri an internal struggle to compliment him.

"Samir isn't a warrior. I see Samir." She paused. "He is Ventus." She prickled.

Realisation struck Ceto in her stomach. She braced herself to deliver more bad news that could amount to more hostility.

"He's looking for his wife and child." Ceto gently explained, trying her best to sound soothing and not judgmental.

"I know." Nuri whispered.

There was a short silence between them.

"I was wrong, I spoke without thinking." Nuri apologised and strode back to the door. Ceto was struggling to keep up with the conversation and Nuri's emotions. She wondered if this was because she didn't have the tools for this sort of thing, or if the confusion was on Nuri's side.

"Quidel is different towards you than Ignis women. If you truly feel that way, he should know." She warned.

Ceto smiled reassuringly in response, although her stomach did a sickening somersault.

"I'll leave you. I'm next door to Daylah if you need anything." She said as she made her way to the doorway, stopping just before she left and turned.

"Talk with Quidel, he may have Fixed with you." She finished with a knowing look and walked away.

Ceto watched Nuri stalk across to the other side of the house in a few easy strides, to see which room she was in.

Ceto closed the bedroom door, the bottom of it sliding against the plush carpet.

She perched on the edge of the bed, pushed her knotty hair back with her fingertips, giving it a gentle tug as she did. More than anyone, she longed to find where Oscar was staying, to talk this through with him, but she couldn't do that without admitting to him how she felt. At least she felt a small relief at figuring out how she'd offended Nuri. She ticked Nuri off her to do list in her mind.

She heaved her body to stand and set out to find Quidel, it was the next right thing to do.

She placed herself in front of a mirror on her way out of the room, her fingers clawing at her hair, trying to make herself look more presentable.

She couldn't deny to herself that she found Quidel attractive on the surface, but Nuri was right, it was apparent that he felt more for her than she did for him. Maybe if she could clear the air, it would make the last part of their journey less strained.

She glanced out into the wide corridor, wondering which room Oscar had found himself in. Oscar, safe, loving Oscar. She sighed at the thought of him and wished he was here to help her. She could be herself with him. She felt equally in charge and out of control with him. He excited her, he challenged her. He was the other half of her.

She forced herself to push him to the back of her mind and concentrate on the task at hand.

With a steadying breath in, and a slow breath out, Ceto made her way to the bedroom she assumed Quidel had taken.

As she made her way across the house, a figure in the kitchen caught her attention. She was a little surprised to find Samir sat at the kitchen table, colour returning to his tanned face and a sparkle growing in his vibrant eyes. He nodded in her direction in a way of a greeting, but his face didn't move. He didn't seem angry at this moment, he looked calculating.

"Did you not find a bed? I assumed there would be enough?" Ceto asked.

"I found one, don't worry." He waved his hand up at her to waft away her worries.

"I hate to see this food go to waste after…being so hungry for so long." Samir admitted, a little embarrassed.

Ceto felt a shift in their dynamic. He wasn't being friendly, but he was talking to her again, and that was progress.

"Eat what you need, and get some rest." She smiled and made to turn back towards Quidel's room.

"Can I ask you a question?" Samir asked quickly at Ceto's back. She turned back around, slowly, unsure of where this would lead. Was she about to find out how she had offended him?

She leaned on the door frame, arms folded, but gave a nod for him to ask his question, she felt tensed and uneasy.

He seemed to struggle to form the question he'd wanted to

ask but finally he, ineloquently, asked, "What are you?"
Ceto had definitely not expected this question and it caught
her off guard.

She was taken back to when she'd asked this question of
Khepri.

"You have eyes of water, hair of fire, the magic of the forest
but the magic you create is Ventus?" He didn't fumble over
his words, he'd obviously been working on this question for a
while now. It was rehearsed.

"Oh!" Ceto replied, a little relieved that it wasn't something
too personal or difficult, but she took a few seconds to
contemplate on how best to approach the subject.

Daylah had been very accepting of who she was, but on the
other hand, Amaru was utterly disgusted at her very existence.
She decided on the truth, and that Samir could react exactly
how he needed to.

She unfolded her arms and pulled out a chair opposite Samir,
slowly taking a seat and pulling the sleeves of her jacket over
her hands.

"Nature created me, my only purpose is to defeat Krokar.
His dad is from Ventus," She paused to gauge his reaction,
but his expression didn't change, "his mum is from Earth."
There was still no expression change, this surprised Ceto.
"This match resulted in his soul to become blackened.
Nature brought my mum, who is of Azureus, and my dad,
who is of Ignis, together and here I am.
I'm here to balance out the mistake it made in Krokar.
I'm nature's design." She said this proudly, finally feeling
ready to accept her purpose in life.

There was silence whilst Samir processed this but his face
gave nothing away. He stared at his hands that lay clasped on
the kitchen table.

"I will help you." And with that, he flew from the kitchen and
to a bedroom at the front of the house, his hands balled into

fists as he marched away, leaving Ceto a little dazed and flustered.

She regained her bearings and headed on her earlier trail, towards Quidel's room. She was still feeling unsure as to whether she had figured out Samir's anger or not.

She stopped abruptly in front of Quidel's door that stood slightly ajar.

Raising her hand to knock, she hesitated when hushed angry voices travelled to her ears. Amaru and Quidel.

She lowered her hand.

"That decision shouldn't have been made." Amaru was hissing.

"It wasn't my decision." Quidel replied. "It's for Ceto to decide, we can't interfere with her path. We are here for protection, not to take the lead, we must follow."

Amaru scoffed, "Ignis? Follow?" He sounded offended to his very core.

"Yes, Ignis must follow…this once." Quidel explained with authority in his voice.

"Ignis do not follow." Amaru spat. "We lead and we *fight*."

"There will be time to fight…"

"When?! Ignis are being taken from their beds and there is *nothing* we can do. Nothing but follow *her*?"

"There will be time to fight." Quidel repeated, his voice steady and unchanging.

"For now we must trust. My father trusts her and so do I."

"You don't think I see? Your judgment is blinded." Amaru criticised.

"Do not over step, Amaru. I may be following Ceto but I am still your leader, you forget your place." Quidel had a sternness in every word and it seemed to land with Amaru.

"I'll leave you, I can see there is nothing more I can say on the matter."

Knock. Knock-knock. Ceto quickly rapped her knuckle on the bedroom door before Amaru swung it open to find her there, listening.

"Oh," She feigned surprise as Amaru pulled open the door. "I thought this was Quidel's room, I'm sorry."

Amaru gave Ceto a disgusted look and stormed past her to the room Nuri had entered previously.

This concerned Ceto a little, but she already had a task for now.

"Ceto? Is everything okay?" Quidel was standing in the doorway when she looked back.

"Yes, everything is okay." She replied, her heart hammering at the base of her neck again, her hands growing damp the harder he inspected her. He looked very impressive stood before her. Tall, dark and undeniably handsome.

"I was hoping we could have a word?" He didn't answer but pulled the door open wider and held out his arm for a fraction of a second, inviting her inside.

Once inside she could see Quidel had chosen the most basic room she'd seen so far. The floor was tiled and cold, there was a free standing bath in one corner and what looked like a camping bed in the other. Multiple mirrors covered the walls in an odd way, making Ceto feel a little uneasy. Ceto wasn't surprised at Quidel's choice in room.

She was getting the sense that who had lived here previously had brought odd items they had found interesting from Earth and filled their home with oddities that really didn't make sense in her world.

"Nuri came to me earlier, a little upset with me." She began.

"I can speak with her, if you'd like?" Quidel offered.

He spoke in a tone so soft, Ceto hadn't heard him speak in this manner before and wondered if it was because they were alone.

Ceto waved her hand to stop him from speaking and swallowed hard

"No, we've spoken. We're fine. She brought my attention to something…" Her brain seemed to have hit a wall and she struggled with the words she wanted to say.

"I think you may feel differently towards me, than I do to you." She blurted and instantly regretted it, she sounded foolish and immature.

"Urgh." She sharply bent her head to glance at the floor, "What I mean is…" But Quidel had placed his finger under her chin and lifted it so their eyes met. A part of Ceto ached for him to kiss her. But there was no electricity at his touch, simply an understanding in the pit of her stomach.

"Okay." Was all he whispered, his lips pulled down a little, but not enough for Ceto to be sure that he understood her.

"Okay." She agreed, her brows pulling together as her mind cleared of its fog.

"Was that all?" Quidel asked, dropping his hand and clasping them behind his back. His expression had become passive.

"Yes, I suppose that was all." Ceto replied and for a fraction of a second, disappointment flooded her features as she realised she'd quite enjoyed his attention. She rearranged her face and smiled, but it didn't reach her eyes.

"Good." Ceto nodded.

"Good." Quidel replied, with a mocking nod, his dark eyebrows raising for a beat.

Ceto turned on her heel and swiftly made her way back to her own room, her footsteps quick and close together.

She closed her door, leaving it open a crack. She sighed and tried not to think about what had just happened from fear of dying of embarrassment.

Throwing herself down on her fluffy bed, arms and legs spread wide at her sides.

"Is that how they sleep in Natus?" Her heart sank at the sound of another visitor, when she longed to be alone. But it quickly raised again when her ears realised it was Oscar's voice.

"Do you feel 'good'?" He asked.

She slowly turned to sit on the edge of her bed, whilst trying to figure out what he was talking about.

He'd been listening to their conversation.

"I don't feel *good* Ceto." There was a pleading in his voice now as he made his way over to the bed, closing the door fully behind him.

"Oh, Oscar, I…" But how could she explain? Surely if he was listening, he would figure out that she didn't feel a connection with Quidel.

She knew deep in her soul that she loved Oscar, that she would only ever need him. How could she begin to express this?

"Do you love me?" He interrupted, cutting right to the chase. As if he'd wanted to ask the question for a long time.

She stared at him, her eyes wide, her lips parted slightly.

Yes. She wanted to shout at him, but it was too much.

"Ceto, I *love* you." He filled the silence with uplifting words. He shook his head, his bright hair falling into his eyes.

"Maybe I imagined it, but before all of this," he shot his long arms out wide around him, "I thought you felt the same. When it was just me and you."

There was silence from Ceto as her mind raced through everything she wanted to say to him. He was talking too quickly for her, she needed time to answer him, to tell him that she felt exactly as he did. But the words needed time to catch up with her brain.

"Maybe I imagined it." He repeated, in a whisper this time, and turned towards the door.

Ceto leapt from her seated position and grabbed his arm, pulling him back and leading him to sit on the bed next to her.

They sat there in comfortable silence. Oscar studied Ceto's

body language and expression, hoping they would tell him what she couldn't.

Ceto kept her gaze on his hands as they rested gently on his leg.

Be brave. She willed herself.

Ceto slowly took her hand and slipped her fingertips under his. Oscar's fingertips reacted instantly with an explosion of electricity, letting her hand in as she slipped it further under the weight of his.

She shifted her gaze up towards Oscars.

His face was close to hers, she could feel his breath as it shifted her hair slightly.

"I've loved you for a very long time." She whispered.

Oscar's tight expression immediately softened. His shoulders dropped and he let out a short sharp breath.

"I need you and nobody else. My mind hasn't been right since I found myself here." She was taken aback to feel a tear drop down her cheek and under her chin, she wasn't aware she'd been crying.

The pent up confusion, tension, fear and constant thought process had been weighing on her mind, and now with Oscar next to her, the rest of the world and responsibility closed off for a moment. She felt the release as she allowed herself to feel everything.

He pulled her into a large embrace, his long arms wrapping around her small frame.

She let her body fall into his torso whilst the tears stopped. Eventually, he pulled his arms back, placing them on each of hers and pushing her away a little. He stood up and made his way to the door.

"That was all I needed." And he made to leave her room.

"Don't go." She blurted.

He grinned widely at her request, closed the door again and took one large stride back to Ceto where she now stood by the bed.

He scooped her face up in both of his hands and fiercely pressed his lips to hers.

She closed her eyes, blissfully taking the moment in with her other senses; his familiar scent, the way his lips gave the right amount of soft pressure she needed.

His kiss felt a little desperate, as if he'd needed to do this for a while. As if he couldn't get close enough to her.

He broke away, placing his forehead on hers.

"I know you've been through a lot. I know there are more important things you need to think about right now.

But there is nothing more important to me in this world or the next, than to be here with you like this."

And Ceto knew he did know, they weren't empty words. She'd known him long enough to notice his sincerity.

"Stay with me." She pleaded.

They made their way to the bed, synchronized, laying their heads on the soft pillows. They took each other in, a new light shining on the other. Each knowing that they had closed the chapter on their friendship and entered an intense new chapter; one much more than anything either could have hoped for.

She seemed to have been cleared of her fog, she was in control of her own body and thoughts again. She felt elated at the fact. She had been cured by Oscar.

Their bodies close and warm against each other. Ceto's mind forgot everything, the peril that faced them, questions she'd had that were unanswered, insecurities and anxieties; she was completely in the moment and the moment was, at a loss for a better word, good.

Chapter 22

Ceto woke to the soft sounds of muttered conversation, crackling fire and the clanging of cutlery. The sounds of breakfast.

She didn't open her eyes at first, she could feel a source of heat cradling her from behind. She smiled to herself as memories from the night before came to the front of her mind.

As she lay there, revelling in her pleasant thoughts and rested body, a familiar hand made its way from her exposed shoulder and slid down her bare arm, resulting in their fingers intertwining.

Little sparks of electricity happily danced from one hand to the other. Ceto's heart began to hammer against her chest again.

This should feel awkward. She thought, but there was no awkwardness between Ceto and Oscar, simply a need to be close to one another.

Ceto smiled down from her now seated position at Oscar. His head cradled in the pillow, his mass of intense hair satisfyingly askew.

"I've never slept so well, especially considering..." Ceto gave a shy smile.

"Do you find yourself on the eve of battle a lot?" Oscar chuckled, pulling her back down to lay beside him. Both ignoring the angry growls from their stomachs, the waft of food and coffee trying its best to break them from their bubble.

Their laughter subsided.

They lay in their comfortable castle, letting their silence fall gently around them.

"What are you thinking?" Ceto hadn't noticed that Oscar had been examining her profile.

"I was just wishing that we could listen to music like we used to. God! That seems like a lifetime ago, doesn't it?" Ceto replied to his stares.

But Oscar had leapt from the bed, pulling his arm from under her head.

"What?" She asked impatiently. But he didn't reply.

He picked up his jeans that were strewn on the floor and delved into the pocket, pulling out his music player, a grin on his soft face.

He bounded back into bed, passed Ceto an earphone, placed the other in his own ear and tucked his arm under her head again.

"What shall we listen to today…" He trailed off as he got lost in his extensive music library. "Ah!" He announced as a soft piano filled Ceto's ear.

She watched him close his eyes as the percussion grew louder and the music became more desperate.

Ceto propped herself up on her elbow and watched his face as he let his mind delve into the feelings of the music.

She tucked her hair behind her ear and bent to touch her lips on his.

When she pulled away, she noticed he was watching her again, enchantment in his eyes, and joy in his smile.

Ceto's heart jumped, she felt as though all the pieces were beginning to slot into place. She felt ready to take on the threat hanging over her head. She felt ready to avenge her mum. With the strength of Oscar, her best friend, behind her, she felt unstoppable.

"Breakfast." She whispered, unable to ignore the rumblings anymore, or the smell of warm food.

Reluctantly, they peeled their way from their cocoon, dressed and made their way across the hall to the kitchen.

Quidel. She felt sudden panic at the uncertain way he would react to the shift between herself and Oscar. Had she been clear enough when they last spoke? She was sure he understood in the moment, but now, as the kitchen grew closer, she felt less certain.

Oscar sensed her hesitation and swooped her hand up into his own.

Together they entered the kitchen, already full with the other members of their company.

Ceto expected glances and shocked noises, but instead they were greeted with mumbled hellos as they busied themselves with eating.

Ceto let her shoulders drop and gently pulled her hand from Oscar's, each grabbing a plate and filling it with food.

They sat around the table, eating and making small talk. Nuri, Daylah and Samir were even laughing amongst themselves.

Oscar brought his plate of piled high food and sunk into the chair next to Ceto, inching it closer to her own, to fill the gap between them.

Quidel twitched his head as he witnessed their bodies' inches apart. She saw his head bend a little lower over his plate, the fork in his hand held in his entire fist.

In her new blissful state, Ceto tried her hardest to ignore his negativity and instead refocused on the laughter before her. She'd always assumed that her life would be lacking of friends, becoming content with the company of her mum and Oscar. She certainly didn't expect to find herself in a new world with enough friends to fill a kitchen! But here she sat, glancing around at the different faces; an assortment of coloured eyes, various shades of hair colour and different shades of skin tone, conditioned to despise each other, yet here they all were, ready to do what it took to help Ceto. To help a stranger. Working together to save their world.

It filled Ceto with delight to know that there was goodness in this world and that people were willing to change what they had been taught by their elders.

Ceto was brought out of her happy musing by the *tap tap tap*

tap of Quidel's foot below the table.

She turned her head to his glare and smiled back in response. Oscar was none the wiser as to the shift in mood at the other end of the kitchen table, he had joined in with the others in laughter.

Ceto longed to switch off her mind from the angry energy being emitted from the two Ignis men, to instead join in the light hearted laughter.

But she couldn't.

"Is there enough food for you? I can see if there's something different to eat if you'd prefer?" In her uncomfortable state, Ceto had become formal, careful to not say something to upset anyone. It was an empty offer, she could plainly see that the two men had plates full in front of them.

Amaru grunted, whilst Quidel grabbed his fork harder in his fist and shovelled scrambled eggs into his mouth.

Attractive. Ceto thought, whilst internally rolling her eyes but keeping her outward expression pleasant.

Waiting for the day to pass was going to be strained.

"How are the preparations for the night? I'm not even sure what time it is in here." She changed the subject to something she knew both men couldn't resist.

Surprisingly, it was Amaru who answered between mouthfuls. "Provisions have been packed, we have enough food for two days. We have fresh water and I have scouted outside. There doesn't seem to be any disturbance of Raven tonight. It is midday. Judging by the cloud movement and the dry air, it will be another bright full moon."

Ceto was stunned into stuttering as Amaru reeled off his report. She expected Quidel to answer, and Amaru to ignore her as usual.

She was also trying to figure out how long she and Oscar had stayed in their bubble for. Over 24 hours? No wonder she felt rested.

"I…I can help with the moon." She offered, dropping her head into her plate of food.

Ceto pulled her elbows in, hunched her spine and concentrated on shifting food around her plate, her appetite evaporated with her elated mood.

"You okay?" Oscar pulled his head in close to Ceto's, in a weak attempt to block out the rest of the world.

"Yeah." She breathed. "I'd do anything for a wash." She faked a chuckle. Suddenly feeling dirty; she hadn't realised how much she had hurt Quidel until this moment.

"You can bathe in my room." Quidel grunted, not taking his eyes off the table.

"Oh, th-thank you." As much as she tried, Ceto felt she would never figure this man out. A familiar unease swam through her, one she had become to associate with Quidel.

After everyone had eaten, Ceto, Daylah, and Oscar cleared the table whilst the others busied themselves with various activities, mainly, ignoring the monstrous job of clearing the remnants of the feast.

"Go take that bath." Oscar nudged at Ceto, with his arms stacked high with plates. "We can sort this." He smiled at Daylah, who nodded brightly in response.

She couldn't deny that she was secretly relieved to get away from the prying eyes she felt boring into her shoulder blades.

"If you're sure?"

"Lock the door." Oscar winked. She wasn't surprised there was still some hurt in him regarding Quidel, but she hoped he knew what he meant to her.

She exited the kitchen with eyes following her.

As she sunk into the soothing water, her body feeling lighter as she bobbed a little off the bottom of the bath, her mind grew heavy.

Why couldn't she have what she wanted? She'd felt an

250

attraction to Quidel, however real those feelings had been, they had been there. But she'd loved Oscar for many years. Her love for him had grown as they had. Maybe if there was no Oscar, maybe then she could see herself with Quidel. The match didn't seem so farfetched to her; but there would always be Oscar.

Finally, by giving into her feelings, she feared that she had brought an unnecessary strain on their task ahead.

Could she have waited until Krokar was defeated?

Was she sure she would live to see Oscar again after facing this evil?

Her eyes snapped open as she heard the handle on the door move.

"I'm in here." She said as loudly as she dared, still aware of the danger that awaited outside.

The door opened a crack. Ceto panicked and sunk further into the bath, her chin touching the water, her hands wrapped around her body as best she could.

It was Quidel.

"Excuse me. Could you leave, please?" Her voice high pitched from horror.

"I have to talk to you." Was his reply, as he refused to avert his gaze.

"Now's not really the best time, Quidel." She spat his name furiously.

He turned his body, suddenly realising that Ceto was embarrassed and angry.

"I won't look."

When she was certain he wouldn't turn back around, she leapt from the bath, water spilling over on to the floor. She grabbed a large fluffy towel she had found and wrapped it around her body, scooping her hair up into a messy bun, wet tendrils sticking to her neck.

"Well?" She snapped impatiently.

251

Quidel turned around and was greeted by Ceto, her face furious, her hands planted firmly across her body.

"You spent the night with *him*." It wasn't a question.

Ceto's arms slackened for a second and then crossed firmly again.

"I'm not sure what business it is of yours." She'd hoped that she could be sensitive towards him but her words came out harshly.

She regretted her response immediately.

Quidel dropped his gaze but she could still see his face; he was hurt. She hadn't seen this side of him before, it broke her heart. She dropped her arms.

"I'm sorry, you have to understand that it's always been Oscar." She took a step closer to him, careful to still leave a large gap between them.

"I understand that there has been…*something*…between us, but…" He nodded, able to fill in the end of her sentence. Bits of hair falling around his face as he bobbed his head sadly.

"I thought…when I came to your room…I thought you understood?" She spoke softly now.

He shook his head, unable to meet her gaze.

Ceto was shocked at his vulnerability, she hadn't expected it. She supposed if she'd allowed herself to get to know him, without the threat of the end of the world around them, she might have seen this side of him and she might not have broken his heart.

She had thought that all they had was attraction, that once he understood that she didn't like him in that way, he would admit defeat and move on. His feelings didn't seem to have changed in the night as hers had.

"Quidel, I…" She took a few steps forward now, reaching her arm out to touch his. But he yanked his body away and stood up to his full height, head held high and proud.

"I will not let this hinder our orders." He announced. Ceto

took half a step back, taken aback by his sudden change in demeanour.

"The sun will be setting soon. We are getting ready to depart. I suggest you do the same." And he flew back through the door, closing it firmly behind himself. The candles in the room flickered from the gust.

Ceto was left alone, cold and in the dark, able to let the shame of what she had done fill her lungs.

And she began to cry, silent tears.

She only allowed herself a few. She then splashed her face with water from the bath, dried herself and dressed. Ready to walk out into the night, possibly her last night.

Back in the kitchen, the mood had lowered from the hours previously.

Everyone busied themselves with checking their packs for supplies, checking their weapons, nibbling at bits of food and wrapping themselves up ready for the cold that awaited them. Ceto was wrapping herself up in her scarf when Amaru came down the hall and into the kitchen, drenched as if he had been submerged in water, his dripping face full of anger.

"Rain." He growled.

"We can't go in the rain?" Ceto asked. It sounded like a silly question from the look on his face, but she didn't want to wait any longer. She was ready to go *now*.

"Heavy rain. So heavy, you can't even see through it. Sheets and sheets of rain." He reported.

Ceto sunk into a chair, clearing her mind and pushing it through the walls around her and up into the clouds.

She was vaguely aware of Samir talking to the group, but Ceto was too busy concentrating to take in what he was saying.

She asked the clouds to gently bring its rain to a stop until they reached the top of the mountain. She was careful to ask them to not stop abruptly, as this would cause suspicion to anyone watching the mountain.

"We should be good to go in a few minutes." She told the group, unknowingly breaking Samir off midsentence.

All of their faces turned to hers.

"The rain will stop soon." She explained.

"That's not possible, I haven't even begun the ritual yet." Samir prickled at Ceto.

"Samir was just saying how he could try to stop the rain, or at least divert it from us." Oscar explained, having watched Ceto grow quiet as Samir was speaking.

"Oh, well, I've done that. I've asked them to stop slowly so we don't draw attention to ourselves. I've asked them to give us cover from the moon." There was quiet in the room. "I assumed we still wanted that to happen too?" Ceto found herself growing infuriated at the lack of action around her. They could go now. She stood up out of the seat, hoping to prompt the same urgency in her company.

Samir took a great stride towards Ceto and stopped with his face inches away from hers.

"How is it, that *you* can command the rain? You are not Ventus. There are rituals…" He spat in her face.

This sudden surge of anger from someone she had found meek until now seemed to ground Ceto, and she began to question how good her judge of character was. So this was how she had offended Samir. The realisation crashed like glass around her.

"I first did it in the meadow coming back from Azureus. I was already angry at something else and it began to rain. I told it to stop and…it stopped."

Samir was still breathing harshly on her face. Oscar hovered by her elbow, Nuri not far behind Ceto either.

"I'm sorry." She whispered.

"You shouldn't do that. It is sacred to Ventus." He spat, but he backed off a little.

Silence fell around them as Samir and Ceto composed themselves. Amaru went to check outside again.

"The rain has stopped. The moon isn't bright." He nodded at Ceto, who felt gratitude towards him. The feeling felt strange. They each swung their packs on their backs and adjusted their warm clothes. Ceto pulled her scarf up to her nose and her hood over her eyes, wanting to hide from the world. And they silently made their way out to the mountain's path for the last time.

Up the mountain's path they sneaked, careful not to slip on the beautiful stone floor as a fine mist of rain drenched them, just as much as a heavy storm would have.

Ceto had half a mind to ask Samir if he could do anything about the mist; she didn't want to exhaust herself before they reached Krokar. But when she turned her head to ask him, she was met with his glare as he brought up the rear of the group.

She buried her face in to her scarf once more, happily feeling the warmth of her breath as it spread through the material. Oscar took her hand in his, the sturdiness of the act filled her with courage as she poked her head out and smiled up at him. Nuri had taken Ceto's place as protector of Daylah, and although it warmed her heart to see Azureus and Ignis behave this way towards each other, she felt a pang of jealousy and made the effort to widen her steps to fall into pace with them.

They weren't speaking, nobody was, they had all reverted back to a frightened silence. But to be in close proximity of each other seemed to calm their nerves, if only a little. Amaru and Quidel had been leading the group as usual, but in the mist they had made quite a large gap between themselves and the others.

After some time, Samir advised that they should take some shelter from the rain and have a little food before they reached the very top of the mountain. They could see now that they were just minutes away from their end goal.

Ceto's stomach gave an uncomfortable lurch.

She was positioned in a huddle with Daylah, Nuri and Oscar off to the side of the path, whilst Amaru, Quidel and Samir lunged around, trying to open the doors of the extravagant houses now around them. They were truly beautiful here, and had it not been a ghost town, Ceto would have loved to have taken in all of Ventus' beauty.

After all the doors and windows were tried and found to be locked, they took refuge from the wind and rain under a ledge of rock, half full of chopped logs.

It was a cramped space, but they managed to squeeze in. Ceto made a conscious effort to separate Oscar and Quidel.

Daylah pulled tins of tuna from her pack. Ceto was sure she didn't know what she had picked up from the pantry, but assumed she'd probably picked them for the picture of the fish on the packaging.

She turned it over and over, trying to get to the food inside.

"You need a tin opener." Oscar whispered, kindly.

Quidel grabbed the tin and stabbed it with a small knife he'd pulled from thin air.

One after the other. Stab. Stab. Stab. Until they each had a partly opened tin of tuna, its brine pouring onto the stone floor beneath their feet.

They used their fingers to place flakes into their mouths, some eating more than others.

Daylah seemed to really enjoy her meal.

Ceto couldn't think of anything worse than eating right now, except maybe imminently facing Krokar.

The rain seemed to have passed, leaving the night air feeling crisp and damp.

Ceto risked a little light for them and asked the clouds to show them a tip of the moon. They moved over slightly to reveal the top of the moon; it looked as though it was sitting comfortably in an arm chair of cloud.

The moon was bright yellow tonight, casting an almost golden glow on the protection of the clouds. Its beauty filled Ceto with a hope she didn't have moments ago.

She took a deep breathe, filling her lungs and standing from her crouched position.

"If I don't go in there now, I never will. I don't expect anyone to come with me, you can take refuge in one of the lower down houses." As she said this, she selfishly hoped that they would ignore her advice. Ceto knew she was supposed to unite them, but she couldn't bring herself to lead them to their deaths.

She still had no idea as to how she was going to defeat Krokar, and she had a strong feeling that a spear or two wouldn't hurt.

Samir was the first to stand with her, which surprised her considering a few hours ago, he had been a completely different person. She nodded at him, confusion in her wrinkled brow.

"I overreacted earlier, I'm sorry. M-my wife, she was trained in the rain rituals. She spent most of her time and energy on them. To see you achieve it with ease…I miss her." Samir dropped his head slightly.

Ceto cocked her head a little, her face softening. She disliked being spoken to in that manner, but here this broken man stood, having gone through much more than any of them, apologising.

She placed a hand on his arm and smiled warmly.

Daylah jumped up and Ceto's heart sunk. Out of everyone, she'd hoped Daylah had come to realise how fatal this could turn out to be and head for safety. Ceto didn't say what she felt. Daylah had proved herself time and time again on this journey, feeding them, warming them, healing them, saving

Ceto from an icy death. They wouldn't have gotten very far without her, and yet, she was so *small.*

The three Ignis moved to a standing position almost immediately after Daylah.

Only Oscar stayed in his seated position, nibbling at his tuna flakes.

Ceto should have felt relief that he had decided to stay out of harm's way, but she felt fear. He was the one to ground her, make her feel like she could do anything.

She needed him.

"Good, well hopefully we'll find you again..." She began, but he cut her off with an outstretched hand.

He reached for his music, scrolled for a long silent minute whilst he searched for the song he needed, smiled and handed it to Ceto. She placed the earphones into her ears as the others watched, confused.

Playing into her ears was the familiar short notes of the introduction to a boxing film they had once watched together.

Ceto gave out a laugh, all fear of the Raven gone.

Oscar joined them, scooped up Ceto's face and kissed her fiercely.

Together, in a tightly packed formation, they took the last few steps that led to the very top of the mountain.

Chapter 23

After a short while, the ground below their feet became flatter. Their calves and thighs singing out gratefully as their backs grew straighter from the level ground.

The moon had turned into a new day; the rain had stopped and the air became crisp in the morning's sun. The wind still whipped around them at the very top of Ventus, the highest point in Natus. But it was an encouraging gust, Ceto could feel it, and she could see that Samir felt it too.

She wondered if the air was thinner up here, she felt a strange relief and happiness for reaching the top, regardless of what faced her now.

The group around her became motionless, their gazes positioned upwards.

Ceto tilted her head back and let it rock on her shoulders as she took in what the others had seen.

A grand structure stood tall before them, it had characteristics of a cathedral, with its large curved entrance walls joining at the top in a point. Its many long thin windows, missing glass. Its roof made up of pointed turrets as they reached for the sky. It was made from the mountain, as the other buildings were in Ventus, but these walls had been carved and smoothed intricately and perfectly. Pictures and words that Ceto couldn't make out ran along the front wall.

Ceto glanced around to see Samir, his eyes closed, a tear escaping his eye, he looked as though he was praying.

She quickly realised she was staring and turned her attention back to the building. As she did she noticed a flurry of black feathers soar from their perch high above, gliding easily through the open entrance.

Amaru, Nuri and Quidel fluidly posed defensively, their spears pointed to where the Raven had flown past them.

Ceto's pleasant state came crashing down around her, like crumbling walls.

"Well, he knows we're here now." Ceto said. Her voice sounded strange to her ears. She felt as if she had been set to auto pilot, and she couldn't say that she minded. She didn't feel fear, worry or anxiety. She had a goal and she was going to see it through.

Her feet carried her body towards the building, following the Raven.

Their feet echoed on the high cold walls as they entered in a close huddle. Daylah in the centre guarded by Oscar, the others in a messy circle around them.

Daylah turned her head to the stream of sunlight, still visible through the tall door they'd entered through.

"It's not too late to turn back, Daylah." Ceto whispered to her small friend. But she shook her head stubbornly, her blonde hair falling around her wide eyed face. She trembled as she moved forward with everyone else. Ceto wondered if she would ever not be surprised by Daylah's fierce bravery.

They slowly made their way through a long thin entrance way, a Raven here and there sat perched up high; their black eyes piercing the group, always watching. The bright sun outside growing fainter as it grew further away.

They passed a second doorway, a similar design to the first, but considerably smaller; just tall enough for everyone to fit under.

When they emerged on the other side, they each gasped at what stood before them. Only Samir stayed silent having seen the building before.

They had entered a great hall large enough to seat tens of thousands of people, comfortably. It was longer than it was wide.

Along each of the side walls sat tiered steps, seating overlooking the long flat walkway. In this seating, perched thousands of Raven. They were still, not one so much as rustled their feathers. They simply *watched.*

Ahead sat an altar. Candles could be seen fluttering in the darkness, dancing around a silhouette, unmoving.

Krokar.

Ceto made the first move, watching the Raven as she moved towards the candles, ready to form a protective dome if they began to attack.

The others followed closely behind.

Ceto stopped suddenly, unaware of the progress she'd made across the room as she watched the Raven.

The silhouette hadn't moved as they made their way closer. Why wasn't he attacking?

His head was bent over, his hands neatly clasped in front of him.

"Ceto." He whispered, his voice raspy and deep.

"Krokar." She replied. The greeting would have been civil if it wasn't for the atmosphere around them; a breath waiting to be released.

His body tall and thin, stood before a stone throne, high above them atop a few stairs. His movements were fluid, as if he was made of air himself. Krokar began to descend the stairs, the loose black pants he wore seemed to billow with his movement. His loose fitted white shirt moving in a similar way. Every step he took was calculated and smooth, he was almost dancing down the stairs.

He slowly raised his arms, his shirt rolled up to the elbows showing his dark arms, hairy and sturdy. They rested at either side of his ears, outstretched.

The Raven raised their wings in the same manner.

Ceto desperately glanced around the room for an escape if they needed one.

To their left, she felt relief at a small wooden door. She wondered if it was locked.

She closed her eyes and asked the wind to try the latch. She breathed a sigh of relief when it gave a satisfying *click*.

"Join me, Ceto." Krokar said. It wasn't a question.

This took Ceto by surprise and she ineloquently answered, "What?"

Growing anxious, the others had noticed the small door too. Daylah, finally losing her courage, edged little by little towards it.

Ceto sensed this and asked the wind to give her a little nudge back to the safety of the centre of their formation.

Daylah pushed back against the wind and through it, falling to the floor with a loud, "OOF."

Krokar snapped his sharp face towards the commotion. His sharp long nose pointing at Daylah. His yellow-green eyes narrowing as he took this small child in.

He twitched his index finger towards her.

No.

It all happened too quickly for Ceto to respond, for anyone to respond. Except Amaru.

As a dozen Raven leapt from above and soared towards Daylah. Ceto desperately tried to create a dome around them, but in her panic, it was patchy.

Nuri ran from the furthest point but Amaru, standing closest, sprang from where he stood. Strangely, he disregarded his spear and with both hands, pushed Daylah with enough force to send her rolling across the dusty ground and hit the wall by the door.

The Raven didn't stop.

Amaru pulled his arms and legs in towards his body, trying to protect his head.

They pecked and they clawed. A wall of black preventing them from being able to see Amaru anymore.

They knew he was still behind the black feathered wall, only by his screams. A sound so full of pain that it didn't sound right coming from his masculine form.

It was over quicker than anyone could react.

A trickle of blood made a path to the centre of the room as his screams faded with the echoes.

Ceto watched, her eyes wide, taking the savage attack in. Wishing she could close her eyes, but unable to look away.

Nuri yelled his name from behind. The only sound over the squawks and screeches, the rustle and the clawing.

Krokar gave a high pitched screech of a laugh as he raised his arms higher and brought them down in one fluid movement. The remaining Raven moved to the air and began to plummet to the ground, beak first.

A hand grabbed hold of Ceto's arm and dragged her towards the small wooden door. She looked over to where Daylah had been pushed, but she wasn't there anymore.

Panic and despair set in and Ceto's thoughts shut down.

This was not going well.

The door was slammed shut behind them. A few bangs came from the other side as the Raven tried to get through, but they stopped as a high pitched whistle sounded.

Then there was silence.

Quidel placed an open flame on an empty shelf to cast light on where they now found themselves.

They had taken refuge in a small room, empty shelves lined the walls, thick with dust.

Nuri grabbed onto the nearest shelf and bent her head below her shoulders.

Ceto wanted to comfort her friend but she was consumed with the possibility that Daylah was lost to them and the shock and sadness from the loss of Amaru.

Oscar placed his arms around Ceto as she collapsed into his chest. She sobbed as her knees gave way.

"I can't…can't…" She gasped.

Oscar held her at arm's length and peered into her soul as only he could. His brown eyes intense.

"She's not gone, we'll find her." He soothed.

263

"Are we to forget about Ama…" Nuri's voice caught as she had to bite back a sob.

Ceto shook her head and dropped her gaze to the ground.

"He saved her." Samir pointed out, a twinge of disbelief in his voice.

"I know." Ceto whispered. "He was changing. He was beginning to accept us."

They grew silent, in thought of Amaru, for a few seconds.

"What now?" Oscar asked. They looked to Ceto.

She opened her mouth to say something, and then thought better of it.

She didn't have a plan, she was feeling hopeless and helpless.

"I…can't." She glanced up at Oscar, her arms and shoulders held up in a sharp shrug.

"I think, up until now, I've relied heavily on fate. Fate brought my parents together. It was my fate to grow up on Earth. Fate brought me here, it brought me you. And now I'm starting to realise that I've got to put some effort in to win this. I don't know if I can do that?" She paused for a breath. "What if its fate that I'm supposed to lose?"

Oscar took both her hands in his again and moved her to the corner of the room.

"I've watched you grow numb when Adara died. I've watched you cringe away from strangers. I've watched you ignore your feelings for me for years and I stood there and watched it all. Encouraged you when you needed it, a shoulder to cry on if you needed that too.

But now I'm telling you to have courage, because that's what you need in this moment. You can't shut down now, you don't have that option. The only option you have, is courage. The only option you have is to go on." His eyes flickered in the flames light, powerful but supportive.

There came a slight tap on the wooden door from a beak or a claw.

Ceto looked to the door and then back up at Oscar.

"Do this." He urged. His expression, usually kind, was full of determination, he was out of patience.

Ceto turned towards Samir, Nuri and Quidel, who had been listening, unable to escape in the small room.

"Can you all listen to me, for once? Stay here until I'm ready for you...*please*." Ceto pleaded.

Quidel, leaning on his spear, shook his head down at the ground, as if he'd anticipated this plan.

Nuri took a step toward Ceto, tears betrayed her and made her cheeks damp. "No." She whispered.

Ceto held her hand up, it shook slightly. She tensed in the hope that the shaking would stop.

"Hear me out. I promised Maia I would try to find a way to not kill…"

"Oh, Ceto!" Oscar sounded exasperated behind her. "He's insane, he's dangerous. You can't be serious?"

Ceto turned her head towards him.

"He will kill you without hesitating." He took her hand and moved to face her. "Some people can't be saved."

"I have to try." She took in his face, it had turned to anger. He was *angry* with her for trying to find another way than murder. She looked around the room at the other faces, they were a mix of worry and sadness.

Quidel nodded, stoic.

Ceto grabbed Oscar by the neck and pulled him down a little in a great hug.

"I love you." She whispered into his ear and she felt his body mould itself to hers. Without a second look at her friends, she opened the door slowly.

There was no sound of Krokar or the Raven, it was unnervingly silent in the great hall.

She slowly placed one foot in front of the other, keeping her thoughts tensed so that she was ready with a protective dome if she needed it.

Almost at the centre of the room now, the altar came in to view and she gasped. Fear stopping her dead, mid walk. "Daylah."

There Krokar stood, hands clasped behind his back, a smirk on his face. And there stood Daylah, so small and light in contrast, her slight body hunched over.

She was hurt. Ceto's heart sunk to her stomach, she grew cold.

"So nice of you to finally join us." Krokar spoke strangely formal, as if she had been invited round for tea.

When Krokar began to speak, Daylah's bowed head snapped up, her eyes wide with fear.

"What have you done to her?" Ceto longed to run to Daylah's side, as if a rubber band attached them. A force was pulling her in, but she had to resist. Oscar had been right, Krokar was unstable and there was no knowing what he would do if she raced to Daylah's side.

"What?" Krokar feigned innocent shock. "Nothing!" He wrapped his arm around Daylah's shoulders and jostled her into his side.

"Ceto…" Daylah whimpered, whilst she was shook like a rag doll.

Ceto held her hand up to her, as if she could bring her comfort from far away.

"It's okay, I'm here." She tried to soothe.

Krokar rolled his eyes and released Daylah roughly. She stumbled down the steps.

Ceto couldn't help it, that rubber band was tugging at her. She took a few leaps forward before Krokar threw his hand out.

"Stop!" He commanded. The Raven above rustled, ready to take flight and descend on Ceto.

She halted and took in the room. The Raven in the rafters

positioned themselves, beaks pointed towards her.

She glanced down at Amaru's mangled body, lifeless on the cold stone floor.

She turned her head away, the taste of bile rising.

She tried to calm her emotions, willed herself to gather her thoughts, to have a civil conversation with the mad man that stood before her.

"You don't have to do this." She began.

He shot an animated confused expression at her, and threw his arms out into a large shrug.

"Oh, Ceto, but I *want to*." He grinned at her, his teeth yellowing and jagged.

He took the few steps to be on level with Ceto, ignoring Daylah now. Disregarding her as useless. His hands clasped before him, held at his chest.

"Join me." He hissed with a wicked grin. This took Ceto aback, she hadn't been expecting this. He'd wanted her dead. Had killed her mum in place of her.

"These *people,* they don't deserve this life. Always fighting, never accepting what is different." He stopped a little way away from where Ceto stood, in a one handed arm fold. One elbow resting on his other arm, as he absentmindedly examined his nails.

Ceto needed more time to catch on to what he was saying, this conversation had thrown her off course.

"They deserve the darkness. You can help me. Together we can give this world what it deserves." He went on.

"But, your mum, she's in this world." She tried to persuade him, wondering if he knew she was here and not on Earth.

He dropped his arms and held them straight by his sides, hands clenched.

"*She* deserves the darkness more than anyone." His tone had become sharp.

"I met her, she seemed unhappy without you. Maybe if you

spoke to…"

"NO." He thundered. Ceto jumped.

"The way she looked at her son." He began to pace, his hands clasped behind his back. "Such hatred." He spun back to Ceto. "But isn't that the way in Natus?"

Ceto noticed Daylah begin to lift herself up on her hands. *Stay down. Stay down. Stay down. Stay down.* She chanted in her head. Daylah slowly lowered herself back to the floor. Had she heard her?

"Ventus, Azureus, Ignis, Folia; they *hate* each other, so untrusting. Unaccepting. They cannot take in and adapt to *anything* new. They're stuck in their old ways. Well," He gave a manic chuckle, "I will cleanse them. They will live in the darkness, all the same." He raised his hands to the Raven above them.

"But not everyone is like that." Ceto pointed out.

Krokar's sharp eyes snapped back to Ceto's face, a wicked smile slowly growing on his face.

"Really?" He asked. Ceto felt suddenly exposed.

"You've travelled with Ignis, Azureus and Ventus. Have they been accepting? Have they worked together seamlessly? Going out of their way to help others?"

She felt her stomach twist. Amaru came to the forefront of her mind. Not wanting to think poorly of him now, but he had been nothing but an angry problem throughout. Quidel was unaccepting and Samir had shouted at her just a few hours previously.

"Folia are accepting." She threw at him, her finger raised in excitement at the thought of the help Khepri had given her.

"You met *one* helpful Folia. That doesn't mean the rest of them are as keen to help." His tone had become mocking.

"How do you know all of this?" The information he knew was scarily accurate.

"Oh I've been watching you." He flicked his hand at her as if this was not a problem.

He stroked his chin in thought as he examined her.

"You look like her." He looked down at Ceto through the corner of his eye.

Ceto tensed every muscle, she knew he was talking about her mum.

"She put up quite the fight all of these years, keeping me at bay. But I found you." He grinned his wicked grin again, happy with himself for cleverly seeking Ceto out.

She didn't answer right away, she didn't want to say something that would tip the scales. At the moment, they were having a relatively calm conversation. She knew if she said one wrong word, he would instruct the Raven to attack.

He cocked his head.

"You're mad?" He asked, genuinely shocked. She scoffed, unable to hold it back.

"I did you a favour." He leaned back, hurt.

"A favour?! I suppose I'm lucky that you didn't murder me. No, you murdered my *mother* in my place."

Krokar placed his hand on his chest and tucked his chin into his neck.

"I never wanted to kill you. Why would I want that when I wanted you by my side?"

"Then, why did you come to my home and…" She couldn't finish the sentence.

"Adara trapped you in a bubble that you couldn't escape. My mother did the same to me. She kept me from the world, scared at how they would react to me. She gave me no affection. The world is lucky to have people like us."

Ceto was not expecting that, it took her a few beats to compose herself.

"I wasn't trapped." She whispered.

"No? You led a full life? You did everything you ever wanted? Had lots of friends, did you?" He mocked. How long had he been watching her?

"I had love. She loved me. I had a friend."

"*Love?*" He screwed up his face.

He raised his hand and brought it down in a slicing motion. Ceto raised an arm to the side of her face. As quickly as she could look up, Krokar had ordered a Raven to plummet towards her. It had clawed her from her temple and down to her arm, ripping the shoulder of her mum's cloak. A searing pain firing from her face, hot and wet from blood as it poured from the two parallel wounds down her cheek.

"Ceto!" She heard Oscar shouting from the room to her left, but she was struggling to see through the blood as it dripped over her eyebrow.

She held her hand out to the side, instructing them to stop and to not come any closer.

She couldn't do it, she couldn't defeat Krokar. She wasn't quick enough. She needed more time to perfect her defences. She was out of time.

She bit her tongue, not wanting to shout out in pain. She didn't want to give him the pleasure of her pain.

He clapped his hands together in a slow clap. The noise echoing off the high walls and ringing in her ears, making her dizzy.

"They won't save you. If they cared for you, they would rush to your aid." He poked at her.

With what little energy she had left, she asked the wind to blow towards her friends, warning them to not take the bait.

"They don't care for you. They don't understand you, you're too different. They're *scared* of you. They deserve the darkness." There was a pause as Krokar let his information sink in.

"Join me." He whispered. He'd become closer as Ceto grabbed her head and tried to blink through the blood.

"He saved her." She whispered in her dizzy state. She blinked towards where Daylah had been lying, but she was nowhere to be seen. Had she gotten away? She turned her head and forced herself to look at Amaru's body.

"Amaru, he risked his life to save Daylah's. He is Ignis, she is Azureus." She began to straighten up and drop her arm. "Daylah is the most accepting person in Natus. Nuri is my friend. She knows what I am and she's my *friend*."

"You're *wrong*." Krokar growled, letting his calm exterior crumble away.

He raised his arms high and brought them down with such power, all the while never taking his eyes away from Ceto. She felt a gust of wind as thousands of pairs of wings took flight.

She threw her left arm out, summoning her friends. *Daylah*. She worried in her mind. She needed them close, to protect them.

Within seconds, Oscar stood close to her shoulder, almost touching her. Nuri and Quidel stood a little ahead of her, poised for a fight, spears held strong by their sides. Samir stood at her other side, a little behind, ready to fight off as many Raven as he could with a small glittering knife.

With the strength of her friends, she created a dome around them.

A few Raven made it through the defence by hopping underneath it. Nuri, Quidel and Samir saw to these.

Ceto scanned the room for Daylah's small form. As her heart tried to pound out of her chest, she spotted Daylah behind a pillar at the far right of the room. Her face a sheet of petrified white.

Krokar was too busy instructing the Raven to notice what Ceto was doing.

Daylah and Ceto locked eyes and Ceto beckoned her with her hand.

Daylah, bent low and with her hands over her head for

protection, quickly made her way across the great hall and towards Ceto.

Out of nowhere, a single Raven shot like an arrow from the rafters and aimed straight for Daylah.

Before Ceto could call out, the great black bird, talons at the ready, clawed from Daylah's forehead to her cheeks. Thick gashes poured with blood down her face. She couldn't see. She was panicking. She dropped to the floor and began feeling around on her hands and knees. The screaming unbearable.

Ceto couldn't form words. She had gone in to shock. The pain in her own face, mixed with the pain before her was too much.

Daylah. She weakly thought. As soon as she thought her name, Daylah stopped feeling around and her head snapped up in the direction of Ceto.

Daylah! I'm here! She screamed in her head. As she did, Daylah wobbled to her feet, arms held out in front of her, and inched her way towards the centre of the room.

Finally feeling slightly in control with Daylah tucked under her arm, Ceto closed her eyes and concentrated on her protective dome once more.

She felt a new power surge through her, a liquid power. It was strong. She used this to strengthen the dome. As the power surged stronger and stronger and the dome become more powerful, her strength became too much. The dome exploded and threw her and Daylah apart to opposite sides of the great hall. She felt the exploded dome shattering around her.

Hitting her head on the hard stone floor, she lay there motionless for a moment. Watching the massacre happening above her. A new perspective as she witnessed every Raven breaking through her protection and edging closer and closer to her friends. And there was nothing she could do about it.

She had nothing left.

She heard Krokar laugh manically in the distance. A laughter filled with glee and victory.

"Ceto!" A voice called, but it seemed far away.

A large hand wrapped around her upper arm and pulled her to a standing position. It was Quidel. He had left Samir to fight by himself to save Ceto.

The Raven noticed Samir on his own and they gathered as one, high above them. There they regrouped and aimed directly at Samir now. For a moment, Samir was lost as a wall of black feathers sped past him, but they could hear his pained screams. When the mass cleared and twisted in the air above them once more, Samir wobbled and fell to his knees with a bang, weakly jabbing his knife into the empty air above his head. A pool of blood gathering around him. He finally fell to the ground.

The Raven were preparing for their second attack on Samir. Ceto ran to his side and flung her body over his. If she couldn't protect him with her abilities, she was going to protect him with her life.

"Ceto! Don't be stupid!" Krokar laughed, his voice echoing of the high walls but getting lost in the rustle of feathers.

Daylah. She thought once more, in the hope that she could follow her thoughts and be protected by Ceto's body too. Ceto closed her eyes tightly, trying to think away the pain on the side of her face. Reaching out her arm for Daylah to grab hold of.

She heard the Raven, but they weren't attacking. She dared take a glance above her. They were circling, whipping the wind into a storm as they did.

She turned her head to Krokar.

Quidel was stood before Krokar, his spear pointed under his chin. He was still smiling manically, his arms held up in surrender.

"Cetoooo." Krokar sang. Ceto slowly got to her feet whilst whispering for Daylah to stay with Samir, who was breathing shallowly.

"We can stop this." Krokar bargained. "You want your friends to live, and I want *me* to live." He flashed a toothy grin in Ceto's direction.

She edged closer to Krokar.

"All you have to do, is join me." Krokar jolted his head back further as Quidel shifted his spear. "Join me, and your friends can go about their lives."

No one spoke, the only sound came from the Raven cawing and fluttering high above.

"So they can live their lives in darkness?" Ceto shouted to Krokar. "I don't think so."

Krokar growled and twitched one of his hands. A Raven broke from the others and headed straight for Oscar. Talons outstretched, it ripped down Oscar's back, from top to bottom. He didn't make a sound. His body arched and he fell to his knees, eyes wide. Before the Raven could join the others, Nuri rammed her spear straight through the creature.

"NO!" Ceto yelled. Krokar laughed and clapped his hands together in delight.

Anger bubbled up inside Ceto and she let out a great surge of energy upwards as she let out a scream.

The Raven, looking flustered and unsure, began to fly in different directions.

Nuri helped Oscar up and together they made it to where Ceto stood over Samir and Daylah.

Oscar used the last of his strength to watch over Samir's motionless body on the floor. Daylah lay huddled next to him, her hands over her face. Loud screams of pain could be heard muffled through her fingertips.

Quidel had abandoned Krokar to help the others. He placed his hand on Ceto's shoulder as a gesture of support, before joining Nuri as they readied their spears for the inevitable onslaught of Raven. But as he did, she felt a great hot power surge through her. Much like she did earlier when she touched Daylah.

Unite Natus.

"Nuri, Quidel, come here." Ceto commanded. They glanced at her, confused, and then back up at the Raven who were beginning to create a formation once again.

Nevertheless, they did as they were commanded, loosened the grip on their weapons and came close to hear what Ceto had planned.

"Hold hands." She told them breathlessly. They glared back at her, mistrust in both of their faces.

"Please, trust me." She hurried, daring a glance above them. The Raven were about to charge.

Ceto took Quidel's hand, who took Nuri's, who took Oscar's, who took Samir's and with Ceto's other hand, she pulled a still screaming Daylah up to take her hand.

As they were interlinked, she felt all of their power surge through her, mixing together and making her stronger. Hot, liquid and light as air.

She sent an outpouring of force upwards. The Raven froze mid-attack, in unison. They plummeted to the ground, hitting the hard stone floor around them with a great force.

As they lay, strewn on the ground, they began to change. Men, women, children. Tanned faces and grey hair.

She felt Samir gasp on the floor, his eyes open slightly.

The people of Ventus.

"NO!" Krokar thundered, not beaten yet.

Ceto quickly dropped Daylah and Quidel's hands and turned to Krokar, encircling him in a twist of wind. His arms pinned to his side, slowly running out of air.

Ceto walked slowly towards him, trying to not see the people around her. She couldn't think of how many she had killed just yet, she had one last task to take care of.

"We…we belong together. We've been…designed to be…together." He gasped.

"No, I was designed to right your wrongs. You're wrong, Krokar. The way you want the world. You're wrong."

It felt good to have found her power and to gain control of the situation around her.

She felt her mind asking the wind to grow tighter and tighter. To squash and crumple.

She heard Daylah behind her, still screaming out in pain. Ceto's heart leapt at the agony her small friend was feeling. She loosened the wind and Krokar fell to the floor in a pile. His hand held up in a plea to stop as he tried to grasp his breath back.

"Quidel!" She shouted, not taking her eyes off Krokar. Distrust on her face.

In half a second, Quidel was straight backed at her side, waiting for instruction.

"What do we do with him now?" She tried to sound authoritarian, although she was really asking him what she should do.

"We could kill him." He replied without emotion.

"And if we don't want to kill more people?" She prompted. He turned his head to hers, disbelief on his face.

"We can hold him in Ignis." He offered. Ceto nodded.

"No, don't take me there." Krokar pleaded, kneeling on the floor amongst the bodies of Ventus.

Maybe he shouldn't live? Ceto questioned herself.

Quidel gave him a firm kick to the stomach. Krokar bent in on himself from the force.

"Stop!" She yelled. She'd had enough of violence for a whole lifetime.

Krokar began to laugh, broken as he was from defeat and physical pain, there he lay, laughing.

"You see how they treat me? Why would they treat you any differently? You'll always be *different*." He tilted his head upwards so that Ceto could see him sneering.

Ceto crouched down next to him, her hands between her legs, steadying herself.

"You're *wrong*." She forcefully whispered. She then straightened up and began to walk away, feeling brave enough to face the bodies around her.

Chapter 24

Ceto made her way to where the others huddled, injured. Daylah whimpered for her pack.

"I need...someone...to heal." She said between sobs.

Oscar silently shuffled to fetch her pack lay strewn on the ground and followed her instructions.

First he dipped a cloth in a jar of liquid and wrapped it around Daylah's eyes. As soon as the cloth was secured, her body began to relax and her whimpering slowed.

Together, Daylah and Oscar began working on Samir. A combination of dripping a medicine into his mouth and dabbing his scratches had him sitting up and glancing around the room in no time. He muttered his family's names as he searched frantically, whipping his head one way and then the other, waiting for enough strength to stand.

Next, Ceto was instructed to see to Oscar's large wound on his back.

Finally, after Nuri and Quidel had refused ointment for their scratches, Oscar turned to help Ceto.

He smiled sadly at her and held his hand out for hers.

"Does it hurt?" He examined her face. The bleeding had mostly stopped but it was throbbing. She was afraid to touch it.

"What's happening?" Daylah asked as bodies around them began to wake and stand up, a little confused.

"The Raven were the people of Ventus, they've turned back now and they're starting to wake up." She tried to sound as upbeat as she could, but she was still very aware that a lot more bodies hadn't moved yet.

Daylah felt around on the floor for her pack and delved into it, biting her lip as she concentrated on using touch rather than sight.

A lump grew in Ceto's throat as she fought back tears.

Daylah pulled out a strip of white cloth and a glass jar with an odd muddy ointment inside, she sniffed it first and then handed them out for Ceto to take.

"I can't see to do it myself." Daylah tried to joke. "Dab the ointment on the wound and place the cloth over the top until the ointment has been absorbed." Daylah instructed. Her formal tone seemed strange. Ceto felt as though she was talking to an old doctor, not a young girl. But she gratefully took what was offered.

"Daylah? Will you see again?" Ceto asked, a little wary. Daylah didn't seem troubled by her loss of sight.

"No." She said, bluntly. There was silence around them. Daylah sighed.

"I've heard of seers losing their sight for one reason or another, but it usually always ends with them becoming more powerful." She shifted the cloth over her eyes a little. "It's an honour really." Daylah said, almost back to her cheerful tone. "Although I can't see, I have better *sight* than the others. I can hear some thoughts." She fiddled with the ends of her hair. "I'll probably rank higher than Nahlah." She gave a nervous chuckle.

"Have you applied the ointment yet?" She changed the subject.

"Oh, no. I…" She couldn't do it, the pain was too much, she couldn't bring herself to touch her face, afraid of what she might find there.

"Here, I'll do it." Oscar offered, taking the ointment from her.

He guided Ceto to a wooden bench at the side of the room. Daylah followed the sound of their feet. Ceto wondered if she could *see* that they'd moved.

As Oscar gently applied the ointment, it smelt of pond water, she finally let herself take in her surroundings.

She had been putting this off, compartmentalising.

She let a little relief seep into her lungs at the sight of some Ventus stirring, seemingly with no memory of what had happened to them.

The room was full of Ventus as they made their way around the room, checking to see if those that lay still on the ground were breathing.

Some took it upon themselves to gently move those that couldn't be woken to the side of the room. Laid out side by side in straight lines.

Others weaved in and out of each other, trying to find loved ones.

"Daylah, there are Azureus here." Ceto brightly told her, between winces of pain from her face. For amongst the sea of grey hair, she could pick out a few blonde, their eyes black as Daylah's had been.

"Yes, I feel them." She replied, sitting back onto the wall behind her and seemingly relaxing, hands clasped together on her lap. Her remedies worked rapidly.

Samir could be heard shouting for his family.

"Almas? Coralie?" He shouted over and over again.

Ceto's heart lurched. She'd killed so many Raven. So many Ventus. So many innocent people. Whatever lightness the sight of Ventus and Azureus getting to their feet had given her, her heart grew heavy again at the sight of Samir's anguish.

"Ceto?" Oscar asked. She wasn't aware, but her breathing had become shallow and quick. She moved her eyes to his, trying to find comfort in their familiar sight.

"I killed them." She whispered. Her heart pumped cold with a sad ache.

Oscar lowered his eyes. She expected him to soothe her as he always did. She had come to the conclusion slower than he had.

Having finished applying the ointment, he gently placed the

cloth on her face and held it there. She instantly felt the thick substance find its way into her open wounds.

They locked eyes again.

"Krokar was orchestrating them…and you." His expression softened, his brow furrowed. "What choice did you have?" It wasn't entirely rhetorical. He wondered what Ceto could have done differently.

She dropped her eyes and then forced herself to look at the lined up bodies near her.

"I don't know."

She then found Nuri in the crowd of Ventus. Her dark mass of curly hair and her beige clothing stood out amongst the sea of grey.

She and a Ventus woman were carrying Amaru. Nuri with her arms hooked under his. The Ventus woman cradling his feet. They placed him down softly with the Ventus dead and then the woman went away to help somebody else, whilst Nuri stood at Amaru's head as if she were standing guard.

Ceto noticed Nuri locking eyes with Quidel across the room as he stood guard of Krokar. Neither had much emotion on their faces.

"I expected Nuri to be upset." Ceto said, more to herself, but Daylah replied.

"From what I've read, Ignis believe their dead will rise again in another form."

"Reincarnation?" Oscar added.

"Mmm, I haven't heard of that before. Ignis call it 'the spark'. They have rituals, they burn the body and believe that the spirit will ignite in another. I'd like to see that…" She trailed off, realising that she would never see an Ignis ritual.

"And what do Azureus believe?" Ceto changed the subject.

"Our beliefs are similar. We send our dead out to sea, and their essence enters the fish that we catch and eat."

"Khepri once told me that when Folia die, they become part

of the forest." Ceto added.

"And Ventus?" Oscar asked, swallowing hard at the sight of the lifeless bodies.

"They also burn their bodies, but they believe their souls become part of the wind." Daylah explained. "I suppose each belief aren't so different from one another." She mused.

The conversation grew quiet. Daylah rested her head on the wall behind her, whilst Oscar carefully pulled a corner of cloth away from Ceto's face.

She winced. It felt as if the cloth was stuck to her, pulling off bits of skin with it.

"Sorry." He muttered. "It looks a lot better under there already." Ceto took hold of the cloth so he could sit next to her.

She let her gaze settle on the crowd around her, as they were desperately seeking loved ones. Rather than settling on the bodies on the ground beside her.

Her stomach was heavy with grief and remorse.

She glanced over to Krokar, his face smug for some reason. How could he feel no guilt?

"Don't." Oscar's gentle tones danced into her ear. She glanced down at her hand on her lap, her clothes growing stiff as her blood dried.

He placed his hand on top of hers.

"He doesn't have the same mind as us. You can't figure him out, he doesn't work the same." Oscar tried to convince.

Ceto knew he was right, and Oscar's fresh outlook on the situation loosened the knot in her stomach a little. She nodded, knowing she had to find a way to live with this.

"He won't be a problem for much longer." Daylah chimed in from Ceto's other side, head still resting on the wall. A knowing smile on her face.

Ceto was too tired to ask. Instead, she turned her attention to the crowd before her again. The atmosphere had changed as more and more families found each other. Some complete, others huddled around still bodies on the ground.

She noticed Samir still weaving in and out, shouting his family's names, his searching becoming more frantic.

Please. Please. Please. Please. Please. Please. Ceto chanted.

"Don't worry." Daylah soothed.

Are they alive? She asked, desperation in her tone. Daylah didn't say anymore, the edges of her mouth pulled down. Ceto looked back to Samir, panic in his hollow face, his clothes hanging off him. He'd been through so much mental torture to find them.

They have to be here. She willed.

Her heart lifted into her throat as she watched Samir's entire body change.

"Daddy!" A little girl bellowed, running towards Samir. He crouched down and caught her, wrapping her in his arms, his cheek resting on the top of her head. He wailed with relief and they collapsed onto the ground, still embraced.

Ceto's vision grew blurry with a rush of tears. She glanced around to see if the girl would be followed by her mum, but there was no one.

"Momma?" The girl asked over and over, trying to look up at her dad, but Samir held her in his embrace. His gaze hovered over the bodies at the edge of the room as their numbers grew.

Chapter 25

After some time, the families of Ventus began to make their way out of the great hall and to pick up the pieces of their lives.

When the crowds thinned, Ceto noticed a small girl at the other end of the room. She was younger than Daylah.

She sat with her back against the wall, her arms hugging her knees.

She had deep black hair, straight and long. Long enough to sweep the floor as she sat, huddled.

She was Ignis.

Ceto slowly made her way to her feet, her tired body stiff. She made her way to the young girl and crouched in front of her.

The girl looked up at Ceto and flinched, tears falling off the edge of her chin.

"Seraphine?" The girl nodded in response.

"I can take you to your mother." The girl let out a sob and leapt forward, clumsily engulfing Ceto in a shaky hug.

Ceto winced at the pain in her face as the girl grazed her wound with her arm, but she recovered quickly, embracing the child.

Ceto took Seraphine by the hand and they walked back to the wooden bench.

As they made their way past the centre of the room where Quidel stood with Krokar, she glanced over at the monster.

He was still smiling, he lifted one hand and wiggled his fingers in a wave.

Ceto looked away and reminded herself of Oscar's observation about Krokar's sanity. A shiver running down her spine.

Ceto sat on the ground, her back rested on Oscar's legs as she people watched.

Daylah straight backed, against the wall, her head tilted back, her eyes still covered in blood soaked bandages. Ceto wasn't sure if she had drifted into sleep.

Seraphine lay in a foetal position, her head resting on Daylah's lap as she slept surprisingly peacefully.

The hall had almost completely emptied of Ventus; the bodies still remained in neat rows. Samir sat cross legged on the floor next to the body of a woman whilst his daughter, Coralie, lay on his lap. Her eyes gazing off into the distance, not really seeing. Samir had the same expression on his face whilst he absentmindedly stroked Coralie's silver hair.

The warm sun leaked in through the entrance, but the air hung limply around them, full of a gloomy exhaustion.

They had succeeded in what they set out to do, Krokar had been stopped and they'd even managed to find the missing Ventus and the taken Azureus and Ignis.

But this still felt like a failure, everyone felt it.

Krokar didn't seem to think he'd failed, which made Ceto feel unease in her stomach, coupled with a bubbling anger.

"Why is he still *smiling?*" Ceto forced out through gritted teeth.

Ceto's tone awoke everyone up from their forlorn thoughts. Even Nuri, still standing guard of Amaru a little distance away, seemed to feel her frustration and turned her head slightly in Ceto's direction.

Ceto harshly rubbed her eyes, trying to wipe her frustration away.

"I can...see...it's not over." Daylah pulled her eyebrows towards each other as she tried to see Krokar's plans.

Samir propped his daughter on his side, she buried her head in his neck and continued with her vacant gaze.

He came closer to the group.

"Maybe we should just *kill* him and be done with it?" He hissed.

"How many more people is he going to k-" His voice caught

in his throat and he hugged Coralie closer.

Ceto instantly wished she hadn't said anything. She hadn't meant to, but the frustration forced it out of her and now they were on edge and riled.

"We can't kill him." Ceto noticed Nuri turn her head back to the front at that, her neck moving as she gulped back tears. Ceto glanced at their faces in turn.

"I couldn't take a life, no matter what they'd done." She tried to persuade them, finally moving her body around so that she could see Oscar who had become silent and still.

He shrugged at her when they locked eyes.

"You agree with Samir?" She asked, hurt. They hadn't always seen eye to eye through the years, but they did on the big things. And this was big.

She turned on her heel and made her way to where Krokar sat on the steps, Quidel standing guard next to him.

She walked with purpose, her arms swinging at her sides. Her hair in a ponytail, whipped side to side with every step.

Finally, she stopped dead, inches away from Krokar. Her foot slapping the floor as it came into line with the other.

"Cetooo." Krokar greeted as if they were old friends, his arms held out before him, welcoming her.

She flicked her eyes up to Quidel quickly, checking he was paying attention, checking he would spring into action and protect her if she needed it.

"Do you have any remorse?" She asked.

He tapped his chin and looked to the ceiling, in mock thought. His finger nails long and blackened as they scraped against his dark stubble.

"I do have regrets." He lowered his eyes to the ground, rounding his shoulders.

Ceto's breath caught; was it that easy?

"I regret not killing you when I had the chance." He kept his head low, his eyes finding Ceto's. "I should've killed you both." He began to laugh a low throaty chuckle.

She felt rage bubble in her chest. Her hand raised, and in one swift motion she slapped him hard across the face.

When he brought his head level again, he was *still* smiling.

She slapped him again.

His smile grew wider.

She brought her hand into a fist and made contact with his jaw.

His smile temporarily gone, but laughter remained in his eyes. A trickle of blood escaping his bottom lip.

"Tell me, Ceto. Do *you* feel remorse?" He asked calmly.

She brought her arm back again to take another blow.

Her mind acknowledged Oscar shouting her name in the distance, footsteps hitting the floor and echoing off the walls. But all that mattered to her in this moment, was to cause Krokar pain until he felt something for the people he'd killed. The people she had killed.

For Samir's wife, for Amaru, for Khepri, for the Ventus lying still behind her. For her mum. She needed to cause pain, as much pain as she felt in her chest.

Before her hand made contact, Quidel had taken hold of Ceto's arm. His hand engulfing her small wrist.

"Don't." Was all he offered.

She let her shoulders un-tense as a sense of foolishness washed over her. She looked down at Krokar and let her brain take in what she had done to him.

His grin returned.

Quidel stepped between Krokar and Ceto, blocking her view of the mad man.

"You will regret this. I do not think this is you." He spoke softly, but bluntly.

"Ceto?" Oscar timidly spoke from behind her.

This wasn't her, he was right. She wasn't violent.

"CETO!" Daylah shouted from the far wall.

287

All heads turned to her shouts, and as they did, Krokar leapt up from the steps and transformed into a Raven.

Ceto's heart sunk into her stomach. He was escaping and she didn't know how to stop it from happening.

A spear cut through the air towards the bird. It sang as it made its way towards Krokar.

In the blink of an eye, he plummeted to the ground. A great spear through his chest.

Krokar's human form lay askew on the hard ground. Nuri's spear embedded through his centre.

He lay on his side, his arm draped over the weapon as if in an embrace.

Nobody moved, nobody made a sound.

Nuri showed no remorse; she stepped back to her post next to Amaru's body, her arms clasped behind her back.

Ceto's stomach twisted with regret as Maia's face forced its way to the forefront of her mind. Tears in her eyes, asking her not to kill her only son.

Oscar made his way over to Ceto, wrapped his arm around her shoulders and pulled her in close.

Ventus were making their way back into the hall, their solemn faces low.

Some dragged a piece of white cloth stretched over a wooden frame behind them, whilst others held candles.

They were collecting their dead.

A young woman, straight silver hair falling behind her all the way to the bottom of her back, strode towards Samir and Coralie. She handed him a frame for his wife, and she handed his daughter a basket of purple flowers. She walked beside them with a candle.

Quidel, no longer standing guard of Krokar, took the same stance as Nuri, placing his gaze before him, a strangely tranquil expression held on his stern face.

"Ceto?" Oscar asked as they stood beside Krokar's body.

"Don't." She replied, fighting back tears.

"He killed people. He killed Adara." He pushed.

"I know." She breathed.

She couldn't explain it to herself. She expected to feel as though justice had been done, but as she stood over Krokar's body, the side of his face visible, his smile gone, she felt sadness.

He needed help, maybe a friend, someone to love him. Was it true? Had his mother and father treated him without affection? If he'd been treated differently, would he have grown up to be a different person? Ceto had wondered if she had grown up in Natus, rather than hiding on Earth, would she be a different person today.

"We'll have to take him to Maia." She croaked.

"We will." Oscar said, his voice breaking a little.

They watched as the dead were placed carefully on white cloth, one by one. Children came with baskets of flowers, and placed them around the bodies. Then they were gently pulled towards the exit and out into the afternoon sun. Each body followed by a candle.

Samir was one of the last in the hall, falling behind to speak to the others.

Amaru had already been hoisted onto a cloth, Krokar lay abandoned in the middle of the hall, small against its vastness. The others huddled closely together, ready to make their way down the mountain.

"Join us outside, it would mean a lot to me if you were there for this." Samir asked.

Ceto nodded.

"Samir?" Nuri spoke for the first time, her voice unsure and low.

He turned to face her, kindness in his emerald eyes.

"Would it be okay if Amaru lay with your Ventus?" A tear finally fell down her cheek. But she quickly wiped it away.

Quidel snapped his head towards Nuri, but she ignored him.
"Do you think he would want this?" Samir asked, a little
taken aback.

"You burn your dead?" She asked.

"We burn our loved ones." He corrected. She lowered her
head, worried that she had offended him.

"You burn your Ignis too?" He prompted. She nodded.

"That would be fine." He reached his arm forward and placed
his hand on her shoulder. She looked up through her
eyelashes and gave him a smile.

Nuri then looked to Quidel for blessing, he nodded in
response.

Quidel and Samir carried their loved ones towards the exit,
Nuri and Coralie followed with a candle each.

Ceto gave them a reassuring smile as they left. The men
nodded in response but Nuri still seemed to be holding a
grudge against her.

"Nuri, can I have a word?" She interjected as they turned
their backs.

She nodded, let the others leave without her and the two girls
moved a few steps out of ear shot.

"I wanted you to know that I've spoken with Quidel and I've
made it clear that we're just friends." Ceto picked the side of
her nail as she spoke.

Nuri's stern face turned to one of pity, which Ceto wasn't
expecting.

"Just friends?" She cocked her head a little to the side.

"Quidel has Fixed with you. All he can do now is wait for
you, he has no other choice." She shook her head
disappointedly and made to walk away.

"Wait...I don't fully understand what Fixed means?" Ceto
asked.

"When Ignis Fix, fate has brought them together. Once we
do this, we can have no one else." Nuri paused to let this sink

in. "Quidel will be alone until you decide you want him too."
She shrugged. "He has no choice."
"I'm sorry, I didn't know." She risked a glance towards
Oscar. It had always been Oscar. If she was honest with
herself now, she had never entertained the idea that she
would have other friends, let alone other love interests.
Perhaps she hadn't given Quidel a chance.
Ceto let out a long breath as a pang of shame ran through her
body. She had led Quidel on; she didn't realise how much she
craved the attention.
"I'm sorry, I didn't realise." Ceto said as she hung her head.
Nuri placed her hand on Ceto's arm and smiled sadly at her.
"We have more important things to do for now." Her eyes
filled with tears as she said this, but they didn't spill over.
Ceto nodded back and let the beautiful Ignis woman walk
away.
Ceto glanced over to Krokar.
"We'll come back for him." Oscar reassured her.
"He'll be left alone here." Daylah offered her wisdom.
They left the hall together, back out the way they had come
only a few hours previously; although it felt like a lifetime
ago.
They followed a few Ventus stragglers out into the open air.
The heat hit them and one by one, they stripped their coats
and scarves off.
"Summer!" Daylah exclaimed, a relieved smile on her face.
She was right, it had turned to summer and the summer sun
was high in the sky as the day grew warmer.
They followed Samir down a pathway that led round to the
other side of the mountain, behind the great hall.
Ceto's stomach twisted at the sight of piles of bodies
wrapped in white cloth, lying still. A queue of Ventus, making
their deposit, could be seen in the distance.
Ceto was reminded of a line of ants as she watched.

As they turned a corner to bring them to the back of the mountain, she gasped at the sight before her.

Ventus wasn't a singular mountain. It was a vast rocky landscape that seemed to go on into the horizon. Houses could be seen dotted here and there, hollowed out into the rocks. Many even had greenery surrounding the dwellings. Ceto had never put much thought into mountains and rocks before, she had found them cold and jagged; but looking out onto this great landscape, she could see its beauty. Its paths made from precious gems as they sparkled under the suns watch and lay intertwined amongst the houses and rocks. Ceto breathed in the clean mountain air and let it settle in her lungs, calming the racing guilt in her mind.

When all of the bodies had been placed together, Nuri and Quidel stood side by side, muttering words that Ceto couldn't make out. Heads tilted back, eyes closed, arms held out at their sides.

"They must be doing a part of their ritual." Daylah whispered. A hushed excitement in her tone.

Samir stood a little ahead, Coralie on his hip as they watched the fires being lit.

"It seems a little impersonal to me." Oscar muttered, not wanting to be overheard and offend.

"I think, usually, there is a stone table where the body is laid and words are said. But whilst...whilst there are...so many..." Daylah didn't need to finish her sentence, they knew what she was saying.

"They have to do it immediately too. I think I've read that, the longer they burn after death, the weaker their force on the wind." Daylah added, tilting her chin as she tried to recall what she had learnt.

In a matter of minutes, the mountain of bodies were alight with a strong flame, dancing around each other, guiding souls to the sky above.

If she let her gaze settle on the top points of the flames, she could see flecks breaking away from the heat and escaping up into the clouds.

She was peacefully reminded of the way her mum had escaped the world after her death. She wondered if she had found peace in the wind or in the water. Either way, she knew she was watching over her now.

Ceto quietly turned and headed back to the hall, to where Krokar lay.

She turned him onto his back and pulled the spear from him, crossing his arms on to his chest and asking the wind to lift him from the ground and to follow her down the mountain and across the meadow.

On exiting the great hall, Krokar following as they walked, cradled in mid-air by the wind, the Ventus people were beginning to make their way back to their homes from the burial in dribs and drabs.

She noticed Nuri and Quidel in the distance, Seraphine stood close to Nuri, almost touching her. They still seemed to be in the middle of their ritual. Ceto thought better of disturbing them.

"They'll head back to Ignis when they've finished." Daylah spoke matter-of-factly. Her new *sight* growing stronger.

Ceto grabbed her arm and laced it through her own, offering comfort and guidance down the path.

As Ceto made her way down the mountain, green eyes peered at them as they stopped to let her past.

The news had gotten around of what Krokar had done to them and of how so many of them had come to lose loved ones.

Disdain, rage, pain, fear, just a few of the emotions on the faces of the Ventus people as they walked past.

Ceto felt the glares between her shoulder blades as she

moved forward.

She spotted Samir in the doorway of a small house, Coralie with her arms hugging his thigh tightly, afraid that she would be left alone again.

He nodded, but his arms were crossed firmly against his chest.

"Where will you take him?" He asked, a bitter note as he referred to Krokar.

"To his mum, she lives in Azureus." This was the right thing to do and she knew it. He was a living being, he had a mum, and she deserved to say goodbye.

"Quidel and Nuri are still at the top." Samir lifted his chin to the top of the mountain, where a blaze of fire could still be seen dancing.

Ceto nodded, grateful for the information she already knew. "Seraphine is with them. We'll meet them in Ignis. I have someone I need to say goodbye to myself first." She replied.

Samir's arms fell to his sides, his hand brushing the crown of his daughter's head.

"You're welcome here any time. You all are." He glanced to the top of the mountain again. "Thank you." His eyes grew shiny, but no tears fell down his exhausted face.

She placed her hand on his shoulder, smiled at Coralie and carried on with their decent.

Chapter 26

Ceto, Oscar and Daylah made their way through the meadow towards Azureus, Krokar gliding behind them. No one spoke. Exhaustion had caught up with them and they each hovered in their own thoughts of what the immediate future held. Bees buzzed lazily from colourful flower to colourful flower, unaware of what could have transpired in this world. Happy that the sun was shining and the bitter cold had been defeated. Ceto envied their ignorance as she waded through the grass.

With Azureus in sight, a flap of feet could be heard running along the walk way.

It was Maia.

She stopped suddenly at the top of the small wooden incline as Ceto made her way towards her; her son still on the air. Ceto's chest clenched, anxious to know Maia's reaction. She had pleaded with Ceto to keep her son alive. She knew she had tried her hardest, but did Maia know that?

Maia fell heavily to her knees, finding it hard to catch her breath.

Nahlah could be seen making her way towards where they stood from the opposite walkway, a crowd of Azureus following her.

There was a silence whilst the people took in what they were seeing. The only sound coming from the tranquil waves below as they lapped softly against the wooden poles holding them up, and the low sobs of a mother who failed her son.

"Help me." Daylah sprang into action, an authority in her voice.

As soon as she spoke, a handful of Azureus made their way from the crowd and placed their hands under Krokar.

Ceto let the wind go. Feeling herself relax without the strain, she let her body lean on Oscar's gently.

Silently, they carried Krokar towards the edge of Azureus, the crowd making way for him and then following.

Ceto helped Maia to her feet and Nahlah took her hand, guiding her after the crowd. She nodded towards Ceto and smiled broadly towards Daylah.

"Come, Daylah." She said softly. Daylah quickly reached her arm out to where she sensed Ceto to be.

"You will see each other soon." Nahlah continued, there was no edge to her voice. "You will have to rebuild this world together. For now, we need you to lead us in this." She gestured to the back of the crowd, knowing Krokar was somewhere amongst the throng.

"I'll see you soon." Ceto whispered into Daylah's hair as they embraced.

Without a word, Daylah took Nahlah's other hand. The three walked away, before finally falling out of sight.

"What now?" Oscar asked, his arm wrapped around Ceto's shoulder.

She felt a chill on the air and pulled her scarf from her pack and swung it around her neck.

"I have a friend to say goodbye to." She said sadly, casting her eyes towards Ignis, where she knew Khepri was waiting for her.

Ceto and Oscar strolled hand in hand, there was no urgency now. For the first time in a long time, she didn't feel rushed. She took this opportunity to let herself feel her surroundings. The air, so clean, filling her lungs with a slight floral hint. The fire at the top of Ventus had finally died down. A pair of tall silhouettes could be seen making their way across the meadow towards Ignis, a small silhouette dragging behind a little.

Ceto let her mind wander away to what her life would look like if she gave in to her feelings towards Quidel. She squeezed Oscar's hand, reassuring herself that he was still there.

She watched as her remaining Ignis friends got lost between the huts and she and Oscar made their way to Khepri's stone body.

"This is Khepri." She explained to Oscar, looking up to the great Folia before her.

"They were my first friend." She smiled, sadly.

Oscar looked down at her at the comment, pretend shock on his face.

"My first friend in Natus." She corrected.

"What happened?" His demeanour matching her serious one.

"Krokar happened." She shrugged sadly. He pursed his lips in reply.

They stood in silence for a few beats.

"I'll be honest," Ceto looked up puzzled, "I expected them to wake up when I defeated Krokar."

More silence. Ceto's heart beat faster and fluttered as a thought penetrated her mind.

"What if we killed the only person who could help Khepri?" She spun her head to see Oscar's reaction, her eyes wide as she awaited his response.

"Ahh, Ceto, I…" He rubbed his hand up and down on her arm. She knew what he was going to say before he said it.

"Krokar is gone, and that's what was *supposed* to happen. He was never going to stop."

She knew he was right.

She had no more tears left. She pulled away from Oscar and stepped towards Khepri.

Looking up at their angular face as it was set as despair in stone, she reached her arm as long as it would go and gently placed her hand on their chest.

"I'm sorry, goodbye." She sighed.

A crack started at Khepri's forehead and ran quickly down the centre of their long body. The sound of stone rubbing against stone penetrated her ears.

"NO!" She yelled. She had broken them.

Oscar pulled her back as shards of stone broke off in all directions, releasing Khepri from within as they used their outstretched wings to soar above Ceto and Oscar, blocking out the late afternoon sun.

"Khepri!" Tears of overwhelming relief burst from her eyes as she ran to where they were landing softly.

"I knew you could save us." They sang confidently. Ceto let her lungs fill at the joy of knowing there was someone that had complete faith in her.

She internally vowed not to doubt herself again, to be confident in the human she now found herself being.

Khepri cast their eyes behind Ceto and towards Folia. The corners of their mouth dropped slightly at the sight of the line of dead trees.

"We have much to do." Khepri glanced down at Ceto and then let their gaze land on Oscar as he nervously stood slightly behind her.

"Oscar." They nodded, as if greeting an acquaintance.

Oscar squirmed a little at a loss of how to respond, this made Ceto giggle.

Khepri turned their attention back to her, hinging at the hips, their back straight. Their face coming into line with hers.

"Oh child, your face." Khepri made to cup their hand around the long scar on the side of Ceto's face, but didn't make contact.

"I see sacrifice in your eyes. You did well." A crystal tear dropped down Khepri's perfect cheek.

Ceto lifted her hand and swiped it away with her thumb.

"Not all tears are sad." Khepri smiled wildly at Ceto.

Then, they straightened up and gazed out towards the middle of the meadow.

"You still have work to do, and maybe one more sacrifice."

They turned their head to lock eyes with Ceto, an apologetic expression on their beautiful face.

"Oscar doesn't belong here." They gently said.

She'd known it. Whilst ambling through the meadow, she had ran through scenarios in her head. She couldn't face going back to Earth and picking up her life there. Back to an empty house. She knew she belonged in Natus and she knew there was still more work to be done. But, with a heavy heart, she had to admit that Oscar didn't belong here. She had wondered how it would play out if Oscar was allowed to stay in Natus. What would their life look like? But when she allowed herself to think on that life, it seemed far away and hazy, like a dream.

She then wondered what her life would look like if she stayed here and Oscar went back to Earth. That scenario was laced in pain. That, also, was not an option.

She supposed she would leave it up to Oscar, to what he decided, and she would be happy with his choice.

"Come Ceto." Khepri called as they lunged their long legs through the grass towards the archway of branches.

She took hold of Oscar's hand, possibly for the last time, and together they followed Khepri.

At the archway, Khepri placed their delicate hand on the branches and the scene between the branches changed from Ignis in the distance, to the path that stood beside Ceto's old home.

"I will leave you to say your goodbyes?" Khepri said as a question.

Ceto brought her eyebrows together. Were they suggesting that they didn't have to say goodbye? She turned to Oscar, awaiting his decision. Had he noticed the question in Khepri's voice?

"Do not be too long."

Then they took off into the sky, making their way through

the air and into the trees.

Ceto kept her eyes on Khepri, watching as they flew out of sight. Unable to look at Oscar, knowing that he would want to go back home.

How could she tell him that she *was* home.

"You still have things to do." He tried to joke, repeating what Khepri had said.

She still didn't look at him, but kept her head held high, her gaze off in the distance to Folia.

"I understand if you need to go back home." She said, gritting her teeth slightly, willing herself not to cry.

"Will you remember me?" She whispered.

Oscar placed both of his hands under her chin, forcing her to look up at him.

"My home is with you. There's nothing for me back there." He replied, with complete sincerity on his face.

He released her chin when he was certain that his words had landed in her mind.

His face turned jovial again.

"I had hoped that this was the end of the story." He glanced at her, not turning his face fully, a grin on his lips.

"This is just the beginning!" She matched his grin, unable to contain herself for the pure joy she felt in her chest.

He was staying. He'd chosen her.

They watched as the scene under the archway turned to Natus once more, as Earth slipped away.

"What now?" Oscar asked.

Ceto thought about that for a while.

"Now? Now our life can begin." She grinned up at him.

She took his hand and together they made their way across the beautiful meadow towards Folia, and the beginning of their new life.

Printed in Great Britain
by Amazon